OUR FATHERS

Rebecca Wait

OUR FATHERS

Europa
editions

Europa Editions
214 West 29th Street
New York, N.Y. 10001
www.europaeditions.com
info@europaeditions.com

Library of Congress Cataloging in Publication Data is available
ISBN 978-1-60945-571-2

Wait, Rebecca
Our Fathers

Book design by Emanuele Ragnisco
www.mekkanografici.com

Cover photo by Victoria Borodinova/Pexels

Prepress by Grafica Punto Print – Rome

Printed in the USA

CONTENTS

Our fathers sinned, and are no more;
and we bear their iniquities.
—LAMENTATIONS 5:7

OUR FATHERS

If she had survived, Katrina would have said what people always say: that it had been a day like any other. That everything was normal. She might have said, too, how strange it was that you only noticed normality after it ended, that by its nature it was invisible as long as you were in it.

It was March, and outside the sky was washed white like the bleached wood the tide left on the beach. She sent the boys to collect it so they could dry it out and use it as firewood, but some days it was hard to get warm. Spring came late to Litta. They had many days like this, of piercing cold and little colour. Sometimes the isolation of the place appalled her. Even on the clearest days, you could not see the mainland, thirty miles distant to the east. To their west, the Atlantic stretched out blankly, nothing but a lighthouse standing between them and Canada. When they'd first moved to the island, Katrina had found herself feeling as muted as the landscape during these endless winters. But John had said that she'd get used to it, and she supposed she had.

On this particular Tuesday in March, the sea had been rough all day, hurling itself against the rocks in an explosion of foam, then sliding back to gather force before it surged forward again. The wind was up already, laying the grasses flat across the machair and buffeting the sheep on the cliffs. It would grow in strength as the afternoon wore on, but on the island their houses had to be coming down around their ears before they were willing to call it a storm.

The boys had arrived home from school and were playing round the side of the house. Beth was in her playpen, occupied for the time being with Joe Bear and her cloth book, so Katrina could move around with relative freedom as she completed the housework. She had been dusting the skirting boards, because John's brother and his wife were coming round the following evening, and although Katrina always kept a clean house, she never noticed the skirting boards until she tried to look at each room critically, as if through the eyes of somebody else. John minded if things weren't perfect when Malcolm and Heather came, though you would think with family it would matter less.

John had been working from home that day. He had mostly remained in his study, emerging only to make a wordless cup of tea at eleven and to collect the sandwich she'd laid out for him at one. Katrina had known from the moment they woke that it would be better not to disturb him today. Impossible yet to say if it would be a bad one.

She completed the skirting boards in the living room, dusted the top of the piano and the windowsills with the same damp cloth and got her long-handled feather duster to do the corners of the ceiling. Then she laid down the duster, sneezed three times in quick succession, and went to crouch by Beth's pen.

"All right, love?" she said, and Beth stared up at her with that mournful, contemplative look that babies sometimes have, as though they have come from another place. Then she put Joe Bear down and pushed out her fat little arm for her mother's earrings. Katrina moved out of reach, took off her earrings—dangly silver ones she didn't much like, but which John had bought her years before—and leaned in again to tickle Beth under her arms. The gappy, delighted smile appeared immediately, and Beth gave her full, surprisingly throaty chuckle that always made Katrina laugh too.

"Have you been having a nice time?" Katrina said, and

Beth said, "Ba-rat," which was a fairly new one that Katrina hadn't worked out yet. Then Beth added, "Mama," and gave a smile so wide it screwed her eyes shut, as if practising how far she could stretch all the muscles of her face.

"That's right, my darling," Katrina said, reaching into the pen to lift her out, sighing with bliss at the familiar, warm weight of her child.

Outside, Nicky and Tommy didn't venture far from the house, taking refuge from the wind in the shelter of its walls. In an hour or so, the light would start to fade. Soon, they knew, their mum would come outside to ask them to watch Beth while she made tea, so they had to make the most of their freedom while they had it. Tommy had his hands pushed into his coat pockets and thought that he'd rather be playing inside today, but Nicky had ushered him out of the back door after their milk and snack, saying self-importantly, "We need to keep the noise down," which annoyed Tommy, even though he knew Nicky was right. Nicky always thought he knew best because he was ten, and Tommy especially hated it when Nicky used words that weren't his own, pretending to be a grown up.

But they were so good, both of them, at sensing the tiny currents in the air inside the house. They knew when to keep out of the way.

Tommy wanted them to be Vikings because that's what they'd been studying at school, and he liked the Vikings a lot, how fierce they were and how far they'd travelled, though Nicky said the Vikings were their enemies. Tommy himself hardly ever left the island, and even then it was only to get the ferry to Oban once a month to go shopping with his mum. Apart from that, he'd only been to Loch Lomond on holiday, which didn't count, and never even once to Glasgow or London or anywhere on a plane. Almost nobody he knew had been anywhere interesting. But Angus, who was the only other boy at school (though the Wilson twins were as good as boys), had been to Portugal with his grandparents from Dumfries the summer before and wouldn't stop talking about how hot it was and how bright. When Nicky finally told him to shut up, Angus had just given them both a pitying look and said maybe they'd be able to go one day, and Tommy had been so enraged that anyone should talk to Nicky like this, especially someone who was two years younger, that he'd hit Angus on the arm. Angus had cried even though Tommy knew he wasn't really hurt, and Mrs Brown had made Tommy apologize and miss out on playtime. But Tommy was pleased to have restored balance, because though he'd had to apologize, Angus had still cried. He'd thought Nicky would thank him after school, but all Nicky said was, "You shouldn't hit people," and Tommy was annoyed again because here was Nicky pretending to be a grown up, just like always.

When Tommy suggested, shyly, the Viking idea, Nicky said no. He said two wasn't enough to play Vikings, which made no sense to Tommy because they always played with just two, unless Angus or the twins were round. You could do almost anything with two. You just had to imagine the other characters you needed in the game, or each take on more than one part. Occasionally they even made Beth stand in, but she was never much use. Either she sat on the ground chewing anything she could get her hands on, or she hauled herself to her feet and tried to toddle unsteadily away, so that they had to break the game and give chase.

"Well, what do you want to do then?" he said to Nicky, trying to sound sulky enough that Nicky would know he was annoyed, but not so sulky that Nicky would call him a baby.

"Star Wars," Nicky said.

This was a game they played a lot, though Tommy wasn't sure Nicky liked it that much either. They both claimed to love Star Wars because their dad did. He had shown them all the films, which he had on video, even sitting between Tommy and Nicky on the sofa to watch with them, an arm round each of them. The films had bored and baffled Tommy, seeming old and clunky and silly, although he'd tried hard to believe in what was happening. But he knew he would never stop pretending; his dad was always in a good mood when they watched the films. "Star Wars changed my life," he'd said to them once. "It showed me there was a whole world out there beyond my own small one on the island. I knew your mum was the one for me when she said she loved Star Wars too. Most women don't get it."

Young as he was back then, Tommy had had the disquieting thought that perhaps his mum was pretending too.

Now, Nicky said, "I'll be Luke Skywalker and you can be Darth Vader."

Tommy drew himself up for the familiar battle. "I don't want to be Darth Vader. I'm always Darth Vader."

"Well, you have to be or it doesn't work."

"I want to be Han Solo."

Nicky shook his head in disbelief. "You can't be Han Solo fighting Luke Skywalker. That *doesn't make any sense.*"

"Well, why don't you be Darth Vader then?"

Nicky looked at him patiently. "That's not how the game works, Tommy."

Tommy had decided he disliked being called Tommy. He'd expended a lot of effort over the past couple of months trying to insist that everybody call him Tom, which sounded older. But in truth, he still thought of himself as Tommy. He had already realized in a vague way that you got your idea of yourself from other people. You didn't choose it yourself.

"I want to be Luke Skywalker," he told Nicky stolidly.

"You can't." Nicky gave the matter some thought. "If you really, really want to," he conceded generously, "you can be a stormtrooper."

"I don't want to be a stormtrooper."

"Tell you what," Nicky said, "I'll be Luke Skywalker for a bit, then we'll switch and you can be Han Solo and I'll be a stormtrooper. That's fair."

Tommy considered. It sounded fair, like most things Nicky suggested, but he had a suspicion it would be almost teatime before Nicky allowed them to switch, and then he'd hardly get a turn at being Han Solo. He could see, though, that there was no point arguing any longer; he never won. "O.K."

They spent a while looking for the sticks they used as lightsabers, and found them at last about ten metres from the house, where they must have thrown them down a few days before.

Tommy lifted his own lightsaber up, held it poised above his shoulder for a few moments, and then took several exploratory swings. He loved the feel of the weapon in his hands, the sense of power and purpose it gave him. One day he would do something brave and daring like the Vikings or like Han Solo. He decided to pretend secretly that he was Han Solo now and that Nicky was Darth Vader, and felt very pleased once this idea had come to him.

Fiona McKenzie, who had turned forty the previous day and was feeling unexpectedly wretched about it, caught sight of Tommy and Nicky playing with a couple of sticks outside the house as she walked past on her way to the bins, a little further up the lane. She wondered what game they were playing—pirates, perhaps? She raised her arm to wave and the boys waved back, Tommy not noticing her at first, until his brother pushed his arm and made him wave too. They were nice children, Fiona thought. You had to give Katrina that. Island boys through and through. As Tommy and Nicky turned to resume their game, Fiona saw Katrina herself coming out of the back door with Beth in her arms. This time,

Fiona didn't wave. Katrina wouldn't have seen her; she was intent on handing Beth to Nicky. Katrina's hair was loose this evening and hung down her back—all that lovely red hair. But it would start to go grey soon enough, Fiona thought, shifting the rubbish bag to her other hand as her arm started to ache. It came to us all, and Katrina wasn't so very much younger than Fiona herself. That is, unless Katrina decided to dye it when the time came. But surely not, Fiona thought, as she walked on.

Forty was no great age really. She wondered if she should buy herself one of those expensive face creams she'd seen advertised—anti-wrinkle, firming and so on—though as soon as the idea came to her she felt it would be unbearable if Gavin made a joke of it. But she could keep it quiet: get one in Oban next week, smuggle it upstairs and never mention it. Not that they really worked, probably, but it might make her feel better.

Rounding the bend in the lane, Fiona wondered what the Bairds were having for tea. It was the sort of little thing she liked to know. She and Gavin would finish the chicken casserole she had made the day before, when Kathy and Ed came round. Fiona had been worried it was too watery, but everyone seemed to enjoy it. Gavin had two helpings, and the second had left a bright smear of orange on his chin that remained there all through dessert. Try as she might, Fiona had not been able to catch his eye.

After their mum had disappeared back into the house, Nicky and Tommy sat Beth, carefully wrapped up in a coat and hat, on her blanket next to the wall of the house.

"Well, that's just *great*," Tommy said, delivering a line he'd heard on TV and had liked the sound of. "That's just *fan*-tastic."

"It doesn't matter," Nicky said. "We can still play."

And they did carry on for a few more minutes, but with

their baby sister watching from the sidelines and making her silly laugh-gurgle sounds, the illusion was broken and however fiercely they fought, it could not be restored.

Nicky stopped and leaned on his lightsaber. "Maybe we could make her part of it?" he suggested.

"How?"

"We could pretend she's Yoda," Nicky said, and they both found this so funny that they shrieked with laughter for several minutes, Tommy looking at Nicky from time to time to check he was still going, and then making himself continue laughing as long as his brother did so the moment wouldn't be over. At last, Nicky stopped and said, "We'd better keep the noise down," and Tommy agreed, saying sensibly before Nicky could, "We don't want to disturb Dad."

While they'd been laughing, Beth had hauled herself to her feet and was waddling along next to the wall, stopping to pat the rough brickwork purposefully as she went, as though it were a dog or a pony. Then she turned suddenly towards her brothers and came at them with open arms and her open-mouthed grin.

Tommy knew she was going to fall before it happened. She'd launched herself off with too much momentum and her small staggering steps were out of control from the start. Neither he nor Nicky reached her in time to stop her sprawling on the gravel, sending little pebbles flying up around her. There was a brief shocked pause, then Nicky went quickly to her, picking her up and putting her on her feet, perhaps in the hope of distracting her before she realized she was hurt and started wailing. But it was no good. Beth's puzzled face gave way to screwed-up misery and snot, and she sent out that long yowling sound both boys were familiar with.

"It's O.K., Lizzy-Lizard," Nicky said, dusting her down. "You're not really hurt." He made a show of rubbing and kissing her knees. "There. All better."

"I think she banged her elbow," Tommy said.

"I'll kiss that better too, Lizard," Nicky said. "See? All better now."

Beth kept crying, her face getting red. She looked a bit like an alien when she cried like this, Tommy thought.

"We'd better take her in to Mum," he said.

"She's fine," Nicky said, lifting her up into his arms and jiggling her about in a way Tommy didn't think was very helpful.

"We should take her in," he repeated. He wasn't sure if he was really concerned for Beth, or just wanted to get rid of her.

"No. She's making too much noise," Nicky said. "Wait till she stops crying. Dad's still working."

"You want Joe Bear, Lizard?" Tommy said, so that it wasn't just Nicky taking charge, but Beth carried on wailing.

Nicky swung Beth about in his arms, so quickly that she stopped crying for a few moments, then began again, but more half-heartedly.

Nicky swung Beth again. "You like that?"

Beth had stopped crying now, and was clinging on to the collar of Nicky's coat, the fabric bunched up in her hands. Tommy watched as she kneaded it uncertainly, a frown on her face. Experience told him she was deciding whether to start crying again. He went up and opened her coat and tickled her solid little body in the way she loved so that she started doing that weird deep laugh of hers.

"Good girl," he said. "Good girl, Bethy."

Nicky put Beth down again and knelt in front of her to wipe her face with the bottom of his T-shirt. "You'll get better at walking," he told her kindly. "More slowly you need to go," he added in Yoda's voice, which set Tommy off giggling again, and that made Beth chuckle because she could see that both her brothers were laughing.

The light was going fast by the time Fiona passed the

Bairds' house on her way back from the bins. As the house came into view, she saw Katrina coming out again to pick up Beth and usher the boys inside. The family was illuminated by the light above their back door, but Fiona knew she herself would be invisible on the track in the gathering darkness.

She paused to search through her jacket pocket for the little torch she was sure she'd remembered to put in before she set out earlier. Nice children, she thought again. Those polite, likeable boys. Fiona remembered Nicky offering her a cup of tea when she'd dropped round once while Katrina was having a nap upstairs with Beth, for all the world as if he were an adult, and then little Tommy appearing with biscuits he'd arranged in a perfect circle on the plate. The tea had been so weak it was like drinking hot water and milk, Fiona recalled. But they'd been so eager to please, and so determined to entertain her without disturbing their mother. Fiona thought of her own son Stuart, who seemed to become more uncommunicative and disdainful of his parents every day. He was now at Oban High and stayed on the mainland during the week. Sometimes Fiona felt guiltily grateful for his absence. She had thought he might have left something for her birthday—a card or a present, even—but, though she allowed herself a discreet check of the house yesterday, feeling very foolish, she found nothing, and when she'd called him up in the evening as usual, Stuart had made no mention of her birthday until she brought it up herself. Then he wished her many happy returns, and asked politely, as you might address a distant, elderly relative, if she'd had a nice day. Fiona found herself in a rage after she'd hung up the phone, not with her son but with her husband, who, she felt, should not have allowed this to happen. When it was Gavin's birthday, she always ensured Stuart had a card for him at the very least. Men were not considerate like women. She wondered how Katrina's sons would turn out, if they too would grow hulking and hostile overnight. Stuart used to pick wild flowers for her on his way home from school.

Fiona retrieved her torch at last from the inside zip-pocket of her jacket and watched as Katrina and the children vanished inside the house. Nicky was the last to go, pausing to lay two long sticks carefully by the back door, presumably so he and Tommy could resume whatever game they were playing the next day. The back door closed behind them and a moment later the outside light was switched off. Fiona pictured the Baird family cocooned together in the brightness and warmth of their house. She hoped Gavin had remembered to leave the porch light on for her when she got back, but he often did not. The wind was rising. She knew it would be a rough night.

Later, when questioned by the police, Fiona gave the time she passed the Baird house on her way to the bins as around 5.35 P.M., and the second time as six P.M. She hadn't looked at her watch during the walk, but she did remember looking at the clock in her kitchen shortly after arriving home, and it was 6.20 P.M. It was about a fifteen-minute walk between her own house and the Bairds'. Fiona's information proved important. She was the last person to see the family alive.

When Nicky and Tommy Baird didn't turn up for school the next day, their teacher, Aileen Brown, tried to call Katrina at home. There was no answer. Aileen tried again at intervals throughout the morning, but still nobody picked up. As the single permanent teacher in a school with only five pupils, Aileen had no one to consult, and as the morning wore on, she became more and more uneasy. It wasn't like Katrina Baird to keep her boys home and not call in.

During the last lesson before lunch, while Angus and the Wilson twins were working on their Viking longboat models, Aileen dug out the number of the firm in Oban where John worked as an accountant. But the receptionist who answered sounded surprised. She said John hadn't worked there for some time.

After lunch, Aileen cracked and rang her husband at his surgery, asking if he could drive round to the Bairds' house to check everything was all right. Greg Brown thought his wife was overreacting, but he didn't want her worrying all through the afternoon—once she'd got an idea in her head, it tended to get stuck there—and although he was the island's only doctor, he had no patients that day. He set off immediately. It was a twenty-minute drive to the Bairds' house on the other side of the island, and he arrived there shortly after two P.M.

Later that day, once the worst of his shock had worn off and he'd had several cups of sweet tea and was sitting with two police officers in the McKenzies' house, Greg would try to reconstruct very carefully what happened upon his arrival at the Bairds' house. Still, there were some parts he was unable articulate, even once Aileen had arrived and was sitting next to him, ashen faced, holding his hand. Some things you could not put into words.

When there was no answer to his ringing of the doorbell, Greg had waited for a couple of minutes and then rung again. It occurred to him that perhaps the doorbell was broken, so he tried banging the knocker a few times. Still there was no answer, and Greg concluded that the family must be out for the day. Nevertheless, and mainly so he could tell Aileen he'd done a thorough job, he decided to go and knock on the back door.

Passing round the side of the house, he happened to glance through the kitchen window. What he caught sight of within made him stop dead, though at first he couldn't process what he was seeing. They're decorating, he remembered thinking (this part was so absurd he never shared it with anyone). But why choose red?

Then he felt his whole body go cold. The sun was nowhere

to be seen, but it was a bright day beneath a white sky and reflections against the window broke up his view. However, Greg could see enough to realize that the kitchen was awash with blood. For a few moments, he didn't move at all. Then he made himself put his face closer to the window, and cupped his hands round his eyes to block out the reflections. A red room. Blood all over the floor, glossy and bright around the bodies where it must still be wet; darker, dryer-looking near the corners of the room. Blood sprinkled and spattered in bright patterns across the far wall in a way that reminded Greg of his children's efforts at abstract art.

In the middle of this explosion of red, Katrina was on the floor on her back, legs bent, one arm above her head as though she'd collapsed in a faint. Greg knew it was Katrina by that purple jumper she often wore, dense and heavy now with blood, and by the red hair which fanned out around her like she was floating underwater. It took him a few moments to absorb the fact that half of her head was missing, replaced with empty space and dark pulp and glistening red. "Obscene" was the word that came to Greg afterwards when he thought about this moment, seeing a human body as it wasn't meant to be seen, even by a doctor, as a carcass, a lump of bloodied meat.

But it was Beth whom he would never afterwards be able to get out of his mind, even though he barely saw her, barely allowed himself to see her. He had caught sight of her immediately, lying not too far from her mother, closer to the kitchen door, but he didn't let his eyes do anything more than drift quickly over her and away again. He had time to observe that her eyes were open. Her chest open too, a dark red sinkhole in her small torso. What kind of man turns a shotgun on a baby?

Greg knew that if he entered it, the room would have that heavy smell of raw meat, of blood, of the abattoir.

All the same, he forced himself to try the back door, his hands shaking so much they kept slipping off the handle. It was locked and he could have wept with relief. The only thing he had grasped in his shock was that whatever else was inside that house, he couldn't bear to see it.

Greg stumbled back to his car and drove to the McKenzies', the Bairds' nearest neighbours, to call the police and an ambulance. As he heard himself telling Gavin McKenzie what he'd seen, Greg wondered if this high, panicked voice was really his own.

Since there was no permanent police presence on the island, it was over an hour before the helicopter arrived from Oban and police broke down the door of the Bairds' house.

Inside, they found the bodies of thirty-four-year-old Katrina Baird, her one-year-old daughter Elizabeth, her ten-year-old son Nicholas and her thirty-seven-year-old husband John. All had died from shotgun wounds. There was one survivor, eight-year-old Thomas, who was found crouching in the wardrobe of his parents' bedroom in a pool of his own urine, in a state that appeared almost catatonic.

Greg would afterwards say to Aileen, over and over, "I should have gone in and got him. He had to stay there for another hour. Alone in that house. I should have got him out."

And Aileen would say, "You couldn't, my darling."

And Greg would say, "I should have broken a window."

And Aileen would say again, "You couldn't."

The Browns sold their house and moved to Harris two years later, where Greg joined the thriving Harris GP practice. Escaping the claustrophobia of Litta for a much larger island was a relief. They didn't say they left because of the Bairds, even to each other, but Greg knew he would never get little Beth out of his head if they stayed put, and Aileen knew it too. (Greg never did anyway, not even after their teenage boys finished high school and the Browns left the Hebrides for good and moved to Edinburgh.)

There were many details about the killings that remained a

mystery afterwards, but some central facts were established during the early days of the investigation. They were these: some time shortly after eight P.M. on Tuesday, 8th March 1994, John Baird, described by all who knew him as a quiet man who was devoted to his family, took a double-barrelled shotgun and used it to murder his wife and two of his children, before turning the gun on himself.

Tommy, when he was finally able to speak, was unable to provide a coherent account of events, but he was able to identify his father as the killer. John's brother Malcolm, who lived with his wife three miles away to the west of the island, was brought to identify the bodies and to take charge of Tommy.

There had never before been a murder on the island. There had never been any serious crime at all. In that tiny community, everybody knew everybody else, and everyone had liked the Bairds. John, it was agreed by all, had been a decent family man who'd gone out of his way to help his neighbours, and had always been considerate and polite. Nobody, at first, could believe he was responsible, and rumours circulated about an outsider breaking in and staging the killings. But the police were quick to stamp this out. The evidence against John was overwhelming, even without Tommy's confirmation, and the police didn't want panic spreading about a fictional killer still at large. They were clear with the public: nobody else was being sought in connection with the deaths. Besides, the islanders themselves had to concede that there was no way a stranger could have made their way across Litta without being seen, and widely discussed, within moments of their arrival.

But something must have happened, people said. Something must have made John snap. Nobody could say what, beyond the fact that, as it came out later, he had lost his job a few months before and was in some debt. Plenty of men lost their jobs and didn't go on to murder their wife and children. Perhaps Katrina had been having an affair, some people suggested, but how could this possibly have been the case? Nothing stayed hidden on the island. Still, he must have been driven to it somehow or other; ordinary men don't suddenly go off the deep end like that. Not without provocation.

Some things you could never get your head round, however many years passed. Perhaps it was true, the islanders conceded at last, hardly sure if they meant it or not, that you could never really know anyone else, not even your own neighbours, not even your own family.

PART 1

1

When Gavin McKenzie came home from the pub, wiping his boots on the mat with that slow deliberation that meant he was half-cut, he said to his wife, "Tommy Baird's back on the island."

It wasn't that she didn't recognize the name; no one would forget a thing like that. But the mention of it was so unexpected that for a few seconds Fiona's mind was blank. Then she saw him again, his serious little face as he stood in the shop with his mother, those bright cagoules he and his brother wore. Fiona was sixty-three, but her memory was as sharp as ever.

"Wee Tommy Baird?" she said. "Surely not."

"He's not so wee now," Gavin said, taking off his wet coat and disappearing for a moment as he went to hang it up. "Must be thirty or more," his voice came from the hallway.

Fiona was silent, calculating. Her own Stuart was thirty-nine this year. Already on his second marriage, the one they hoped might stick, though they'd liked Joanne very much. "Thirty-one," she brought out. "I think he must be thirty-one." She stopped, trying to take it in. Then, "What's he doing back here?"

Gavin, coming into the room, shrugged. "I know no more than you," he said, which was absurd given that he was the one telling her the news. "Ross saw him on the ferry this morning, coming over from Oban."

Fiona allowed herself to relax a little at this. "Well, if it was only Ross! Are we to take his word for everything now? He'd barely know his own wife if she was standing beside him."

"He spoke to him," Gavin said, leaning against the door-frame. "Ross spoke to Tommy. There were only the two of them on the ferry. You know how Ross is, seeing a stranger, especially this time of year. Went up and introduced himself. Asked Tommy if he was on holiday."

"And Tommy—he said who he was?" Fiona said.

"Aye. Though Ross said he'd worked it out already, soon as he got closer, before Tommy even spoke."

Fiona couldn't explain why she suddenly felt hot and cold all over. "Ross is all talk," she said. Then, as another thought occurred to her, "He might be lying. The stranger."

Gavin did that frown of his she hated, and which he seemed to reserve especially for her; it wasn't contemptuous, Gavin was too gentle for that, but his look of utter bafflement felt worse, as though he was still amazed, after all this time, at the silly things she said. "Now why on earth would someone lie about a thing like that?"

Fiona had no answer for this. If there was one thing she'd learned from the Baird tragedy, it was that people acted in ways that could not be explained, that sometimes could barely even be imagined. "But why come back now?"

"I expect he's visiting Malcolm."

"Malcolm hasn't seen him in years."

"Still, family's family."

Fiona thought, but did not say, that 'family' might have a more complicated meaning for Tommy Baird than it did for the rest of them.

Gavin stomped through to the kitchen and Fiona heard him clattering about, making tea. "I'll have a cup too," she called, not holding out high hopes of receiving one; he was getting deafer by the year and he didn't make one for her routinely anymore. Other women her age joked about having trained their husbands up nicely, but with Fiona it seemed to have gone the other way.

However, a few minutes later he did bring two mugs through, placing hers, a little sloppily, on the table beside her before he settled into his own armchair by the fire.

"The funny thing is," he said, as though there had been no pause in their conversation, "Malcolm never said anything about it. He was in the bar yesterday and he didn't say a word about Tommy coming."

"Maybe he wasn't expecting him," Fiona said, further alarmed at this idea.

There was a long silence, broken only by Gavin slurping his tea. Fiona tried to focus on the crackling of the fire and not the wet sounds coming from her husband. It was a technique she'd taught herself years before. And she reminded herself that he was a good man, that he was kind, that he'd always been patient with Stuart. That patience wasn't the same as weakness.

"Tommy Baird," Gavin said eventually, in a meditative way. "I never felt right about him."

"What do you mean?" Fiona said, the hot and cold feeling back.

"I felt like—we should have known, somehow. Don't you think? We should have known. Done something, maybe."

"Don't be stupid," Fiona said, more angrily than she'd intended. "What could we have done?" Firmly, with the air of someone closing the discussion, she said, "It doesn't help to dwell on a terrible thing like that."

She had seen that family almost every day, almost every day for ten years, and she had missed it all. She could never have predicted—but nobody could.

And she remembered Tommy afterwards, too. She saw him at ten or eleven, his face contorted in rage, hurling something at her—a vase, had it been? Something of Heather's, something that had smashed just beside her head. He was a demon by then.

"Shall we have some of the coffee cake?" she said to Gavin, trying to soften the way she'd spoken before, trying to quieten the memory of Tommy. "It'll be stale before we're halfway through it."

"Aye," he said. "That'd be nice."

There could have been no predicting what happened, Fiona told herself again as she went into the kitchen and got the tin down from the larder, cut Gavin a large slice and herself a small one. And in any case, as she always reassured herself (it wasn't very reassuring), nobody ever knew what went on behind closed doors.

2

No, Malcolm wasn't expecting him. When he opened the door in the late afternoon, the darkness already thickening, and saw Tommy standing there, he was so shocked that for a few moments he couldn't even speak.

Of course, Tommy looked different. He was a grown man now, utterly transformed from when he'd last stood there. But Malcolm would know him anywhere, even after all this time. The worst of it was this: the boy hadn't grown up to look like Katrina. No, it was John he resembled, with those dark brown eyes, the hard lines of his jaw. Tommy had the same light build as his father, too. The overall resemblance was uncanny. Malcolm could only hope Tommy didn't realize.

It had been raining, though only lightly—a rare kind of rain for them here. But the man on his doorstep wasn't properly dressed for any kind of weather in the Hebrides, wearing only jeans and a jersey, with trainers on his feet (the thin canvas kind, too). There was a rucksack on his shoulder, but it didn't look to Malcolm like it could have much in it—certainly not proper boots and a waterproof.

"Tommy," Malcolm said, because now that seemed like the only possible thing to say.

And the man said, meeting his eye and then not meeting it again, "Hello, Malcolm."

There was a short silence, then Malcolm said, "Won't you come in?" It was the phrase Heather would have used, and for a few seconds he was breathless with missing her. But he was distracted by this stranger—not a stranger, not really—stepping past him across the threshold, and then Tommy was standing in his house for the first time in twenty years.

Tommy said, "I hope you don't mind . . ." Then he stopped, looking around the narrow hallway as though surprised to find himself there. It must seem even smaller to him now, Malcolm thought—the adult Tommy took up so much more space than the child.

Tommy put his hands in his pockets and rolled his shoulders back. Then he began again. "I know it's weird, just turning up here. I should have called, or written a letter, or . . . emailed or something." He gave a short laugh that didn't sound like a laugh. "Of course, I don't have your email. Not your phone number, either. Couldn't find it."

"I don't have email," Malcolm said, thinking how strange it was to hear a man's deep voice coming from Tommy, coming out from behind a man's face—John's face. Tommy's accent was unexpected too. It was unplaceable, not quite Scottish, not quite English, carrying only the faintest inflection of his past. "Never really caught up with all that," Malcolm added, realizing he'd been silent for too long. "Heather was better at it. She had her own email account, her own laptop." He stopped, aware that now he was only talking to fill up the space around his discomfort.

"Where is Heather?" Tommy said, looking past Malcolm towards the kitchen, as though she might actually be waiting there. And Malcolm realized with a lurch like rising sickness that Tommy knew nothing, knew absolutely nothing, that they had been cut off from one another so completely that Tommy might as well have been laid beneath the earth all these years, to now suddenly reappear, to come back from the dead and stand calmly in Malcolm's hallway, brushing off the dirt and asking about Heather.

No way to soften it, not for either of them. "She died,"

Malcolm said. "Almost six years ago now." The words weren't so worn around the edges that they didn't hurt him. He had made a final attempt, after Heather's death, to contact Tommy, but found that the only number he had, which was for Tommy's cousin Henry, no longer worked. He had been too bound up in his own grief to feel much dismay at the time. Anyway, he had given Tommy up long ago.

"A stroke," he told Tommy now. "Two, in fact. Both bad. She survived a few years after the first, but then she had another." Then he added, because Tommy was staring at him without speaking, "She was still herself though. Right up to the end."

"But—she must have been *young*," Tommy said, and Malcolm was surprised to see him stricken like this. Because what had Heather been to Tommy in the end?

"Aye," Malcolm said. "Too young."

Tommy was silent.

Malcolm remembered himself and said, "Come on into the kitchen. You'll have a cup of tea?"

"Yes. Please."

"Put your bag down there for now," Malcolm said, nodding towards the boot rack by the door, and Tommy did as he was told before following Malcolm through to the small kitchen.

How long would he be staying? Malcolm wondered, trying not to feel panicked. He'd have to stay two nights, at least; there wasn't a ferry back to the mainland until Friday. The spare room was in a state—full of dust, with books and clutter piled up to the ceiling. Malcolm tried to think what Heather would do. Nothing could ever fluster his wife. She would tell him to take it one step at a time and make the lad some tea. So while Tommy sat at the table, Malcolm steadied himself with the familiar routine of filling the kettle, getting out mugs and the tea bags, fetching the milk from the fridge. He was grateful for the noise as the old kettle came to the boil;

impossible to have any kind of conversation over the top of that.

He risked a glance at Tommy. He was sitting quietly, both hands placed in front of him on the table, as though he were a child making a conscious effort to keep still. But his eyes slid around the room, coming back to rest on his hands only when he seemed to sense Malcolm was looking. Malcolm wondered if the place appeared different to him. He cast his mind back, but couldn't recall whether it had changed since Tommy had left. Probably not. He and Heather had never really gone in for—what was it you called them?—*home improvements*. They'd always had plenty of other things to be getting on with. The room must look old fashioned to Tommy, dated and drab, with its ancient gas stove and the cheap laminate, which had chipped off the counter in places. Malcolm wasn't used to seeing his own home through the eyes of an outsider.

"How do you take your tea?" he said.

"Just milk. Please."

Malcolm brought the mugs over and sat across from Tommy. His *nephew*, his mind threw out.

He said, "I was so sorry to hear about Jill. It was a terrible loss."

"I was a long way away," Tommy said. There was a silence, and just when Malcolm thought Tommy wasn't going to say anything else, he added, "I got back in time, though. Just in time. Saw her before she died."

Malcolm nodded. "We were sad not to be able to make it down for the funeral," he said. "Heather wasn't well enough."

"It's fine."

The funeral would have been their first opportunity to see Tommy in years. Heather had so badly wanted to go. They'd eventually got through to Henry on the house phone, who'd come back from Canada for the final stages of his mother's illness. He said he'd ask Tommy to ring them back, but for whatever reason, Tommy never had, and their letters had gone unanswered.

"Poor, poor bairn," Heather had said, almost in tears, when they first learned the finality of Jill's diagnosis. "Hasn't he lost enough people already? And poor Jill. She's still so young." Of course they didn't know then that Heather herself would die at the same age.

Malcolm wondered if there was anything they could talk about besides death. But what was there to say? You couldn't ask someone why they'd come, could you, when it was your own family? *No, you could not,* Heather's voice told him firmly. *Leave it to Tommy to explain when he's ready.*

"How's Henry?" Malcolm said after a moment, relieved to have thought of a new topic.

Tommy shrugged. "He's fine. We don't speak much." Then, apparently feeling he had to offer more, he added, "He's married now. They live in Vancouver. Two kids."

"That's nice," Malcolm said, trying to recall Henry's face.

Tommy nodded and once more lapsed into silence. This time, Malcolm could not think how to break it.

But at last, Tommy said, "How's the croft doing?"

Malcolm wondered where the shame came from, sudden and acute, as though Tommy would care that the croft was gone, as though he would have come back for that. He said, "I had to sell the tenancy. When Heather got ill. It was too hard to manage, and it wasn't making us enough money. Not any money at all, really. And I needed to be with her."

Tommy said, his voice low, "I'm sorry about Heather. I really am."

Malcolm nodded. Six years, and he was still no good at knowing what to do with consolation. There was no consolation.

"And you?" he said, stirring himself, thinking of the questions Heather would ask. "Are you married?"

Tommy shook his head, and seemed almost about to smile,

before thinking better of it. "No. Not me." A pause, then he added, "I was with someone. Her name was Caroline."

"Oh no," Malcolm said. "She didn't . . . ?"

And now Tommy really did smile, a strange upwards pull of his mouth that Malcolm didn't recognize. "No, she didn't die. We broke up."

"Sorry to hear that," Malcolm said, hearing the formal note that had crept into his voice. But he felt foolish for assuming relationships only ever ended in death. "Any children?"

"No." There was no smile now.

Malcolm watched Tommy across the table, but Tommy volunteered nothing further, just sat there with his hands around his mug, as though nothing had happened, as though he was still eleven years old and had never left, had just been sitting here quietly all this time while Malcolm went about his business and failed to notice him.

"Where are you living these days?" Malcolm said.

"London."

"How long you been there?"

"While now," Tommy said. He paused, then added, "I've been here and there. Tried Edinburgh for a while. Manchester. Even Lisbon." He squinted, as though seeing the brightness again. "Never did get used to the sun."

"I've never been to Portugal," Malcolm said.

"Have you ever left Scotland?"

Malcolm looked at Tommy, but his face gave nothing away.

"No," Malcolm said. "I never have. Furthest I've been is Edinburgh."

Tommy nodded.

"We were planning a trip to Spain," Malcolm said. "Me and Heather. Not to lie on a beach or anything. Heather wanted to see Barcelona. The—" he couldn't for the life of him remember the name, though it had sounded beautiful, the way it had unfolded and dropped off Heather's tongue—"cathedral. And all the rest. We were all set to book the hotel, but then Heather had the stroke. Her first one."

Someone else might have said they were sorry again, but Tommy made no comment, and Malcolm was grateful.

There was a pause, then Malcolm said, "Did you stay overnight in Oban?"

"Yes. I got the train up to Glasgow yesterday, then on to Oban last night. I wanted to be in good time for the ferry." He hesitated, then said with a sudden stiffness that made his words sound rehearsed, "I'm sorry to drop in on you like this. I was wondering if I could stay for a while. A week, perhaps. If I'm not in your way."

"Of course, Tommy," Malcolm said, hiding his anxiety beneath a heartiness that sounded false, even to himself. "That would be nice."

"Only if it's O.K.," Tommy said, not looking at him.

"Of course," Malcolm said again. "This is your home."

Not exactly the right thing to say. Tommy looked at him, and Malcolm, returning the look, thought, All right, I know.

"Let's sort out your room," he said. "Then I'll get started on tea."

He led Tommy up the narrow staircase and they stopped outside the first door. It was an old crofter's cottage, modernized in the sixties and pretty much left alone since then. It retained its low, beamed ceilings, fireplace and latched doors, as well as its draughts. There were only three rooms upstairs, barely crammed in under the sloping roof: the tiny spare room at the top of the stairs, then Malcolm and Heather's bedroom, and then the bathroom at the end of the short corridor. The spare room had been Tommy's room once, though Malcolm hadn't thought of it that way for many years now. He and Heather used to hear Tommy through the wall during those few years he lived with them, shouting in his sleep. Tommy never remembered his dreams after Heather woke him. Said he didn't, anyway. He'd wet the bed too, not every night, but often, certainly, right up until he left the island. He'd be furious in his shame while Heather soothed him, telling him in her sensible way that it didn't matter, that sheets could be changed, pyjamas could be changed, wasn't that what washing machines were for? It wasn't the end of the world, was it? Heather had said Tommy's bad dreams would stop as he got older and the past got further away, but Malcolm thought differently (he had identified the bodies; he had nightmares of his own).

Reaching out to open the door now, Malcolm wondered how much of this Tommy remembered. The room looked even more of a mess than he'd feared. It had been a long time since they'd given up thinking Tommy might come back to see them, and of course they'd never had children of their own. They'd kept the single bed, mainly because it had seemed too much bother to get rid of, but it hadn't been made up for years, and now the mattress was hidden under stacks of books and old magazines. Boxes covered the floor, packed with things they didn't want but had never got round to throwing out: a broken radio he had once thought he might fix, the Dairy Diaries Heather's sister used to send her each Christmas that Heather kept afterwards for the recipes (which she never used), an old train set from Malcolm's childhood that he felt oddly sentimental about, travel brochures that Heather had held on to because she said she liked to look at the pictures. All the detritus that came from living so long in one place.

There were a few boxes of Heather's things too: her clothes and some of her jewellery that Malcolm had kept, plus an unfinished bottle of scent; he still crept in here from time to time to hold this bottle guiltily to his nose, overwhelmed by the sense of his wife's simultaneous presence and absence. He could never have thrown it all away, but he had felt more recently that it was strange to keep everything in its usual place in their bedroom, her dresses and shoes still in the wardrobe, her hairspray and moisturizing cream on the dresser. Perhaps, he thought, it wasn't "healthy", that word people seemed so keen to use these days. That had been the view of Fiona McKenzie, at any rate—a kind woman, but someone who always thought she knew best. Packing it up into the spare room had seemed like a good compromise.

The whole room smelled musty and airless—*old*, Malcolm thought. Like him, he supposed. He was sixty-two, and felt older.

"I'll have to clear a few things out," he said, and then almost laughed at the understatement.

"I don't mind the mess," Tommy said.

"We can put some of it in the shed. Not too damp this time of year, and I can cover it with the tarpaulin."

For the next half hour, they worked silently together, carrying boxes and carrier bags downstairs and outside in the dark to the small shed by the back door. Stealthily, while Tommy was outside, Malcolm transferred several of the Heather boxes, including the one with the scent, into his own bedroom, placing them carefully at the bottom of the wardrobe.

By the time most of the floor was clear and the bed was bare, both men were sneezing. Malcolm went over to the bed and knelt on the mattress to wrench open the sash window above it—it was stiff, the wood warped, and it took him a few hefts to get it open. The night came into the room, bringing with it the damp of rain.

"Get some air in here," he said. "Sorry about the dust." He looked around again. "Needs a good vacuum."

"I'll do it," Tommy said.

"Right, O.K.," Malcolm said. He fetched the vacuum cleaner from the airing cupboard and while Tommy was occupied with that, went in search of fresh sheets for the bed, and the spare duvet and pillows he knew Heather had kept somewhere. Finally he tracked it all down, crammed into the top of the cupboard in their bedroom. He'd been afraid everything would have a faintly mildewed smell, but Heather had packed it all away carefully, the duvet and pillows folded into a large plastic bag. The woman had been a wonder.

Tommy had turned off the vacuum cleaner and was leaning on it, surveying his handiwork, when Malcolm returned to the spare room. "Not so bad now," Tommy said.

"No. It's much better," Malcolm said. He remembered Tommy as a child then, dusting for Heather or doing the washing up, always wanting his work to be noticed. Malcolm looked around the room again, feeling faintly ridiculous to be making a show of it. "Almost unrecognizable."

Tommy unplugged the vacuum cleaner and wound up the cord while Malcolm took the bedding over to the bed. But when Malcolm began to spread out the sheet, Tommy said, "I'll do it," and came over as if to take the sheet from him.

"It's all right. Leave it to me."

"No, it's fine. I'll make it up."

Malcolm stepped back, surprised at Tommy's insistence. He wondered if Tommy was remembering how many times Malcolm or Heather had remade this bed for him as a child, and hoped it wasn't that.

Taking the vacuum cleaner downstairs, he spotted Tommy's rucksack in the hall, lying by the boot rack. When Malcolm picked it up, it felt very light. Hadn't Tommy brought anything with him apart from the clothes he stood up in? They seemed inadequate enough.

Back in the spare room, Tommy was kneeling by the bed, tucking the sheet carefully under the corners of the mattress.

"I brought your bag," Malcolm said unnecessarily, putting it down just inside the door and feeling as though he'd overstepped the mark, had somehow invaded Tommy's privacy.

"Thanks," Tommy said.

There was a short silence.

"Bathroom's just along the hall," Malcolm said.

"I know. I remember."

"Of course." There was another pause, then Malcolm said, "Well, I'll go and see about tea. Come down whenever you're ready. No rush."

He left the room, closing the door gently behind him.

In the kitchen, Malcolm surveyed the contents of his fridge. He was still so shocked by Tommy's arrival that it took him a while to get his thoughts in order. He'd been going to heat up the remains of the chicken pie he'd made a couple of days ago, but there weren't really enough leftovers for two. He had potatoes, he thought, with sudden inspiration: with a baked potato each and some vegetables, the pie would stretch. From upstairs, he heard the clatter and churn of the water pipes as the shower started up, and was grateful to know Tommy wouldn't reappear for a while.

The meal was almost ready and the table laid by the time Tommy came in. His hair was damp from the shower, but he was wearing the same red checked shirt, jersey and jeans as before. Tommy hovered awkwardly at the door for a few moments, until Malcolm said, "Have a seat." It occurred to him then that he ought to offer Tommy a drink, but not being much of a drinker himself, he only had a bottle of whisky and some very old sherry from before Heather died. The whisky, he supposed, would have to do, but when he made the offer, couched in apology that there was no beer or wine, Tommy swiftly declined.

Malcolm busied himself putting food on the plates, saying, "It's not much—just leftovers. You're not a vegetarian, are you?" he added, the idea only just coming to him.

"No."

Malcolm watched his nephew touching the cutlery in front

of him, shifting the fork slightly, running a finger down the handle of the knife, though whether out of nervousness or absent-mindedness, Malcolm couldn't tell. Tommy seemed to become aware of himself, and stilled his hands on the table, placing one on top of the other. He looked exhausted, Malcolm thought. The shadows under his eyes were almost livid, but the rest of his face had that paleness that wasn't quite natural, that made you think of the sick or the dead.

Malcolm brought the plates over. Tommy probably needed a decent meal and a good night's sleep, he thought, unsure whether these were his own words or Heather's.

They sat across from each other and ate in silence. Malcolm didn't mind this. He'd never distrusted silence the way Heather had, never felt the need to speak for the sake of talking. But he wasn't accustomed, anymore, to eating with someone else present. He felt conscious of the failings Heather used to point out, which must surely have grown worse in her absence: hunching over his food, elbows on the table, not laying his cutlery down between mouthfuls as Heather had always insisted was polite.

But Tommy's table manners weren't exactly refined either. He ate quickly, head down, as though completing a chore as swiftly as possible. Or else he was ravenous, Malcolm thought.

Tommy said eventually, his food almost finished, "Did you make this yourself? The pie?"

Malcolm nodded, mouth full.

"It's nice," Tommy said.

"It was better a couple of days ago," Malcolm said, swallowing. "Doesn't reheat so well."

"I don't remember you cooking much," Tommy said. "I remember Heather doing it all."

Malcolm was surprised at how intimate this comment felt, how swiftly and painfully the past rose up between them. There was Tommy as a child, sitting right where he was now,

Heather fussing around him, Malcolm silent, letting her get on with it.

"I learned after Heather died," he said. "Had to. Wasn't so hard in the end. You just find a recipe and follow the instructions. There's no magic there." He paused, feeling as though he'd been disloyal to Heather without meaning to. "But I can't cook the way she could. I get by, that's all."

Tommy nodded and said nothing else. He'd finished his food and put his cutlery down on the table. After a moment, he seemed to remember himself and picked up his knife and fork, aligning them neatly on the plate. Then he leaned his head on his hand. He looked like he was falling asleep at the table.

Malcolm finished the remnants of his own meal and glanced discreetly at the clock on the wall. It was only eight thirty. Usually now he'd make a cup of tea and read a book in the living room or put the TV on. He wondered how Tommy spent his evenings, but couldn't begin to picture it.

He stood up to clear the plates, but Tommy said, in a way that was swiftly becoming familiar, "I'll do it."

"Just leave them on the side," Malcolm said. "I'll wash them tomorrow morning." Leaving the washing up until the next day was one of the small luxuries he'd allowed himself since Heather's death. Other than that, he'd been fairly strict about keeping to her routines.

Tommy rinsed the plates and cutlery carefully and put them by the sink. Then he stayed where he was, leaning against the counter.

Malcolm said, "Would you like a cup of tea? We could see what's on the TV, or I have the papers to look at . . ." (Three days out of date, he remembered, which wasn't bad for out here, though he wasn't sure Tommy would see it that way.)

But Tommy said, "Actually, if you don't mind, I think I'll go to bed. It's been a long day."

"Of course," Malcolm said, careful to hide his relief. "Have you got everything you need?"

Tommy nodded. "I'll just take a glass of water up."

He'd done that as a child too, Malcolm recalled. But it was a habit for many people. "You know where everything is," he said, unsure whether this was a question or a statement of fact.

"Yes."

"Well. Goodnight."

"Goodnight," Tommy said. He paused a moment longer, then got himself a glass of water and left the room.

Alone at the kitchen table, Malcolm breathed out a slow sigh. He was glad Tommy was turning in early, avoiding the awkwardness of their carrying out their bedtime routines at the same time, stepping politely past each other on the narrow landing on their way to the bathroom, taking it in turns to brush their teeth, each clad in pyjamas.

He went to put the kettle on and longed again for Heather. She would have known what to do; she would have made all this feel easier. Malcolm allowed himself to admit, just in this moment, just while he was alone, that he did not want Tommy in his house. He knew—he would be the first to say it—how many ways he'd failed that boy. How many ways they all had. But still, he did not want Tommy here, this young man he did not know but who looked so eerily like John. He did not want to talk to him and he did not want to remember. Most of all, he didn't want to acknowledge that by the time Tommy had left the island, Malcolm had started to feel afraid of him, however much he'd battled the feeling, however much he'd hated himself for it, reminding himself that Tommy was just a child, and such a damaged one at that. But there had been violence in Tommy by then. He had already started to hurt people.

Nevertheless, Heather would have been desperately glad Tommy had come back, and so Malcolm tried to see it this way too. Heather had always been so much better, so much kinder and braver, than everybody else. It must have been a terrible blow to Tommy, Malcolm realized, to return here and find Heather gone. Of course it had not been Malcolm he had come to see.

But besides Tommy's cousin in Canada, they were each other's only living family now. That counted for something. And perhaps family still meant something to Tommy as well, even now, even after everything that had happened. What else might have brought him back here, twenty years later, all this way across the sea? *Blood runs thicker than water.* The phrase came unbidden into Malcolm's head. It was not an expression he liked. He had spent many years trying not to think about blood.

3

Malcolm had been awake for almost five hours by the time Tommy emerged the next morning. Two of these hours, granted, had been spent lying in bed, where he'd jerked awake a little after five A.M. and lain panicking over what to do about Tommy. But since seven, he'd been in the kitchen drinking tea and reading the paper. There was no work to do that day. He'd helped Robert Nairne on his farm ever since giving up the croft, but the silage was made—they'd grabbed the two dry days last week and worked through the night—and Robert's son was staying for one more day, so he could help his father round up the last of the lambs. October was a relatively quiet month. The next day, Malcolm would go round to help with repairs. He had originally set aside today to catch up on various odd jobs around the house and do his shopping. Now here was Tommy.

Malcolm tried to be as quiet as possible as he showered and dressed—all the rooms felt so close together in the cottage—but by eight thirty there were still no sounds from Tommy's room. Malcolm resumed his seat at the kitchen table, but found it hard to settle.

Finally, around ten, he heard Tommy's door opening, footsteps along the landing, and then the sound of the bathroom door opening and closing. Malcolm winced at the intimacy of this set-up. He got to his feet quickly and ran the taps, washing his mug and cereal bowl, and was relieved when he turned them off to hear the sound of the shower starting up.

Fifteen minutes later, he heard Tommy on the stairs, and steeled himself to appear casual when his nephew entered the kitchen. Tommy was dressed in the same clothes as the day before. Malcolm wondered if he should offer to lend him something, but wasn't sure how. Tommy did look a little better than he had the previous evening, his face less pale, the bruises beneath his eyes less pronounced.

"Did you sleep well?" Malcolm said.

Tommy nodded, running his hand across the stubble on his chin. He said, "I forgot how you hear the weather out here."

Malcolm nodded. "The wind was up last night."

"I listened to it as I was falling asleep. You feel so close to the wind and the rain. You don't notice it so much in cities."

"More traffic noise instead, I expect," Malcolm said. He paused, then added, "Cars and so on." He wondered if all their exchanges would be like this, if in the absence of Heather he had forgotten how to make normal conversation. He said, more briskly, "I have to visit the shop this morning. Do you want to come? We could go in the car, or perhaps get a bit of a walk."

Tommy shrugged. "Sure. A walk would be good."

Setting out together an hour later, Tommy now wearing Malcolm's old waterproof and a spare pair of boots, they followed the track from Malcolm's cottage until it joined the island's single road, which circled the middle of the island in a loop. Once you ran out of road, you were reliant on finding your own way across the rocky hills and moorland, but the island was only eight miles by three miles across, and its crags and heaths, its cliffs and beaches and black rocks held few mysteries for its inhabitants.

Malcolm and Tommy followed the bottom of the road's loop from the west to the east side of the island. The walk was only an hour and the weather was damp but mild. For a while they continued in silence. Malcolm found himself looking around him more than he normally did, trying to see his home through Tommy's eyes. Hills rose up on either side of them, bracken and heather only half covering the protruding clusters of rocks. As they passed the sheep grazing on the croft that used to be his, Malcolm felt a greater pang than usual.

"How's Angus MacIntyre?" Tommy said at last. "Is he still on the island?"

Malcolm had to think for a few moments before he could place the name. "The lad at school with you?"

Tommy nodded.

"The MacIntyres left," Malcolm said. "Went to Mull, as I remember it, when Angus was a teenager. Don't know if they still live there now." He stopped, trying to dredge up more from the depths of his memory. "I think Moira left Joe in the end. Or perhaps that was just a rumour. Heather kept in touch for a while, but eventually . . . you know."

He felt Tommy glance round and then pause fractionally beside him, but it took him a few moments to work out why. They were on the east side of the island now, two thirds of the way through their walk, and were approaching the rough track that led to Tommy's old house.

Malcolm wasn't sure whether or not to comment, and decided to take his cue from Tommy. The house had been sold within a year of the murders. John had been in financial difficulties. All of that came out afterwards, Malcolm becoming caught up almost immediately in legal wrangling that bewildered and distressed him. The estate, he was told, was insolvent. The house had to be sold to pay off John's debts, and to pay the funeral bills; there was nothing left, in the end, for Tommy. It had been bought by an investor at auction and had lain empty for another two years, until it was sold again to Chris and Mary Dougdale, incomers who moved to the island from Stirling. They didn't arrive until Tommy had already left, though they knew the story, of course. But it didn't have the same reality for them as for the locals. Before the house was first auctioned, professional cleaners had to be hired to get out the blood.

When Tommy started to speak, Malcolm thought he would say something about the house. But all he said was, "What about the Wilson twins? Sophie and Millie. They were at school with us too."

"The Wilsons are still here," Malcolm said. "Una and James, at any rate. The girls both left after they finished school. Millie lives in Glasgow, married with a couple of children of her own." They were safely past the track now and he felt it disappearing behind them. "Sophie's down in London, working for a magazine or a newspaper. Happy, her parents say." Malcolm remembered the twins when they were young, with their matching plaits. Nice lasses. They still came back to visit their parents occasionally, Millie with her family in tow, Sophie sometimes with a boyfriend, and it was always good to see them. He said, "Young people don't stay long here. Not now. Most all of them leave as soon as they have the chance."

Tommy shrugged. "No jobs."

"Aye." But it wasn't just that, and Tommy knew it too.

"Does nobody work on the mainland?" Tommy said.

"No. You know how long the ferry takes, and it's not reliable."

There was a short pause, then Tommy said, "My father used to do it."

Malcolm took his time in replying. He did not look round at Tommy. At last he said, "Your father had his own ideas about how things should be done."

They finished the walk in silence.

The island's single shop was located opposite the port in Orsaig, halfway down the east coast of Litta. This was the most populous area of the island, with fifteen houses within half a mile of the port, spread at intervals along the loop of the road that curved north from Orsaig, a scattering along the western approach too, and a few more down several tracks leading off the main road. With the post office next to the shop, as well as the port and the small crafts shop that was opened up to visitors in summer (when few visitors came), there were far more people coming and going around Orsaig than anywhere else on the island, where you could often walk for hours without meeting another soul.

Malcolm was surprised not to bump into anyone as he and Tommy approached the shop.

"You remember this?" he asked Tommy.

"Yeah." A pause, then, "After I came to live with you, I used to help Heather behind the counter sometimes. On her days."

"That's right." How easily Tommy had skimmed over it: *After I came to live with you.* Perhaps it was down to practice. Perhaps this ability to move round the edges of things had become part of his nature. Malcolm thought of Tommy emerging the day before from the semi-darkness outside his door, as though he had simply materialized there.

Kathy MacDonald, grey haired and solid, was behind the counter when Malcolm and Tommy entered the shop, and Malcolm saw the exact moment she recognized Tommy. First there was a faint look of curiosity on her face as she noted Malcolm coming in with a young stranger; then, as her brain worked out who he surely must be, the shock registered before she could quickly smooth it away.

"Malcolm," she said. "Not out on the farm today?"

"No, it's a free day for me."

"And this must be—surely it isn't Tommy?" And she smiled.

Malcolm was impressed by Kathy, as he so often had been in the past. She'd always had a way of carrying things off.

"That's right," he said. "This is Tommy. Back for a wee

visit." He felt reassured by how normal this made the situation sound.

It was unclear from Tommy's response whether or not he remembered Kathy. He said, "Hello," and put his hands in his pockets, his expression unreadable.

"Just stocking up on a few things," Malcolm said.

"And how are you keeping, Tommy?" Kathy said. "It's been a while."

"I'm fine."

"You living on the mainland?"

"Yes. Here and there," Tommy said.

Malcolm wondered if Tommy was aware of how evasive he sounded, as though he'd just been released from prison and was trying to conceal it. Then he thought, What if he *has* just been released from prison? Surely not.

Tommy was staring at the shelves of crisps and biscuits. "Stock's changed," he said, to no one in particular.

"Of course," Kathy said, and Malcolm was grateful again for her cheerfulness, how much more natural she made things feel. "We do make *some* effort to move with the times here."

Tommy nodded, and wandered over to the cheese fridge to inspect its contents.

Malcolm completed his shopping as quickly as possible, feeling absurdly self-conscious. "Is there anything you want, Tommy?" he called, but received a shake of the head in reply.

"Well, it's lovely to see you, Tommy," Kathy said, once Malcolm had paid and packed the shopping away in his rucksack. "Welcome home."

Tommy, already heading for the door, paused at this, and Malcolm saw, or thought he saw, his shoulders tense. But all Tommy said when he turned back to Kathy was, "Thanks."

Outside, he offered to take the rucksack from Malcolm, but Malcolm said, "I'm not infirm yet, lad."

As they began the walk back, Malcolm glanced towards the

coast. "You know, a seal colony's moved in on the rocks further south. Never seen them in that area before. If you fancy a walk another time, we might go and see if we can spot them. You used to have to go all the way down to the southern tip, didn't you?"

"Or north," Tommy said. "Nicky and I used to go north."

"Did you now? All the way up to Craigmore?" The northern reaches of the island were uninhabited.

"Yeah. The rocks were the best for climbing there."

This was the most he'd volunteered in a while, and Malcolm waited to see if he'd say more. But Tommy was silent again, staring out to sea.

As they were about to follow the bend of the road out of sight, Malcolm spotted Fiona McKenzie driving the shop's van down the northern stretch of the road, having finished the day's deliveries. He was grateful, at least, that they'd left without encountering her, although he knew Kathy would be sharing the news of Tommy as soon as Fiona entered the shop, both of them agog. Better, though, to put off any further meetings for now. Fiona didn't have Kathy's ease of manner, and Malcolm hadn't worked out how to account for Tommy's presence yet, even to himself.

And he looked so much like his father.

Sometimes at night Malcolm still dreamed of John, and the worst part of these nightmares was that they weren't nightmares at all. It would be an ordinary day, he and John as boys, kicking a football around or running along the beach; but Malcolm would wake in a cold sweat from these calm, pleasant scenarios, shaken by the knowledge that something terrible was going to happen, and even now he couldn't see it coming, not in the right way, not in a way that would help, even when it had already happened.

4

Later that afternoon, Tommy said to Malcolm, "Would it be all right if I used the washing machine?"

He stood in the doorway of the kitchen, holding his arms across his body: a self-protective gesture, it seemed to Malcolm.

"Of course."

Tommy appeared to hesitate. "I didn't bring many clothes. I'm not sure why. I suppose I was hurrying and . . . I wasn't thinking."

"We can put a load on now," Malcolm said. "But I have some things I can lend you, too."

He saw Tommy hesitating again over this, presumably weighing the awkwardness of borrowing his uncle's clothes against the awkwardness of having no clothes at all. Finally, he said, "O.K. Thanks."

While Tommy sorted out his washing, Malcolm went through the drawers in his bedroom, pulling out old jeans, T-shirts, a pullover, socks, and underwear (this part felt especially uncomfortable, but better Tommy had it than didn't, he decided). He left the clothes in a small, neat pile on Tommy's bed and went downstairs to see how Tommy was coping with the vagaries of his ancient washing machine.

"So connect the two tubes to the taps and check for leaks before you turn the taps on," he told Tommy.

"The kitchen taps?" Tommy said.

"That's right. It's not plumbed into the mains. And check

the bungee cord's securing the door before you switch the machine on. The catch is broken. And sometimes it stops halfway through the cycle, and then you just whack it a few times and it'll usually start up again." He paused, then added, "Oh, and ignore the rattling noise. There's some part loose but it doesn't seem to do any damage."

"Malcolm," Tommy said, frowning at the frayed bungee cord. "I don't want to overstep the mark, but . . . do you think it might be time you got a new washing machine?"

"You sound just like Heather," Malcolm said. "And I'll say to you what I always said to her. If it's getting the clothes clean, then what's the problem?"

"She was a patient woman," Tommy murmured, checking the door was secured, before gingerly turning on the taps and then the machine itself. The kitchen was immediately filled with a deafening rumbling and churning. Tommy leapt in shock and then laughed.

"This is a ridiculous machine," he said.

Malcolm decided not to be offended. He liked seeing Tommy laugh. Tommy was still grinning and shaking his head as he went back upstairs.

By the time Tommy reappeared, Malcolm had made a start on tea. Tommy was now dressed in an assortment of Malcolm's old clothes, and it seemed to embarrass him. Malcolm carefully avoided commenting, but he was glad to see Tommy wearing more sensible clothes, and especially a thick jersey.

"Beans on toast O.K.?" he said.

"Aye," Tommy said. "That'd be nice. Thank you." His accent had thickened slightly, Malcolm thought; he sounded more like a Scotsman now.

While Malcolm heated up the beans, Tommy hung around the kitchen, offering help sporadically, turning the pages of the newspaper that lay on the table without seeming to read any of it, and generally putting Malcolm on edge. Should have picked up beer in the shop, Malcolm thought. Something to offer Tommy, something to ease the atmosphere of awkward formality that seemed to have returned. But when he apologized and suggested getting some beer the next day, Tommy said, "No. Thank you. I don't drink."

"Are you sure you're a Baird man?" Malcolm said, then immediately regretted it. "I don't drink much myself, truth be told," he amended.

"I used to," Tommy said. "Used to drink a lot, actually. I stopped recently. It was . . . getting out of hand."

Oh Jesus, Malcolm thought. So perhaps that was part of it.

"Wise decision," he said, keeping his voice neutral.

After Malcolm had served the food, Tommy said, "This is nice," and then made no further comment for some time.

Eventually, his plate nearly finished, Tommy said, "Do most people . . ." and then stopped, began again. "Do you think everyone round here remembers me?"

Malcolm glanced up at him. "Yes."

"There was a man on the ferry with me," Tommy said. "He lives here. Ross something."

"Ross Johnston, I suppose that'll be."

"He talked to me," Tommy said. "A lot."

"That'll be Ross then."

"He seemed to recognize me. And then when I said my name . . ."

Better get used to that, Malcolm thought. At least they could rely on Ross to spread the news round the whole island within a couple of days, even without any help from Kathy and Fiona, so people could meet Tommy face to face without staring too much. "You don't remember him from when you were little?" he said.

"Not really."

"He can certainly talk, that man."

"Yeah," Tommy said, with feeling.

"We're all used to it now, I suppose," Malcolm said. "He used to drive me mad, though. I got in a fight with him once."

"You didn't."

"Is it so hard to believe? We were teenagers. It's the only fight I've ever been in." He didn't count his father.

"What was it about?" Tommy said.

"I can't remember."

"A girl?"

Malcolm laughed at this. "There were hardly enough girls on the island to have fights over. No, I can't remember what it was over. Something stupid, I'm certain of that."

Tommy took a swig of water and said, "I can't imagine you fighting with anyone."

"Like I said, it was just the once."

Tommy looked away, looked out of the window, though there was nothing to see except darkness beyond it. "I used to get in fights, didn't I? After I came to live with you."

"Aye," Malcolm said carefully. "From time to time."

"I gave Angus MacIntyre a bloody nose. Broke it, I think."

"That's right. You broke it." It hadn't been the final straw, but it had come close.

"Always felt bad about that," Tommy said.

"You were just a child."

Malcolm had enough memories of his own to feel bad about. He had wondered often during that terrible final year with Tommy, and even more so after the boy had left the island, if Tommy had blamed them just as they had blamed themselves, if that was why he was so out of control, why he so often seemed to hate them. Heather had encouraged Tommy to resume his counselling sessions on the mainland during that final year—they had ended when he was nine and had refused to attend any more—but she had been forced to drop it after a lot of shouting and swearing from Tommy, and some hurling over of furniture.

They should have insisted, of course.

"He's not angry with us, Mal," Heather had said after one particularly bad row; they could hear the familiar *thump-thump* from upstairs as Tommy kicked his bedroom wall. "He's just angry. And he's in terrible pain. And we're the only ones here to take it out on. Nobody else is left. He has nobody else left."

And still, *still*, they had failed him.

5

The next day Malcolm went out early, with some relief, to help Robert repair the fencing on the cliffs. He had asked Tommy, "Will you be all right, left to your own devices?" and of course Tommy had said yes.

Up on the cliffs by the west coast, Malcolm and Robert worked for several hours in silence, driving fresh wooden posts into the ground and piling up the old rotten ones in the back of Robert's truck. The wind was up and whipping at their faces, which made conversation difficult anyway. The sheep didn't come too close, clearly not trusting what was taking place.

Mid-morning, the two men sat side by side in Robert's truck, sheltering from the wind and drinking coffee from a thermos.

At last Robert said, as Malcolm had known he would, "I hear Tommy's back."

"That's right."

Robert didn't say anything else for a time. They sipped their coffee from the small plastic cups.

Eventually Robert said, "It's been a while, hasn't it? Since you heard from him." The closest Robert would ever come to prying.

"A long while."

"He O.K.?"

"Seems to be."

"Must be strange," Robert said. "For him, I mean. Being back here."

"Aye."

"Strange for you too."

Malcolm nodded. The men drained the last of their coffee and got back to work on the fence. But Malcolm thought he could feel what was happening. With Tommy's return, people were beginning to look at Malcolm and remember. It hadn't felt like this for years. After Tommy had left, Malcolm had felt himself and Heather drifting loose from the connection. They would never break it entirely, but it had slackened. As the years passed, he felt himself become in the eyes of the others simply Malcolm again, not *John's brother*. Still, though. Just every once in a while he'd feel Davey's gaze on him in the bar, Kathy hesitating fractionally as she handed over his change, and he'd realize they were wondering what he knew.

Heather would tell him, of course, that he was being too sensitive, manufacturing worries where there were none.

They're your friends, she would say. *Nobody's thinking of it.*

The first part was true, Malcolm accepted. But that didn't mean the second part was as well.

"Need some more wire," Robert said, lifting a sagging piece with the end of his hammer.

"I'll get it," Malcolm said, heading for the pickup. Hefting the roll in his arms, he wondered how Tommy was spending his morning. He felt uncomfortable now at the idea of having left this stranger alone in his house. But for God's sake, what was he afraid Tommy might do? Burn it down? There was certainly nothing worth stealing.

He and Robert stretched out the new wire between the fence posts, and Malcolm held it taut while Robert tightened it.

"Gearing up for tupping time now," Robert said. "We'll move the ewes in a week or so. You'll be around?"

"Of course."

They would be moving the ewes down from the hills and

into fields Malcolm had once owned. This fact would never be mentioned between them. Malcolm thought this was due less to any particular sensitivity on Robert's part than to his immense pragmatism; for Robert, things were as they were, and there was no use looking back at how they had once been, or at how they might have been. Malcolm had known Robert a long time and had always respected him. But he couldn't share his attitude, however hard he tried. He himself spent far too long looking back.

Malcolm's father had been a crofter, and his father before him, and his father too, and so on several generations back, all these Baird men working the same swathe of land, give or take a few acres, to the west of the island. Seventeen acres, comprising six acres of covetable in-bye in a shallow green valley, and the eleven acres lying across windswept moorland stretching inland. In addition to this, there was the common grazing, most of it rocky hill terrain, shared by all the crofters in the township.

Malcolm was the oldest son, and had always known the croft would fall to him when his father died, but he hadn't expected it to be so soon, when he was only twenty-two. They had sixty Hebridean sheep then, fifty-six breeding ewes and four rams when Malcolm took over the tenancy, though he would later manage to increase the flock size a little.

It had been a hard life for Malcolm's father, especially in winter. He was out before light, seven days a week, and not back until after dark. There was never enough money. You couldn't really live off a croft, even back then. Malcolm's father did some part-time work as the harbour master to make ends meet. Malcolm sometimes wondered if his father might have been a different kind of man if he hadn't been a crofter, if he hadn't lived on the island. In the evenings, like so many of the island's men, its crofters and its farmers and its ferrymen,

Malcolm's father would drink, and then, from time to time, he would take out his exhaustion and rage on his wife and children. What a cliché that was, Malcolm thought. The drunk, disappointed man coming home to beat his family.

But in truth, the beatings were hardly worthy of their name: a sudden cuff round the head that sent you flying and left your ears ringing, or a backhand to the face that smarted horribly but rarely left a bruise. It was their unpredictability that frightened Malcolm. His father could be in a rage and never so much as lift a hand to you, or he could be smiling one moment and grabbing you roughly by the shoulder the next. His shouting, too. It was mostly directed at Malcolm's mother, who his father said was the most useless woman alive, but sometimes it encompassed the boys as well. Malcolm had only seen his father hit his mother once, but it had always been clear who was the chief object of his hatred.

Malcolm had believed for a long time as a child that he and John were united in their loathing of their father. He was shocked to learn later that this was not the case. When they were teenagers, even during one of their father's black moods, John would defend him, until Malcolm gave up saying anything in case his comments were reported back to their father. As an adult, John would not go so far as to say it had done them good, the way their father had laid down the law, but he would shrug if the subject came up and say, "He was tough on us, just like his dad was on him. Didn't do us any harm, did it?"

Malcolm wasn't so sure. Far from toughening him up, it had only made Malcolm—the eldest son, the one upon whom everyone's hopes rested—afraid; he was conscious all the time of his own weakness, flinching every moment at the blow about to fall.

John had often seemed, if not to admire their father, then at least to understand him better. However many times he was clipped hard round the ear or shoved up against the wall (and perhaps, Malcolm thought later, he was exaggerating the frequency of these incidents in his own memory), John was never resentful. It sometimes seemed to be a point of pride with him, how well he could take it, how little he held it against their father. You might think that if their father had loved anyone (and how strange it seemed to use that word in relation to him), it would have been John, who was so silent and stoical, who even as a young boy never seemed to cry, and whose desire to please their father radiated from him. But their father had been impervious to this. He was disappointed with how small John was, how skinny and weak. "Lucky the croft won't be going to him," he would say. "He's scarce stronger than one of the sheep."

"Leave him be, Jack," their mother would say mildly. "Give him a chance to grow." This was the furthest she ever went in defending her younger son, and in any case she didn't hold much sway over her husband.

For Malcolm, she would risk more, perhaps believing he was in greater need of her protection. Malcolm knew he couldn't keep an impassive face like John while their father raged. He was not brave like his younger brother, even though he was bigger. His father terrified him, and their mother seemed to know this. Many a time when her husband was drunk or furious or both (perhaps the boys had not cleared up after themselves, had not done their chores, had committed some minor misdemeanour at school, or perhaps, as so often, there was no reason at all except that he hated his life and could do nothing about it), she would tell him Malcolm was out of the house, would be out till teatime, when in fact she had simply hidden her son in her bedroom, where he would remain until his father's rage had cooled. She never exerted herself in this way for John, a fact that Malcolm took for granted as a child and only started to question when he was almost grown. He had always known his mother loved him more. She told him, from time to time, that he was her special bairn, that he was like her and that John was like their father. Malcolm could never see this: John was nothing like their father, and Malcolm couldn't imagine anyone being afraid of John. But where their mother was cool and distant with John, she adored Malcolm. She would reach for Malcolm to hug him or ruffle his hair, but he couldn't recall her ever doing this with his brother. It brought Malcolm pleasure and shame in equal measure. He would wonder later if his mother was aloof with John because John seemed so detached himself, so self-contained and difficult to read, even before they were teenagers. It occurred to him later still that it was more likely this behaviour of John's was simply a reaction to their mother's indifference.

Malcolm didn't remember himself and John ever discussing their mother when they were young, except for one time when John came into the bedroom the two of them shared, threw down his bag (this part Malcolm remembered vividly, although he had no idea what age they must have been) and said, "She doesn't like me. She's never *liked* me." Malcolm recalled, too, the rush of guilt he felt at this, of how he had lamely said, "That's not true," while knowing as well as John that it was. John had turned on him at that, shoved him hard and hissed, "Shut up! You don't know what you're fucking *talking* about." Malcolm could still picture the way his face had been screwed up in anger. He really had seemed like their father then. The subject had not been mentioned between them again.

Many years later, after their mother's funeral, he and John had got drunk together in John's sitting room after the other guests had left. Katrina and Heather had come in from time to time to bring them offerings from the cold spread—sausage rolls, crisps, and sandwiches to soak up the whisky—but eventually they'd given up and left their menfolk to it.

This was one of the few times since they were in their early teens that Malcolm had felt close to his brother. They'd laughed as they remembered their mother's obsession with washing the backs of their necks, her collection of crocheted doilies, her gentle eye-rolls in the face of their father's temper (she had been a brave woman, in her way). Then Malcolm had said, sentimental in his drunkenness and trying to grasp at this thread of unity between them, "She wasn't an easy person, I know. But I think she did her best."

"She was an old bitch," John replied, his words only slightly slurred. "I'm surprised Dad put up with it. All her bleating on, her stupid complaints."

Malcolm was so shocked he couldn't think of an answer. He would never again forget that although he and John had grown up in the same house, they had each had a different set of parents, an entirely different childhood.

Malcolm was already engaged to Heather when his father died. He wasn't sure afterwards what he would have done without her steadiness and common sense, how on earth he would have managed the croft. There were times, in fact, especially in the difficult early years, when he had envied John, who had no responsibilities, nothing expected of him, and had escaped to Glasgow as soon as he could to train as an accountant. (Their father had, predictably, been scathing about this, although their mother, for once, had seemed impressed.)

But Heather had been far cleverer than any of the stubborn Baird men, had said straight out in her blunt, practical way, "We won't earn nearly enough to scrape by from the croft, so we need a plan, Mal." Heather had always been one for plans, and Malcolm never got in her way. But he was grateful, too, that she had never suggested, not even once, not even indirectly, that he shouldn't take on the croft. In all else he would have given way to her, but not in that. And since continuing the croft was what he cared about, he was more than ready to listen to her plans.

Heather had a genius for getting by, finding new ways to supplement the meagre income they drew from sheep farming. As well as working behind the counter in the shop, she picked whelks along the shore, which were taken across on the ferry to be sold at fishmongers in Oban, and made craft items to be sold to tourists in the island's gift shop: shell necklaces, beaded earrings, small watercolour paintings and clothes knitted from sheep's wool. Malcolm, meanwhile, like so many other islanders, took on an assortment of extra jobs over the years, including, for a time, harbour master like his father, which he found stressful and did not enjoy, taking him, as it did, too often and for too long away from his sheep. When he was ready to give it up, after Tommy had left the island, Davey McPhee was only too happy to take it on instead. "Had my eye on that one for a while," he told Malcolm. Malcolm in return took on Davey's job of driving the school minibus along the narrow island road in the mornings and afternoons, picking up and dropping off the four or five children who attended the primary school at any given time. By a variety of methods, he and Heather had managed.

After Heather had her first stroke, still so young, only fifty, Malcolm gave up the croft. He might have thought before that it would be a heart-wrenching decision—an impossible one even—but when it came to it, it was no decision at all. He never considered doing anything else. Heather was in a bad way and couldn't manage on her own (whatever she tried to claim), and the doctors said there was a chance of a second stroke. If she had limited time left, Malcolm wanted to spend it with her. He and Heather had long ago come to terms with having no children, and he felt only a little regret now that there was no son—no daughter, even—to pass the croft on to. It had come into Malcolm's head from time to time over the years that Tommy might return one day, might be pleased to find the croft here waiting for him. But even without sharing it with Heather he knew this was an absurd fantasy.

Breaking up the croft hurt more than selling the tenancy itself. Nobody wanted, or nobody could afford, the whole seventeen acres, so in the end Malcolm had sold three acres of inbye to Ross Johnston to become part of his own croft, and the rest to Robert, who had the largest farm on the island and wanted to expand his herd of Shetland cows. The land would be absorbed into their own, just as if it hadn't been worked by Malcolm's family for generations. Malcolm would have given it away almost for nothing, so distressed was he by the whole process, so keen was he for it to be over, but Heather would not have it. "You'll need money to live on, Mal," she told him. "Especially when you get older." It broke his heart that she said "you", and not "we".

"And besides," she went on, "it would be nice to have a little something left over, at the end, for Tommy. God knows he won't get much, but it would be nice to leave him something, wouldn't it?"

And as always, Malcolm gave way to her, as always knowing she was right. He got a fair price for the land (a high price, Ross was heard to say in the bar afterwards, but without any real rancour), and would have a bit of money left to fall back on in his old age, as well as a small sum to be left to Tommy, should Tommy ever return.

A shock, inevitably, being called Tommy again. And then no longer a shock, which perhaps was worse.

He didn't know what to do with himself, alone in the cottage all day. Malcolm had gone out early to work on somebody else's farm (both of them skirted round the subject). In the silence after his uncle had left, Tom took some time going from room to room in the cottage, laying his hands on things only half consciously. He brushed his fingers along the backs of chairs, touched worktops absentmindedly, trailed his hand up the banister as he climbed the stairs.

He had believed he did not remember the cottage well, but it all came back now. Of course it did. It was all still here, as solid as ever. He had thought himself prepared, but he'd been shocked to find Malcolm an old man, and Heather gone. He wasn't so delusional to think time had stood still in his absence, but somehow this knowledge didn't seem to have sunk in: he'd still expected to find Malcolm and Heather as they always had been, vigorous and tough, Malcolm out all hours tending to the croft, Heather working behind the counter in the shop or making deliveries or knitting in the front room. Tom hadn't been sure he'd receive a warm welcome, given how he'd neglected them over the years, and how he'd behaved before he left. But he had still believed they would be here waiting for him. (He'd wept over Heather's death in his old bedroom that first evening, amazed at how readily the tears came. He hadn't really known her, after all.)

At lunchtime, he went upstairs and retrieved his phone from the bottom of his rucksack. He stared at it reluctantly for a few seconds, then switched it on for the first time since leaving London. One bar of signal. After a moment, a message appeared from Caroline, dated two days back: *Just let me know you're safe, will you?*

Not allowing himself to think about it too much, Tom typed out a quick reply. *Yes, I'm safe. I'm on the island. Hope you're O.K.* Wavering for a moment, he added, *I'm sorry*, then quickly pressed *send*, watched to make sure the message was delivered, and switched the phone off again.

Restless now, he went back downstairs and put on his borrowed coat and boots. No rain today—not so far. He stepped outside into the cold air, not bothering to lock the door behind him as he left; nobody locked their doors here, something Tom had taken for granted as a child but which felt strange now. He could walk straight into any house on the island, take whatever he wanted, give the owners a scare. But there had never been any crime here except for his father's, and why bother locking your door when the only danger was already inside?

Settling on a direction at random, Tom followed the upper loop of the road, going north-east instead of south-east as he and Malcolm had gone the day before. On either side as he walked north, the hills increased in size, shaggy with bracken and moss. But it was the air, most of all, that he noticed. It had struck him first in Oban, the freshness of the breeze and the smell of salt, how different it was from the polluted air of London. He noticed it even more now, as he breathed in air that was damp and cool and even on the clearest days carried the suggestion of mist.

Tom walked for an hour without giving it much conscious thought. Although he stuck to the road, he met no one, not even a passing car. He didn't remember experiencing this kind of isolation when he was a child, but perhaps that was because he'd always been with Nicky.

When he reached the point where the road met the coast and ran alongside it, he stopped. Whichever way you headed, you came up against the barrier of the sea. It was surprising how little interest the islanders showed in it, though their whole lives were circumscribed by water. Perhaps that was what made them narrow. Tom turned away at last and retraced his steps back to Malcolm's cottage, still feeling the sea lapping at his back.

Malcolm returned as the light was starting to fade. Tom was sitting in the kitchen, not exactly waiting for him, but not doing anything else either. Malcolm said, standing in the doorway, "Your day been O.K.?"

"Yes," Tom said. Then, remembering his manners, "And yours?"

"It was fine." Malcolm went to hang his jacket up in the hall. "Do you still like cauliflower cheese?" he called after a moment.

This threw Tom. "I think so." He hadn't eaten it since he was a child. "My mother used to make it."

"Is that so? I thought we'd have it for tea," Malcolm said, coming back into the kitchen. "All right?"

"Yes."

"I'm going to change," Malcolm said, and went upstairs.

Later that evening, Tom sat at the kitchen table and watched Malcolm cook. He had offered to help, but Malcolm said it was a one-man job.

"You can lay the table in a bit," he added, as he stirred flour into the pan of milk on the stove.

"Sure."

"Took me ages to master white sauce," Malcolm remarked. "Hard to get the consistency right."

"Yeah. Tricky getting rid of the lumps."

"You have to keep stirring the whole time."

"That's true."

Tom couldn't think of anything further to add, and apparently Malcolm couldn't either. They fell silent.

Tom studied his uncle discreetly. Malcolm was wearing an old green apron, which had presumably belonged to Heather, and was stirring the sauce with frowning concentration. There was something incongruous about seeing his uncle dressed like this, brandishing a wooden spoon and making a dish which Tom associated with his mother. It seemed unmanly, though Tom realised what an absurd idea this was.

A feeling of shame came over him suddenly, a plunge of his stomach. And there was something behind it: a memory, he thought. Tom used to try to close down his thoughts in these moments, to prevent them bringing back anything he didn't want to see, but often that made it more painful in the long run. It was better, he had learned, to be brave and to face up to the memory at once. So, deliberately, masochistically, he followed the threads of the feeling until he found the memory attached to it. The laundry one, as he thought of it. Back again. It was a straightforward event in itself: his mother had asked him to help put away the laundry and he had refused. Then, later, this had led to a row between his parents. It was the timing of the incident that gave it an unsettling significance, and Tom knew this was why it came back to him so regularly: it had taken place just a couple of days before the murders. And although as an adult Tom could see that the two probably weren't connected, still a sense of horror infused the memory that was far disproportionate to its content.

He turned his eyes away from Malcolm and lived it again. He saw his mother standing by the sink, her hair loose. He was supposed to be going out to meet Angus to play. Tom had never been sure if the scene took place in the morning or afternoon, but he could feel the urgency of the meeting in his body, that tightness of anxiety—not that he was keeping Angus waiting, but something else, something vaguer, perhaps caught up with one of the deeper fears of his childhood—of missing out, of being left behind.

And his mother had said something like, "You're not going anywhere until you've helped me put these clothes away."

Tommy had believed he was going to do what she told him as he always did. He was surprised when he opened his mouth and said, "No." Then he felt the frisson in his whole body at having defied her.

He wasn't sure exactly how his mother had responded, but he knew she had stood firm and, amazingly, he had too. He had hated her in that moment, and he remembered the shock of this feeling. "I have to go and meet Angus," he had told her, over and over, feeling himself a hero in his defiance. "He's waiting for me." And then the bit he remembered most clearly, knowing as he said it that he was going too far, but saying it anyway: "Laundry is women's work."

He didn't recall what his mother had said to that either. She had been furious, he was certain, but her words were lost. He was not sure why he had silenced her in so many of his memories.

Into this stand-off between them his father had entered. Tommy had felt a lurch of fear that was like falling, the certainty now that he had overplayed his hand. His father had looked to them both to explain the noise. He must have been in his study working.

They had told him, or perhaps Tommy's mother had told him, reluctantly, maybe, in her quiet voice. Perhaps Tommy had chimed in shrilly in his own defence, saying that he didn't have time, that Angus was waiting for him, or perhaps he had remained silent, fearful.

He remembered, though, how his father had responded.

His father, standing in the kitchen doorway, doing that half-smile he sometimes did. He had said something like, "Katrina, the boy needs to be outside playing, not tied to his mother's apron strings." Then he had turned to Tommy. "Off you go. We won't let her turn you into a lass."

And Tom remembered how he had slunk out, the mingled sense of satisfaction and betrayal, and how—he believed—his mother had not looked at him as he left. He felt the triumph at having defeated her and the horror of it, and caught up with it all was the warmth that flooded him when she turned her smile on him, how she would crouch down to listen to him when he was trying to tell her something, the feel of her as she hugged him and he slipped his arms around her middle and squeezed. Tommy adored no one as he adored his mother. He had confided in Nicky once, when they were very little, that he loved his mother even more than God and Jesus, and Nicky had told him, "You can't say that," before adding comfortingly, "I do too."

Tom knew that he had not enjoyed that afternoon, or that morning, whichever it was, playing with Angus. He had thought of his mother the whole time, of how angry she must be, and worse, how hurt. Getting your own way, he had discovered, did not feel the way you expected it to. It made you lonely.

Malcolm turned and said, "Almost done now," and Tom nodded and got up to lay the table.

When he had returned to the house later that afternoon, his parents had been arguing. Tommy could hear them from the hallway because the kitchen door was partially open. He didn't remember most of what was said, only his feeling of terror at the savage note in his father's voice, which he'd known instinctively was his fault. One thing he did recall was his father saying, "It's just moan, moan, moan with you. Always fucking complaining about something." Tommy remembered this afterwards because he was so shaken at hearing the f-word in a house where no one was ever allowed to swear, and frightened on his mother's behalf that she was having this violent word thrown at her. His shock was so visceral it manifested in a sickness that moved from his stomach to his throat to his mouth, where he forcefully swallowed it down again.

Malcolm spooned the cauliflower cheese into two bowls and brought them over to the table.

"Looks good," Tom managed. "Thanks."

"Probably not as good as your mum's," Malcolm said. "But it's edible, I hope."

Tom nodded and didn't reply. He hoped they could eat in silence again; the thought of more conversation was unbearable just now.

He remembered how he had waited in the hallway that day, paralysed, unable to creep up to his room for fear of being heard, of drawing attention to himself. What he should have done was go into the kitchen and tell his father it was his fault, that his father should be shouting at him, not at his mother. But instead he stayed frozen where he was, the pressure in his bladder now reminding him painfully that he had needed to pee all the way home. Finally, he heard his father shout, "You can all just fucking forget about the cinema next week," and then the noise of the kitchen door banging. Suddenly, Tommy found he could move again. He hurtled down the corridor into the bathroom and locked the door behind him.

Standing in front of the toilet, he stared down into the bowl and tried to relax enough to pee. It was agony at first, being so desperate but unable to go. At last his heartbeat began to slow and the exquisite relief came, and as Tommy watched his urine hurtle downwards, he reflected on the final tragedy that had befallen them. Clearly the much-anticipated trip to the cinema in Oban would not go ahead after all. It was possible, he supposed, that by the following weekend his father would be in a better mood, would perhaps even have forgotten about the row. But Tommy was aware from experience this was unlikely to be the case. His father didn't forget.

(And later, of course, those words would return to him: *You can all just fucking forget about the cinema next week.* Was his father already planning what he would do? No way of knowing.)

Going to the sink, Tommy thought of how upset Nicky would be about the cinema trip. He knew he had caused this disaster. But it was also true that his mother had caused it, because she didn't give in to his father, even though it was obvious she should, but instead made him angry by arguing with him. Scrubbing at his hands furiously, Tommy thought that anyone could see how stupid she was about it sometimes. So Tommy's rage became spread between himself and his mother, and it was this afterwards he remembered above everything else, that although he had blamed himself, most of all he had blamed her.

D avey McPhee rang Malcolm the next morning. Malcolm was in the kitchen, washing up the plates and pan from last night's tea while Tommy ate cereal at the table.

Malcolm went into the hall to pick up the phone.

"Coming for a drink tonight, Malcolm?" Davey said without preamble.

The bar was attached to the tiny Litta Hotel, which closed during the winter months. The bar, however, was kept open for the locals, at least if you rang up Ross Johnston, who worked behind it, and told him you'd be coming (the disadvantage was you then had to drink with him). The others had long given up making fun of Malcolm for drinking his ale by the half not the pint. "Malcolm's not a big drinker," they'd acknowledge to one another, until it became a statement of fact rather than a criticism.

"I'm staying in tonight," Malcolm told Davey.

"Been a while since we've seen you."

"I . . ." He wasn't sure why he was being hesitant; Davey would know already. "I've got Tommy here staying."

"Bring him along," Davey said. "You know he's welcome." After a pause, he added, "There are people here who'd be pleased to see him. See him grown."

Malcolm took this in silence. He thought it was true that most of the others felt warmly towards Tommy, even felt a protective interest in his well-being. This unease, then, came from

Malcolm himself. He said, "I'm a bit worn out, Davey. I'll come along another night."

"You sound like you're in your eighties, not your sixties," Davey said. "But fine, come along another night. With Tommy, O.K.?"

"O.K.," Malcolm said.

"How is he, anyway?"

"He's fine."

"Married?"

"No."

"I heard he lives in London now."

"Aye," Malcolm said.

"Travelled a long way, Tommy Baird." There was a short, meditative silence, then Davey added, "He was a lovely boy."

Malcolm wasn't sure what to say to this. He presumed Davey meant before, given that most people would not have described Tommy as a lovely boy afterwards.

"Well," Davey concluded, "tell him hello. From all of us."

"I'll do that, Davey. Thanks."

When Malcolm put the phone down and went back in the kitchen, he knew Tommy wouldn't ask who it had been. He had already learned that Tommy was scrupulous about observing privacy, both Malcolm's and his own. But Malcolm found himself telling him, perhaps just for something to say, "That was Davey McPhee. Do you remember him?"

Tommy frowned. "Not really. Sorry."

"He drove the school bus for years. Did it when you were small. Do you remember that?"

Tommy's face cleared. "Yeah, I do. He was always nice to us."

"He was asking if we wanted to go to the hotel bar. I said not tonight." Malcolm remembered suddenly that Tommy didn't drink, that he had given up, that he might even have a problem. "We don't have to go any night," he amended clumsily.

"You can go, Malcolm," Tommy said. "Of course. Don't change your routine for me. I don't want to be in your way."

"It's not my routine," Malcolm said, amused while slightly dispirited at how Tommy seemed to view his life. "It's just a drink. I see them all the time, Davey and the rest. Feel I can't escape them half the time."

"I imagine not," Tommy said dryly, "living on an island." There was a pause, then he added, "You were speaking Gaelic."

"Aye, we were," Malcolm said, feeling oddly embarrassed all of a sudden. "It's Davey, really. Feels we should keep it going. Not many of us left now." Then, worried Tommy might assume they were saying things they didn't want him to hear, he stumbled on, "He asked after you. Just briefly. I said you were well."

Tommy nodded. "I haven't heard Gaelic in a long time," he said.

"Well. It's still my first language, I suppose."

Strange to think of that now. All through Malcolm's childhood, he and John had spoken Gaelic at home, English only at school. Even by the time he met Heather, English had felt clumsy in his mouth. But now, in his old age, it was Gaelic that felt awkward to him; when they lapsed into the old language in the bar, there seemed to Malcolm something stilted and self-conscious about it, a foolish pathos in trying to grasp at what was lost. And at some stage—he didn't know when—it had become Gaelic, not *Gàidhlig*; he always thought in English now. It was only in his dreams, and only rarely, that he was truly fluent again in the first language he had learned. The language of his forefathers, the language of his youth: to Malcolm it felt both ancient and young.

"You learned it at school, didn't you?" he said to Tommy.

"A bit. I don't remember much. We never spoke it at home."

Malcolm had known this already. John had even banned Malcolm from speaking to his children in Gaelic. Malcolm had never been sure whether this was a reaction against their own father, who would hit them if he heard them speaking English, or if John had regarded Gaelic, as he did so much else about island life, as "backward". Always in John there was that need to set himself apart.

"*Tha i fliuch*," Tommy said unexpectedly. His accent was passable.

Malcom smiled. "Always is here."

Nothing like having a stranger stay with you to highlight the immense tedium of your own life, Malcolm thought later that afternoon, after hearing himself offer Tommy a cup of tea for the third time in an hour. Christ, when had he started drinking so much tea? It was amazing he got anything else done.

"No thanks," Tommy said, also for the third time.

"Just me then," Malcolm said, and went into the kitchen.

They'd been sitting together in the living room since returning from their walk, which had taken them south towards Alban Bay and the lower reaches of the island. They hadn't managed to spot any seals. Malcolm was reading a detective novel and Tommy was reading one of Heather's old books, which he'd taken off the shelf with a polite, "May I?"

"Of course," Malcolm had said. He hadn't glimpsed the cover as Tommy took the book over to the sofa.

Now, returning with his mug, Malcolm glanced at his nephew. Tommy was sitting with his legs tucked under him, just as he had as a child, a frowning expression of concentration on his face. The book he'd selected, Malcolm saw, was *The Portrait of a Lady*, which seemed a strange choice. Malcolm could never get on with Heather's old books. Tommy, though, seemed absorbed. He had always been a bright lad, Malcolm recalled. Did well at school. He'd been clever in the same way Heather was, always reading and asking questions (not that Heather would let anyone call her clever). They'd heard from

Jill a couple of years before she died that Tommy had got a place at university, though he couldn't remember where now. Somewhere in the north of England. Manchester, maybe, or Durham. Malcolm and Heather had sent him a card to say congratulations, though they hadn't received a reply (hadn't, by then, expected one). Malcolm didn't know what subject Tommy had studied, didn't know whether he'd even graduated.

He watched Tommy across the room for a few more moments, but wasn't sure how to start the conversation.

"I don't read much these days," Tommy said, perhaps feeling Malcolm's eyes on him.

"No?"

"Used to. Somehow got out of the habit."

"I expect life moves fast, down in London," Malcolm said, unable to imagine it.

"Depends," Tommy said, and then didn't expand on this.

Malcolm returned to his own book, but after a moment Tommy said, "Shall I cook tonight?"

He was looking up at Malcolm now, almost shyly. It was only cauliflower cheese, Malcolm thought. It can't have been *that* bad. But then Tommy added, "To give you a break?"

"I don't mind," Malcolm said. "It's no more trouble cooking for two than cooking for one." Then he thought of Tommy's agonized politeness and wondered if it would make his nephew feel less awkward if he was allowed to cook for them, so he said, "Sure, if you'd like. That would be nice."

"Do you like omelettes?"

"Aye."

"Great," Tommy said, with a small nod to himself. "O.K. then." He returned to his reading.

Tommy made a good cheese omelette. Malcolm tried to take his time eating it to show Tommy he was enjoying it, then noticed Tommy had inhaled his own in about half a minute. In some ways, he hadn't changed. Malcolm had a sudden vivid memory of Katrina leaning over Tommy, ruffling his hair and saying, "No one's going to take it off you, bairnie."

Once they'd both finished, neither made a move to leave the table. Malcolm wasn't sure if Tommy wanted to talk or if, like Malcolm, he simply didn't know what to do next.

When Tommy did speak at last, what he said was unexpected. "I learned how to make an omelette from my father."

Malcolm was careful not to show any reaction. "Is that right?"

"Yeah," Tommy went on, in the same casual, distant voice. "It was the only thing he ever taught me to cook."

Malcolm said, "He was never very interested in cooking, as I recall." Thought it was a woman's job. But so, Malcolm admitted, had he for many years. It was only more recently that he had come to realize how old fashioned he had been. Heather, too, in some ways.

"No," Tommy said. "He never cooked. Wouldn't. But he said my mother didn't know how to make a decent omelette. He prided himself on his. Insisted on showing me and Nicky how. Somehow, through the years, I remembered."

"Not a bad skill," Malcolm said, choosing the most noncommittal response he could come up with.

"But it occurred to me later on," Tommy said, "how strange a thing it was, for a man to pride himself on his omelettes. I mean, was there really nothing else?"

"I think he prided himself on a lot of things," Malcolm said.

Tommy nodded and didn't reply. When he did open his mouth, it was only to yawn and say, "I think I'll get to my bed soon. Maybe read for a bit. What time is it?"

Malcolm looked at his watch. "Just gone eight."

"So early? Christ."

"Evenings can be long here."

Tommy seemed to take this the wrong way, growing immediately awkward. "You know, you could still go out to the bar. I don't mind. Please don't stay in just because of me."

"No, I . . ." It was strange, Malcolm thought, how much time he spent trying to put Tommy at ease when he was so little at ease himself. "I'm quite happy staying in. I just meant that it can be boring if you're not used to it. Not used to such a quiet life."

"I think I've only ever wanted a quiet life."

"Well then," Malcolm said. "You've come to the right place."

And even this comment, innocuous as it was, seemed to go too near something dangerous, to touch too closely on Tommy's motives for being here, which were still a mystery to Malcolm. The simplest conversation with his nephew seemed to be riddled with traps.

"I suppose so," Tommy said, getting up. "Well. Goodnight then."

Perhaps Tommy really did just want a holiday, Malcolm thought after his nephew had left the room. Perhaps he had simply come here to get away for a few days, and it really was no more complicated than that.

In bed that night, he thought of his friends gathered together in the bar and wondered if they'd talked about him and Tommy. He assumed they had. Or maybe not about Malcolm himself—out of loyalty, they would avoid discussing him if they could—but he knew how likely it was they had returned to the old unresolved problem of John. Everyone had come up against it at the time and they continued to come up against it now. There was no getting around it.

Malcolm remembered how often Heather had said it, how she had repeated that old question: *Why did he do it?* She had blamed herself bitterly for not seeing any warning signs, as if John had somehow been her responsibility, though she wasn't even related to him. She wasn't the one who'd grown up with him.

Other people had asked Malcolm too—almost everyone on the island at one stage or another during the aftermath—as though he had some secret knowledge, as though he had somehow been party to it. Oh, nobody accused him, he knew that; nobody blamed him. But they watched him and he felt it. They trod quietly around him, waiting for the moment when he would choose to share his knowledge. Why did John do it? Everybody had liked John. Malcolm must tell them why he had done it. Had he lost his mind?

"He loved them," Heather said. "We all saw it. He adored Katrina and those children."

"The thing is," Davey said to Malcolm at the funeral—John's, which they held separately to the others (it was well attended, out of respect for Malcolm, though he'd have preferred it if nobody had come)—"it wasn't just some stranger, was it? It was John. He was born here. He was *one of us.*"

Malcolm saw these words for what they were: a clumsy attempt at kindness. Davey was claiming John for all of them in order to ease the burden on Malcolm a little.

What could have been going through John's head? people wanted to know. Many of them had seized on the fact of his money troubles, as though this could somehow explain it all. He'd maxed out his overdraft and run up £10,000 of credit-card debt buying nice suits, that fancy car, staying in expensive hotels for his nights on the mainland, and—worse—he had fallen into arrears with the mortgage payments. Then, of course, he'd lost his job; the firm had laid several people off, not just John. It had been a mess by the time it all came out, once John wasn't around to hide it any longer.

Too much pressure, people said. *Must have sent him over the edge.* But even the debt John was in—it appalled Malcolm, but even he could just about see it wasn't a catastrophe. John would have paid it off in a few years if he'd got another job, sold the car, lived within his means.

Still, Malcolm sensed in some people a kind of relief at the knowledge of John's debt, as though that might explain everything. *He must have panicked,* they said. *Probably thought he was protecting his family. Temporary madness.* Later, in any case, they ceased to discuss it around Malcolm, and he was grateful. He did not think they had ceased to discuss it, though it was possible that, for a time at least, they had run out of things to say.

He never had any answers to give people, or not the kind that would make any sense. A monster had been among them, and nobody had seen it. Of course they were affronted. Malcolm tasted again the shock like metal in his mouth as he received the phone call that terrible afternoon, followed soon after by the bitterness of bile. "It can't be true," Heather kept saying in the car. "I don't believe it." She would continue to say this in the days afterwards, then over and over in the weeks and months that followed, long after she'd realized the words offered no protection. Malcolm would nod in agreement, seeming to share her disbelief. And yet beneath the surface, although his shock was real, the greatest shock of all had been finding he had no trouble believing it.

8

When Malcolm said, "Shall we head to Craigmore?" the next day, Tom thought of Nicky. His brother was very clear to him on some days, much vaguer on others. Tom wasn't sure whether he missed Nicky more when he was present or when he was absent. Missing someone long dead was a strange thing. There was so much blankness caught up amidst the pain. All he recalled of Beth now was how warm her little body had felt when you lifted her and how she screwed up her face when she smiled, mouth open, in a way that Nicky said (kindly) made her look like a frog. Tom had no idea what sort of person she would have grown into.

"Yeah," he said to Malcolm. "Craigmore." He saw seals and black rocks.

They set off around lunchtime, walking side by side without saying much. Craigmore lay in the isolated northern reaches of the island, where there were no houses, only farmland and sheep and uneven, rocky hillside. It took them just over an hour to complete the journey along the road and then along the rough farm track before they were finally up on the cliffs. As they tramped across the grassland by the old abandoned chapel, Malcolm said, gesturing in its direction, "Fourteenth century, don't they say? Built by the monks of Iona."

The chapel was squat and roofless: just three ruined walls in ancient grey stone, half decayed and covered in moss and lichen. Tom saw himself crouching within these walls with

Nicky, pausing on their journey to the coast to eat their sandwiches. They had loved this place; it felt like theirs.

"And the chief of Clan MacLeod is supposed to have hidden in it once, right?" he said to Malcolm, this information coming back to him unexpectedly. "Escaping capture by the MacDonalds. Afterwards he claimed he was protected by God." Protected by his own cowardice, more like.

"I've heard that," Malcolm said, "but who knows?"

"There are so many stories about this island," Tom said. "The clans, the fighting, the ships lost. Do you still tell them to each other in the bar at night?" He could hear the hard edge that had come into his own voice and felt Malcolm's eyes on him. Tom didn't look round.

"Sometimes," Malcolm said. "I suppose people like stories."

"People like stories about themselves. Especially the people here."

"Aye, maybe that's true," Malcolm said, his voice infuriatingly measured.

His uncle was a hard man to provoke, Tom remembered, not knowing why he himself was suddenly so angry.

Finally, they reached the coastline and descended from the cliffs, coming to empty stretches of beach. The sand was flat and wet, a faint sheen across it from the weak afternoon light. Dark rocks jutted out into the Atlantic, with the hunched outlines of other islands just visible through the mist: Mull to the north and Jura to the east. Way out west, across thousands of miles of empty sea, Canada. On a couple of rocks within sight of land were gannet colonies, and, on a good day, basking on the larger, flatter rocks near the shore, seals. As far as Tom could see, there were none today.

"Haven't been back here for a while," Malcolm said. "Didn't see any seals last time either. Might be that they've moved on."

Tom looked at the empty rocks and thought that finding

seals had never been the point—not for him and Nicky. It had been an extra triumph to return home with, and their mother always seemed to think they were very clever if they did see the seals. But if they had to reply to her, "No, we didn't see any today," they might feign disappointment—perhaps to themselves, too—but it would not really be a blow.

No, the real point had been the rocks themselves. Tom studied them now, the black rocks biting into the cliffs and stretching out into the sea. They were slippery and treacherous, built up of many slanting layers and jagged edges. He and Nicky had loved to scramble over them, climbing up towards the clifftops or racing each other along them where two parallel outcrops rode out into the sea. Tommy, although younger, had always known he had the advantage here. Both he and Nicky were confident on the rocks, quick and surefooted, using their hands only when balance was especially challenging or underfoot was too slippery. They each had the fearlessness of childhood and a keen instinct for where to put their feet and where to avoid, even when moving at speed. But Tommy was the faster of the two, and the rocks seemed to be his natural element, so that he was swifter and more graceful on the jagged rocks than he was on flat, dry land. Sometimes he had to stop and wait for Nicky to catch up with him.

Tom turned his eyes from the rocks to look at Malcolm.

"Did you and my father play together much as children?" he asked, and saw that look of fear cross Malcolm's face, the one he always seemed to get when Tom's father was mentioned. For a moment, it gave Tom a savage pleasure. *If I have to live with it, then so should you.* But of course Malcolm did live with it.

"When we were very young, we used to," Malcolm said. "As we got older, I suppose we had different interests. And there was always work to be done on the croft, soon as we were strong enough."

"Did you ever come here?"

"Just occasionally."

Tom wondered if he and Nicky had really crossed the rocks as fast as he was picturing in his head. Probably not. But they had certainly been quick. He had felt the value of this skill the most when they were on family walks at the weekend. They rarely went as far as the northern coast of the island, but even on the east coast, only twenty minutes from their house, there were good rocks. They weren't as big or as black or as jagged as the rocks at Craigmore, but this only meant Tommy could take them at an even faster pace, scrambling up a sloping cliff-face before the others had even reached the bottom. Nicky would catch him soon enough, but Tommy was usually first, and he liked to be first. Both children had intuited that their father needed them to be physically courageous. They taught themselves to be hardy and athletic, and if they hurt themselves, slashed open a knee or elbow on the sharp edge of a rock, they did not complain, although they could be sure of ready sympathy from their mother. But more than anything they wanted to be their father's sons.

Tom said to Malcolm, "Nicky and I used to climb these rocks."

"So you did," Malcolm said. "I remember when Nicky broke his arm."

Tom remembered too. "He didn't break it. He dislocated it. His shoulder."

"Ah, that was it. He was, what, seven or eight at the time?"

"I think he was just about to turn eight. I remember it was the week before his birthday, because we were supposed to go to the play centre in Oban with all the trampolines, but then we couldn't because of Nicky's shoulder." Their mum had still taken them, once Nicky's shoulder was better, but it hadn't really been a birthday treat by then.

Tom could see the accident unfolding vividly, even at this distance of so many years, could see Nicky losing his footing and falling, as if in slow motion, down the narrow gully between two huge, slanting rock-faces. They had been high up at that point, level with the midpoint of the cliff. Nicky didn't fall all the way down; the gully was so narrow he ricocheted off either side like a pinball, and landed with not too big a thump on the compacted sand at the bottom. But somewhere on the way down he had dislocated his shoulder and when Tommy finally reached him, Nicky was white with shock, winded and shivering. Tommy was shocked too, and more frightened than he'd ever been in his life, but the strange calm of catastrophe had come over him and he'd taken off his own jacket to put around his brother and told him they had better go home.

For an hour they'd hobbled along together, Nicky starting to cry as the shock wore off and the pain set in. Tommy had hardly ever seen his brother cry, or not for a year or more, anyway. He could almost feel the pain in his own body. He set his eyes grimly on the track ahead, told his brother to lean on him, and tried to distract Nicky by telling him every story from Greek mythology he'd learned from the large illustrated book he'd got for Christmas. Nicky seemed to be making an effort to focus on the stories.

"Then what?" he would pant if Tommy paused for a moment in his telling, and Tommy learned to keep the flow of words moving quickly.

Mercifully, when they were halfway along the farm track, and still nowhere near the main road that led to their home, Robert Nairne drove past in his truck and, seeing from a distance that something was wrong, stopped to pick them up. Nicky was almost incoherent with pain by the time they were deposited home, but was clearly making an effort not to cry too much or too loudly, while Tommy rubbed his brother's good shoulder in useless reassurance. Dr. Brown was called and arrived swiftly to fix Nicky. It seemed like magic to Tommy, who saw Nicky go from agony to being almost pain free in a matter of moments. His mum said Tommy shouldn't stay in the room to watch, but his father said Tommy had earned the right.

"He just sort of *pushed it back in*," Tommy told Nicky afterwards. They were sitting side by side in Nicky's bed, eating white chocolate. Nicky was still groggy, but cheerful.

"What, just like that?" Nicky said. Nicky did not remember anything after the injection Dr Brown gave him, though he'd been awake the whole time, and had cried out when Dr Brown did his amazing trick.

"Yeah, just like that."

"Well, if it was that easy, we could have done it ourselves," Nicky said. "You could've just done it on the beach."

"We'll do it that way next time," Tommy said, though he had some doubts. "Now I've seen how it's done."

Tommy had been granted a share in the invalid's privileges, for being brave and for keeping calm in a crisis, as his father put it. Perhaps the best part of the whole thing (even better than the white chocolate) was how proud their father was of them. Their mum was tearful at Nicky's suffering and relieved to have them home safely, but their dad was proud. They knew because he told them. They were tough lads, he said, to have got themselves home.

"My father . . ." Tom started to say to Malcolm. He stopped, having no idea how to continue. He felt Malcolm watching him, waiting for him to go on. Patient or apprehensive? "My father said Nicky could have broken his neck. He said he'd known a boy who'd fallen on the rocks and broken his neck."

"Really?" Malcolm said. "Someone on the island? I don't remember that."

"I suppose he was trying to make us be careful," Tom said. He didn't believe it had been that. He thought that his father had liked to talk about violence.

"Shall we head for home," Malcolm said, "before the weather closes in?"

"Yeah."

They turned back towards the cliffs, away from the dark sea.

The next day, Nicky had gone to Oban on the ferry with their mum to get an X-ray, but they came back saying everything was fine. As Nicky was in no further pain, and as there was more white chocolate that night, and as they had pleased their father, both boys were glad overall that the incident had occurred, and often discussed it together afterwards. But mixed with the satisfying sense of drama and their own heroism was an aftertaste of fear: the knowledge which was new, but felt old, that terrible things could happen, and did happen, from out of nowhere, under a seemingly blue sky.

9

On the night that everyone died except for Tommy, they had chicken for tea, with broccoli and baked potatoes.

Afterwards, Tom would remember the food in detail, though he would not, as an adult, remember most parts of the conversation, every interaction, every nuance of feeling. He retained a general sense of it, with the ending clear and the rest blurred.

There had been no sauce. There always had to be sauce with chicken because otherwise it was too dry and his father didn't like it. Tommy's mother seemed distracted so perhaps that was why she'd forgotten the sauce. It made Tommy anxious. There was plenty of butter for the baked potatoes, but nothing at all to go with the chicken. Tommy waited all through the meal for his father to notice and say something about it. He could feel the prickle along his arms and in his chest and he glanced across at Nicky, who was eating his food with that expression of concentration he sometimes wore when he was doing maths (Nicky was brilliant at maths). Tommy thought Nicky was worried too.

Tommy wolfed his own chicken down quickly, to show everyone it was delicious and not dry at all. "Slow down, bairnie," his mother said, "you'll make yourself sick," and for a brief moment Tommy was annoyed with her for not seeing how he was trying to help her.

Then Nicky started to talk about Viking longships, which

irritated Tommy further because he was the expert on Vikings, not Nicky. But he thought he knew what Nicky was trying to do: keep everyone happy, keep everyone busy, keep their father from getting annoyed.

And it was true that their father hardly ever got annoyed with Nicky, except for the way his hair wouldn't lie flat on his head before church. Their father liked Nicky best, and Tommy knew this, and so did Nicky, and so did their mother, even if they all pretended they didn't. His father said Nicky would be an accountant like him one day because he was so good with numbers. Tommy thought Nicky should be talking about maths instead of Vikings, but he supposed that Nicky had the Vikings in his head because of the project on long-boats they were doing at school.

As Nicky talked on about how they built their ships— Tommy could see how cleverly he'd chosen the bit most likely to interest their father—Tommy looked at his mother. He thought she would at least acknowledge that the Vikings were his by turning to him at some point, but she kept on watching Nicky, and when she did turn it was only to look quickly at Tommy's father, before she returned her attention to Nicky, giving him that special smile that Tommy loved, and saying, "Did they *really*? That's very interesting."

"So they built the outside first," Nicky went on. "And then put the frame in the middle. It's called . . ." And here he broke off. "I can't remember what it's called. The name for how they make the ships. We learned it today."

It's called clinker, Tommy was about to burst out, but before he could speak his father said, "Carvel."

"It's not," Tommy said, without even thinking about it. "It's clinker."

All of them turned to look at him. Tommy felt the silence pushing at his sides. "The other kind is carvel," he said. "The non-Viking kind."

"Well, I haven't heard of either," his mother said, "so all of you are much cleverer than me."

Tommy waited for his father to speak. He didn't dare look up, and he knew Nicky would be staring down at his plate too, thinking how stupid Tommy was, how he always ruined things.

"Do you think you know better than everybody else?" his father said. He didn't sound angry. He sounded curious.

Tommy shook his head. A throbbing had started up in his ears.

"He doesn't think that, Dad," Nicky said, and Tommy was astonished at his brother's bravery, his loyalty.

Their father held up his hand to silence Nicky, but Nicky added all the same, "It's just that he really, really loves the Vikings. They're his favourite. Dad, will you take us to a museum to look at Viking things sometime? Mrs Brown says they have some stuff in Glasgow."

The cleverness of him. Tommy couldn't look at his father, so he kept his eyes on Nicky instead. Nicky looked entirely innocent.

There was a long pause, and then their father said, "Yes, we can do that." After a moment, he added, "Tommy. Nobody likes a know-it-all."

Tommy nodded quickly, staring down at his plate.

Their father picked up his cutlery and put a piece of chicken in his mouth. "It's dry, Katrina," he said. But he spoke calmly. After a few minutes of eating in silence, he pushed the plate away from him and stood up. "Better get back to work," he said, and left the kitchen.

Tommy felt himself letting out a slow, shaky breath, and thought his mother and Nicky were doing the same.

Their mother said, "Crumble for pudding. Finish up, boys." She reached over to ruffle Tommy's hair, and feeling this, and thinking of the crumble, and of how Nicky had saved him, Tommy felt a surge of joy so pure and keen it was like the rush in your stomach on a swing.

Later, when they were upstairs in their bedroom, Nicky said, "It is clinker, Tommy. I knew you were right."

Tommy nodded. He heard without Nicky needing to say it what lay behind his brother's words: we got away with it this time. Be more careful in future. Nicky went back downstairs and Tommy stayed in their room, reading his book about the Vikings.

They hadn't got away with it, of course. They had got away with nothing. Much later, a succession of counsellors would tell Tommy it was normal for children to blame themselves after a tragedy, to obsess over what they could have done differently, as though they could somehow go back in time and prevent it. Magical thinking. Tommy would nod and pretend to be reassured. But his mind threw it out again: *clinker, clinker, clinker*. If only he hadn't corrected his father. If only he had been clever like Nicky.

It wasn't your fault, the counsellors said.

Clinker, clinker, clinker.

Of course, they didn't know what had happened next. Tommy would never tell them. He knew this even at eight, still knew it at ten, knew it at fifteen and at twenty. Clinker wasn't the real trouble. Clinker was a displacement thought he clung to. The Vikings were bearable—almost, almost bearable—where the rest was not. It was so terrible that most days he couldn't even look at it. Couldn't look away either. Always, he would catch a glimpse of its edges and then the awful darkness rose up in him again.

I'm sorry, he tried to say to Nicky in his head. Often he woke up with the words at the front of his mind. Caroline told him one time that he'd spoken them aloud, still half asleep.

If only he could go back. If only he could go back, and

know what was coming, and do everything differently. Do only one thing differently. It would have taken just the tiniest of whispers, the smallest fraction of a second, a different decision, a different outcome.

Clinker, clinker, clinker.

If only, if only, if only.

10

Tommy had been staying with Malcolm for nearly a week, and their days had fallen into a kind of rhythm. Malcolm rose early, Tommy generally rose late. Some days Malcolm went out to work with Robert, but would mostly be back by the afternoon. Then, before the light faded, he and Tommy would go for a walk. Malcolm didn't know what Tommy did with his mornings. Sometimes he'd find him lounging in an armchair in the sitting room with one of Heather's novels. Tommy had finished *The Way of All Flesh* now and moved on to Thomas Hardy. Most days Tommy would have made lunch and left some for Malcolm: a cheese sandwich wrapped in cling film in the fridge, or pasta and tomato sauce to be heated up.

Once they were back from their afternoon walk, they would sit at the kitchen table, drinking tea and not saying much. Tommy might ask a few questions about the croft in the years before it was broken up, or about the state of farming on the island now. He remained knowledgeable, Malcolm thought, about their ways. You'd know he'd grown up here if you heard him talk about sheep farming. It surprised Malcolm how much Tommy knew, since John had been so intent on distancing himself and his family from the farming life. John had shown no interest in the croft after he left home, not even after their father was dead and Malcolm was working it. In fact, Malcolm had to admit now that John had sneered at it; there had been something self-conscious, something deliberate in the lack of interest he would display if Malcolm or anyone else brought the subject up. No, John was an accountant, John worked with his brain, not with his body, not his muscles and sinews; he was not interested in the rough, gruelling existence the rest of them eked out on the island, breaking their backs day after day in the mud and the rain. Malcolm had heard mutters about this in the bar, how John thought he was better than everyone else. Still, there was no real harm in it; people liked John—were impressed by him even. But now John's son, his grown-up child, sat across the table from Malcolm and talked of foot rot and subsidies and silage.

What they never discussed was Tommy's life over the past twenty years, or his plans for the future. The longer this went on, the more anxious Malcolm felt about it, and the more impossible it became to say anything important. He had asked Tommy so few questions, had been so afraid of prying.

You're both as bad as each other, he imagined Heather telling him. *You never get to the point, you men.* It was the sort of thing she might have said when she was alive.

Tommy had originally mentioned staying only a week. Malcolm wondered when he'd leave, but Tommy hadn't brought it up. Malcolm wasn't sure now whether he wanted Tommy gone or not. He was uncomfortable, and longed to have the quiet of his house restored, to be able to return to his familiar routines. But he worried about Tommy, and he felt responsible for him, even after all this time.

During their walks over the past few days, they had twice come across other islanders. The first time it had been Ken Stewart with his collie Morag. Malcolm had found himself holding his breath as Ken approached, but Ken was naturally taciturn, and he didn't seem eager to chat for long.

"So you're back again?" he said to Tommy once he and Malcolm had exchanged greetings.

"Yes."

"You find it much different?"

Tommy hesitated over this question. "No," he said at last. "I don't think so."

"No, I suppose we're more or less the same," Ken said. He thought for a moment, then added, "We don't have a vicar every other Sunday now. Once a month it is, over from Islay or Mull."

Tommy clearly didn't know how to respond to this.

"Not that there are many people who go," Ken said. "To church."

Malcolm wondered why Ken was talking so much about church. Ken didn't go himself.

"Martha Nairne's a lay reader," he said, not sure if he was addressing Ken or Tommy. "She takes some services."

There was a short pause, then Ken said, "Well, I'd best be getting on. Good to see you," he added to Tommy.

They said their goodbyes and Ken walked on, Morag trotting beside him.

The second time they encountered someone, the meeting was more prolonged. Heading south again towards Alban Bay on the sixth day of Tommy's visit, they met Fiona McKenzie coming the other way. Malcolm recognized her pink waterproof in the distance, but she'd already turned the bend in the road where it curved through a rocky pass, and must surely have seen them. They could not turn back without seeming to flee from her.

"That's Fiona," Malcolm said to Tommy, wanting, in some way, to prepare him. "Fiona McKenzie. You remember her? She lived down the road from you. A quarter of a mile or so."

He thought at first that Tommy wasn't going to reply, but then Tommy said, "Yeah. Of course."

Unbidden, a memory came to Malcolm: one of Tommy's outbursts, quite late on. What was it that he'd thrown at Fiona, standing in the middle of the living room? The poor woman

had only dropped by to return a dish. Heather's crystal rooster—Malcolm grasped the memory suddenly, how it had shattered beautifully against the wall like a shower of confetti, per-
ilously close to Fiona's head, how swiftly he had rushed to get
hold of Tommy's flailing arms while Heather ushered Fiona
out into the hall. He had no idea what Fiona's supposed crime
had been, what on earth she might have said to set him off.
Tommy had wept about it afterwards—not over Fiona but over
the rooster, which he'd loved. But it was just an old ornament,
Heather told him sternly; that wasn't the part that mattered.
She made him write Fiona a letter and then she'd taken him
round to deliver it in person. Tommy had submitted meekly on
that occasion. Perhaps he really had been sorry, too. Malcolm
had seen the letter, drafted in Tommy's rough book and then
copied out in his very best handwriting. He couldn't recall
what it had said.

He wondered if Tommy was remembering this too, or if
those years were a blur to him.

As they drew closer, Tommy said, "She was friends with my
mother."

"Aye," Malcolm said. But Katrina had found Fiona hard
work—Malcolm was sure he remembered Heather passing
that on to him once, a rare indiscretion for both women. And
indeed Fiona *was* hard work, an anxious person. She wanted
too much from other people, that was what Malcolm thought
it was. Every conversation with her felt effortful, as though she
must always be coming up too close to you. But she was a good
sort of woman.

"I daresay she'll want to stop and chat," he said while Fiona
was still out of earshot, wanting to convey the idea that her
chatting would not be like Ken's chatting.

Tommy said nothing. He put his hands in his pockets with,
Malcolm thought, the air of someone bracing themselves for an
ordeal.

"Malcolm," Fiona called out, still ten yards away. "Lovely morning. Nice and bright." As she came closer, she said, "And this must be Tommy, of course." Her eyes were on Tommy the whole time, barely grazing Malcolm.

Tommy nodded, and Malcolm added, feeling more was necessary, "That's right. Tommy, you remember Fiona?"

"Yes," Tommy said. "Hello."

"It's been such a long time," Fiona said to Tommy. "You were just a bairn when I saw you last. Now look at you."

Tommy didn't appear to have a reply to this.

"So what have you been doing with yourself?" Fiona said, as the pause threatened to become awkward. "Where are you living now?"

"London," Tommy said. "The last few years, anyway."

"London." She drew out the two syllables. "Really? Well, that must be an exciting place to live. Lots going on, I'm sure. Very different to here."

She was speaking faster than usual, Malcolm thought. And there was something in her manner—she wasn't at ease at all. It occurred to him then that perhaps she had been no more eager for this encounter than they had. The idea distressed him on Tommy's behalf.

"Aye," he said. "Tommy's used to a different pace of life now."

"And what do you do in London?" Fiona said. "For work?"

"I've done a few different things," Tommy said, and it was brought home to Malcolm again that he knew almost nothing about Tommy's life, or how he'd supported himself over the past decade. He'd finally managed to ask Tommy rather tentatively the night before what it was he did for a living, but all Tommy had said was, "This and that. Admin stuff mostly," and then hadn't seemed to want to discuss it further. He was being similarly evasive with Fiona now. Still, it was true that Tommy's life was none of their business.

Fiona seemed disconcerted by Tommy's laconic response. But she lived here, Malcolm reminded himself. Surely she was used to reticent men.

She said, "And is there a wife back down in London? A family?"

"No," Tommy said.

"Well." Fiona hesitated. "Plenty of time for all that. I suppose we all settle down very young out here. We must seem dull to you."

"No," Tommy said again. "Not at all."

"I think he's just being polite," Malcolm said, feeling the strain of this conversation. "Not much for a young lad to do round here."

"And how long will you be visiting?" Fiona said.

Malcolm was curious about this too, though he wished Fiona hadn't put Tommy on the spot.

"I'm not sure yet," Tommy said. "It depends."

"On work, I suppose," Fiona said. "Doesn't everything always depend on work?"

There was a pause, then Tommy said, "Yes."

The three of them stood looking at each other for a few moments. Malcolm said, to save them all, "Well, we'd better be getting on. It'll be dark soon."

"Of course," Fiona said quickly. "The nights are closing in, aren't they? So nice to see you again, Tommy. You take care."

Tommy gave Fiona a formal smile, said, "You too," and finally she walked on, calling over her shoulder, "Have a good evening."

Malcolm and Tommy continued in silence for a few minutes. Finally, Tommy said, "What was it I threw at her?"

Malcolm gave him a sidelong glance. "A crystal rooster."

"You remember it then?"

"Just barely."

Tommy nodded. "I think she might too."

It's not that, Malcolm almost said, but stopped himself. Better for Tommy to think it was only the rooster.

Tommy didn't speak again for the rest of the walk. When they got back to the cottage, he disappeared upstairs. He was upset, Malcolm knew, but he felt he had no real grasp of the nature of Tommy's distress, or what on earth he might say to comfort him.

When it had got to six thirty and Tommy still hadn't reappeared, Malcolm went upstairs and tapped softly on his door.

"Tommy?" he said.

After a moment, he heard sounds from within, and then Tommy opened the door.

"Would you like a cup of tea?" Malcolm said.

Tommy considered for a few moments. "O.K."

He followed Malcolm downstairs and sat at the kitchen table while Malcolm made the tea. He had the slightly dazed air of someone who'd just woken up, but Malcolm didn't think he'd been asleep.

After taking the first few sips of his tea, Tommy said, "I threw a lot of things, didn't I?"

"I suppose," Malcolm said.

"I remember the rooster," Tommy said, "because I felt so bad about it afterwards. Because of Heather. It was hers. It wasn't mine to break."

"She didn't care about that."

"I suppose I had a bad reputation," Tommy said. "Before I left the island."

"You were just a child, Tommy. You were grieving."

"Everyone must remember it."

"If they do, no one holds it against you."

Tommy drank some more of his tea, then said abruptly, "I know I'm inconveniencing you. Thank you for having me to stay."

Malcolm lowered his own mug and looked at Tommy. "It's no trouble," he said.

Tommy nodded quickly. "And I know I said I'd move on. After a week or so."

There was a pause as Malcolm tried to find his feet in the conversation. "There's no rush to leave," he said.

Tommy met his eye. "I'm not planning on staying forever," he said. "Not for months or anything. I promise."

"It's O.K."

"It's just . . ." Tommy stopped and raised his hand to rub his face. Finally, he said, "I don't have anywhere else to go."

When Malcolm didn't immediately answer—he was trying to decide what to say—Tommy rushed on, "I will have. I just need a bit of time. To work things out. Just a little more time."

Malcolm thought of his wife, and at last, holding Heather in his mind, he found the right thing to say. "You're welcome here, Tommy. For as long as you want."

And although Malcolm asked him no questions, Tommy began to speak. Without looking at Malcolm, he said, "I was living with Caroline in London. We'd been together a while. Four years. I thought maybe this time . . . but in the end it all went wrong. *I* made it go wrong. And after that I didn't know what to do."

When Malcolm was sure Tommy wasn't going to say anything else, he said, with more certainty in his voice than he felt, "You need a rest. That's what it sounds like."

"Yeah," Tommy said. "That's it."

"I'm sorry about Caroline. Did you . . . ? Was she nice?"

"Yes," Tommy said. "I loved her."

Malcolm nodded. He thought of how he missed Heather, of how nothing helped. Finally, he said, "We'd best start tea. Lasagne sound O.K.?"

"Yeah," Tommy said. He got up quickly from the table. "I'll do the onions." He got out the chopping board and knife, fetched the onions and sat back down at the table. Turning an onion in his hand, he said inconsequentially, "A crystal rooster seems like a strange thing for Heather to have owned."

Malcolm was so surprised he laughed out loud. "It was a wedding present from some aunt or other. I think she was glad to see the back of it."

Tommy nodded to himself and began slicing the onions.

11

I saw Tommy yesterday," Fiona said to her husband the following afternoon, laying down her book and watching for his reaction. She had found herself oddly reluctant to mention it the previous day, shaken by the encounter and unwilling to summon up Tommy's presence in their living room.

Gavin said, barely raising his head from the newspaper, "Oh? And how was he?"

"Fine," Fiona said angrily, unable to explain why she was angry. "He seemed fine. We had quite a long chat."

"That's nice."

It isn't nice, Fiona thought. It isn't nice.

"I'm pleased for Malcolm, having Tommy back," Gavin said.

"Malcolm doesn't know him. None of us do."

"Don't be silly," Gavin said, returning to his paper. "He grew up here. He's one of us."

"Don't you remember what he was *like*?" Fiona said. "He was out of control. He was frightening, by the end."

"No he wasn't."

"He *attacked* me," Fiona said.

"Oh hen, no he didn't."

"He threw that thing at me—that ornament. Don't you remember? It could have killed me."

"I think that's a bit of an exaggeration."

She was quiet, furious.

"I know what you're thinking," Gavin said, "and it isn't fair."

"What am I thinking then?" she said.

"You're thinking that he's like his father."

"Well, perhaps he is."

"No, Fi."

There was a silence. Fiona thought Gavin wasn't going to say anything else, but then he let the newspaper rest in his lap and said, "I saw them too, actually. This morning. Down by the harbour."

This was so like him, to bring it up as an afterthought.

"Really?" Fiona said. "Did you speak to them?"

"Aye," Gavin said. "I invited them round to eat with us. I meant to say."

Fiona had been going to pick up her book again, but now she froze. "You did what?"

"Invited them round."

"Without asking me first! Why would you *do* that?"

Gavin shrugged. "It seemed unfriendly not to. And it's only a meal, after all."

"I don't want him here," Fiona said.

Gavin looked at her searchingly for a moment. "Fi," he said at last. "You have to let it go—this . . . *thing* about Tommy. It wasn't his fault."

"I don't have a 'thing' about Tommy," Fiona said coldly. "But I'd have liked to have been consulted first, about the meal *I'll* be cooking, in my own home, for someone we barely know, after all."

"I'm *consulting* you," Gavin said with exaggerated patience, "now. You can name the day. I said we'd ring up to arrange it."

Fiona was silent.

"What do you think will happen, hen?" Gavin said, his infuriating good humour returning. "Do you think he might murder us all when he comes round?"

"It's not funny," Fiona said, her voice rising. "That's a terrible thing to say. I don't understand how you can joke about it."

Gavin was unmoved. "It happened more than twenty years ago," he said. "It was a horrible thing, but there it is. Life goes on."

He didn't feel things deeply, Fiona thought as Gavin picked up his newspaper again. He never had. But wasn't it true that she'd loved that about him once, how easily he took life, how sensible and matter-of-fact he was? Her own family had always been histrionic; it had driven her mad, how everything was always a big drama for her mother, how everything had to be picked over and gone into. Fiona had fled at nineteen into Gavin's no-nonsense embrace. But that was the problem. Almost everything you did as an adult was a reaction against your upbringing, so you ended up marrying your opposite in a bid to escape your family, not realizing that it was already too late. They had already had their way with you, burrowed into you until one day you looked in the mirror and saw your own mother or father staring back at you, having bided their time and then emerged like a well-fed parasite from beneath your skin. Fiona had over-corrected in choosing Gavin, and found as the years passed that rather than growing into each other, their differences had become more pronounced. Gavin must surely be aware of this too, aware that he should have married someone practical like Heather or Kathy. Fiona had enough insight to know she infuriated her husband sometimes, how patient he had trained himself to be with her.

Then there was Stuart (who perhaps took after her more than Gavin), who was moody and thin skinned and never seemed to want to visit them. She worried about him, and knew Gavin did too. His life, she feared, had not been happy. The divorce had been painful, and she still wasn't sure Stuart had recovered. He didn't see his children much, though Joanne was very fair about things like that. Fiona and Gavin saw them hardly at all. Stuart's new wife Lucy seemed to work long hours and didn't want children. Fiona supposed she herself was to blame for many of her son's mistakes, because parents usually were, and most especially mothers (Gavin had not helped her enough; Gavin had been unconcerned). But somewhere deep down she also blamed the Bairds for Stuart's absence from the island, though she knew really this had nothing to do with why her son kept away.

Still, it was true that the Bairds had brought horror to the island. And Fiona blamed them for it, blamed John of course, but also Katrina, and even Tommy, because he was the living reminder, and because he knew things they didn't, had seen things nobody should see, and now here he was again, drifting about among them like a ghost.

"I remember him sitting right here across from me," Gavin said, startling her. "John, I mean. You and Katrina would be in the kitchen, chatting away, and John and I would be in here. Having a whisky."

Fiona saw John's face, as she often did, his considerate expression as he asked her about herself. He listened, too—really listened. No trouble from your life was too small to hold his attention. He'd changed, perhaps, towards the end.

"A strange thing," Gavin said meditatively, and Fiona wondered briefly if she had him wrong, if it came to him too in moments alone, if he too felt winded by how much he had missed.

She waited, but Gavin didn't say anything more. Fiona said, to prompt him, "He loved those bairns so much."

But Gavin only shrugged at this, and she saw she would get nothing else from him.

Their car had broken down, she remembered, hers and Gavin's, about a year before the murders, and for a week while they were waiting for it to be fixed, John had driven round specially on the days he worked from home to pick

Fiona up and take her to the shop so she could still work. She saw John's kind face again, turning to ask her something from the driver's seat. That nice car of his.

So much of it was unfathomable, but what Fiona always came back to was the relentless simplicity of this question: how on earth could a man seem so normal, day after day, then suddenly get up from the table one evening, fetch a shotgun and murder his entire family, leaving one child alive only by accident? Fiona was no fool—she could see there were depths to that man that none of them had understood. Nobody could have predicted what would happen, she reminded herself. But it was unsettling for all of them, having Tommy back here. He was the spitting image of his father. Of course it stirred things up.

12

What on God's earth could prompt a man to get up from the table one evening and murder his family? Some questions, Tom knew, had no answer, and weren't really in the end even questions, but rather an exhaustion you carried with you everywhere, so deep it had sunk into your bones. Some mornings when he woke he felt as though his body was full of concrete and he simply could not move. Some days the heaviness was Nicky. Tom used to be glad that his brother so often came about with him, especially in the early years after he left the island, when he had felt so untethered from everything that he thought without the weight of Nicky he might drift up into the sky and vanish without a trace. But Tom was a grown man now and Nicky was still a child: they had less and less in common.

The light coming in through the slats in the wardrobe, slicing the room into segments.

He blinked it away.

From the kitchen, Malcolm called, "Is fish pie O.K. for tea, Tommy?" and Tom, grateful for the distraction, called back, "Yes—great." Then he got up from the sofa and went through to join his uncle.

Malcolm was chopping vegetables at the counter. There was a newspaper on the table and Tom pulled a section towards himself at random—it turned out to be book reviews—and read for a while.

After a few minutes' silence, Malcolm said, his back to Tom,

"You know, we wrote to you while you were living with Jill. Every fortnight. For a few years, anyway."

Tom was thrown by this comment. He had slept badly the night before, and had a headache. He wasn't in the mood for a heart-to-heart with Malcolm. He said shortly, "Yes. Sorry I didn't write back."

"It's not that." Malcolm half turned. "It's . . . we didn't want you to think we'd forgotten about you."

Tom tried to give him a smile. "I imagine I was pretty hard to forget."

Malcolm didn't seem to know how to reply to this. He said, "Well, I hope you were all right with Jill."

"Yes." To her credit, Jill had always behaved in exactly the same way towards Tom as towards her own son Henry. But she was not the sort of person you could be close to. She had treated both boys more like valued young colleagues than close relatives. Perhaps that had made things easier for Tom, given the state he was in back then.

Malcolm put the vegetables into a pan and switched on the heat. He said, "And do you talk to Henry much?"

"Not really. He's been in Canada for more than ten years and you know—you lose touch. We email occasionally."

Malcolm nodded.

Tom went back to reading, but after a few moments Malcolm added, "And will you stay in touch with Caroline, do you think?"

"It seems unlikely." Malcolm didn't seem to understand what it meant for a relationship to be over. Tom briefly considered explaining all the reasons it was unsalvageable, if only to prevent further questions, but decided he didn't have the energy.

"You're running away," Caroline had said as he packed his bag.

"Yes."

"Do you think it'll help?"

Tom had no reply to this. He didn't think anything would help now.

"You always knew I wanted children," Caroline said. She was crying again.

"Yes. But . . ." But what? He had really thought that when the time came it might be O.K.

"You've wasted my time," she said. "Four years. Wasted."

"I know." He put out his hand to her. "I'm so sorry."

"*Don't* say you're sorry," she said, moving beyond his reach. "I love you. It wasn't wasted."

This was the worst thing: that somebody like her could love him, and still he would find, when it came to it, that he could not feel as he ought to.

He tried again. "I can't do it. I thought I could, but . . ." Children of his own. He should have known it would be impossible. How stupid to have allowed himself to imagine otherwise, and to have allowed her to imagine.

"So what is it then?" she said, and he could hear in her voice that she was looking for a way to hurt him. "You're worried they'll inherit—what? Some kind of family *disorder*?"

"No, it isn't that. I don't know how to explain it."

"You should be more worried they'll inherit your dress sense."

Taken by surprise, Tom laughed unhappily. She'd never been easy to predict.

"Tom," Caroline said. "That place. Why go back there? Won't it make things worse?"

"I have to get away," he said.

"Well, go to Brighton for the weekend like a normal person. Go to fucking Magaluf if you really need a break. Don't go back to that godforsaken island."

"I need to," he said, not sure if this was true. He wasn't sure of anything, except for the terrible heaviness in his body.

"I'm worried," Caroline said, "that you won't be O.K. You don't seem O.K."

Tom shook his head. He'd never been O.K.

Sometimes Tom wondered if there were other people in the world who carried a burden like his, and if so, how it felt to them, how they could bear it. Some days he wished he was dead. Survival had never felt like a blessing.

It wasn't that he wished he had died at the time. Even now, the terror in his stomach felt like a living thing, making him want to run to the bathroom, to throw up, to shit himself, he wasn't sure. His instinct, whenever he thought of it now, whenever he dreamed of it, remained the same: save your life. Animals are programmed to preserve themselves. As a child or an adult, Tom did not wish to be murdered. He did not wish to have his body blown apart by the explosion of lead-shot cartridges in his chest, his legs, his head. He did not want his blood and his brains all over the walls.

So his survival then, he would not undo. But if he could only slip quietly away now, he thought, that would be O.K. Mostly it was a passive wish, a desire to disappear more than anything else, but he had toyed with the idea in the past of taking matters into his own hands. Pills and vodka. Even the brutal immediacy of a train. It made him feel tired. If he could be dead just by wishing it, without effort and without pain, without any action at all on his part, he thought he would choose it.

He could not remember now exactly why Nicky had gone back downstairs that evening. He was almost sure it was because his brother had wanted to watch television, but it bothered Tom that he could not recall this for certain, nor think of what programme he might have been watching. So much was broken and blurred, but what remained clear was that Nicky and his mum were downstairs when it started, and so was Beth because she'd woken up crying some time earlier, and Tommy was alone upstairs in the bedroom he shared with Nicky, reading an illustrated book about the Vikings.

There had been shouting and several shots but he could not say afterwards what order these things happened in, or if they were all taking place at the same time. He could not say either how long he remained frozen, the book still in his hands. Then he was up and running along the landing, and the shouting got louder and he thought he remembered his father yelling, "You did this, you bitch," (Tommy would later repeat this to the police) and the next moment he was in his parents' bedroom, though he couldn't have explained why this was the place he chose. He couldn't have explained any of his actions after the shots began, could not even have said if he knew at the time what was happening, that downstairs everyone was dying. His body simply took over and there he was in the middle of his parents' room. He had closed the door behind him and now his eyes were darting around in panic as he looked for a hiding place.

Most of all afterwards he remembered the cold that had gone all the way through him and the way his heart seemed to have escaped from his chest and now was beating everywhere his body, in his legs and his arms and his head. It was so loud in his head that after a time he could not hear any more shots. He didn't notice he had wet himself until much later, when his soaking pyjamas had gone cold and he started to shiver. It was a strange and rare knowledge, the discovery of what the human body does when it is in terror. He had felt fear before and since, but never like this. Mortal terror was something different. A hard thing, to find you are just an animal, in desperate fright, trying to save itself. He would not forget.

There was a built-in wardrobe along the far wall of the room that his father had installed some years before. Tommy's father was proud of this wardrobe. He said it was "modern".

It was made of light-coloured wood, with several different sections—two big ones in the middle, and two smaller ones on either side. Four wardrobes in one, Tommy's father had boasted. Tommy chose—though there seemed no conscious choice in it—the narrow section on the far left, where old coats and some of his mother's dresses hung. He crawled in and pulled the door closed behind him. The clothes smelled of his mother. He pushed himself as far back as he could. He wanted complete darkness, but there were slats in the door allowing slivers of light through, and allowing him to see thin slices of the room from where he was. For a time he screwed his eyes shut. He wasn't thinking anything at all when the door of the bedroom was pushed open.

Most people got to spend their whole lives never knowing whether they were good or bad. What beautiful safety there must be in that. Walking down the street in London, waiting to cross at traffic lights, sitting at his desk at work, Tom always knew the kind of person he was. Once you knew, you carried it with you forever. Other people might behave badly at times—lie or cheat or manipulate—and then they might feel guilty for a while, but mostly they would still think of themselves as good. Not perfect, perhaps, but certainly not *bad*, not at their core. It would be so peaceful, he thought, to be able to move through the world like that. Tom wasn't sure how many other people were out there who had truly been tested, and who had truly failed; people who, in that crucial moment, had made a terribly wrong choice and then had to live with it afterwards, marked in a way that only they could see, haunted forever by their shame.

13

Y ou know, we don't have to go," Malcolm added, when he told Tommy that Fiona had rung them to ask them round for a meal the following evening. He'd forgotten Gavin's invitation until Fiona called, and found it hard to explain why he felt dismayed.

Tommy's face was, as so often, difficult to read. "It's fine," he said. "No reason not to go."

"She said she's invited the MacDonalds, too. Kathy and Ed. You met Kathy again in the shop, you remember?"

"Yes," Tommy said.

"And the Dougdales. Chris and Mary. They . . . well, they moved into your old house. Not long after you left for the mainland." He stopped, suddenly unable to look at Tommy. *It'll be more fun for Tommy with more people,* Fiona had said. Malcolm was not convinced.

"Right," Tommy said, his voice neutral.

"They're very nice," Malcolm finished lamely.

It was later than usual in the evening, but Tommy had yet to disappear upstairs. They were on the chamomile tea tonight; Tommy had asked Malcolm the morning before if he had any non-caffeinated tea to have in the evenings (he didn't always sleep well, he said), and so Malcolm had picked up the herbal tea in the shop on his way back from helping Robert with the feed buckets. Chamomile was the only option. He was surprised, in truth, to observe that the tiny shop stocked anything other than normal tea, but he supposed herbal blends were becoming all the rage these days. Still tasted like ditchwater though.

Kathy had raised her eyebrows as she rung up the purchase.

"This is a new one for you, Malcolm."

"Aye," he said, feeling it was too much effort to explain.

Perplexingly, he'd opted for chamomile himself this evening, possibly out of a vague desire to be companionable. He wondered what Ross or Davey would make of this scene, Malcolm and Tommy sitting here in the kitchen at nine in the evening, quietly sipping their herbal tea. He tried to work out whether these long silent moments between him and his nephew were becoming more comfortable. Perhaps he was just getting used to the discomfort.

"What time will we go to Fiona's?" Tommy said.

Malcolm realized then that he had half hoped Tommy would say no, that he would save them from having to go. The evening, he felt, would be hard work. More than that: he had an inexplicable sense of dread. But Tommy would never say no. That blankness seemed to have come over him again, expressed as a kind of distant amenability.

"Seven."

"Do you go for dinner there often?" Tommy said. "Do you eat with your neighbours often?"

"From time to time," Malcolm said, wondering why he felt guarded.

"You haven't since I've been here," Tommy said. He was looking into his tea.

It's only been nine days, Malcolm wanted to say.

"I hope I'm not getting in your way," Tommy added.

"What do you mean?"

"Disrupting your life."

This again. "Tommy, I'm not the social butterfly you imagine," Malcolm said. "I don't have much of a life to disrupt."

Tommy laughed at this, and Malcolm thought that something

in him seemed to shift. His nephew leaned forward and put his elbows on the table as he looked at Malcolm.

"There used to be a ceilidh in the hall every month," Tommy said. "Maybe even every fortnight. Does that still happen?"

"Occasionally," Malcolm said. "Every few months now. None of us are as young as we were. Nobody wants Ross dropping dead from a heart attack in our midst."

"No young people to replace you."

Malcolm shook his head, thinking this was rather a bleak thing to point out.

"But it's still a social place, right?" Tommy said. "It always used to be."

Tommy's expression was more open now. Malcolm remembered what a chatterbox he had been as a child, how brightly and quickly he would talk when he got on to a favourite subject (dinosaurs, or was that Nicky? No, Tommy had liked history), how John would raise his eyebrows and adopt an air of forced patience, and how carefully Katrina would listen.

He said, "I suppose it's still fairly social. Tiny place like this, you can't exactly avoid each other."

"Don't you find it claustrophobic?"

Malcolm considered. "Sometimes, I suppose. But I grew up here, remember. Never known anything else."

"You can't do much here without other people noticing."

"You can't do anything here without other people noticing."

"How long do you think I'd been on the island before every single person knew about it?"

"Oh, I'm not sure," Malcolm said, pretending to think about it. "Maybe all of three minutes."

"Three minutes of blissful anonymity," Tommy said. "You'd find London strange. Caroline and I didn't even know the names of the people living in the flats down the hall from us."

"Now that does seem unfriendly."

"I think I liked it. It was peaceful. But . . ." He paused a moment, then said, "I suppose it might be nice having people around you who know you. I remember when I was a kid, you and Heather came round all the time, didn't you?"

"Every few weeks or so," Malcolm said cautiously. It had been once a fortnight, probably. He couldn't quite admit this to Tommy.

"Was my mother sociable?"

"I'd say so," Malcolm said. "She liked people."

"My father said she talked too much," Tommy said. "I remember him saying that to her. Maybe more than once. I don't remember when or why."

Malcolm took this in. At last, he said, "She was fairly quiet, your mother. On the whole. Perhaps he sometimes told her she was too quiet, as well. He wasn't easily pleased."

"He thought she should always do what he wanted," Tommy said.

"He never knew what it was he wanted."

They were both silent. The conversation had taken an unexpected turn, and Malcolm looked for a way to draw it back to safer territory while knowing he had no right to do that.

He wondered how much Tommy knew, or had guessed, about the events leading up to the murders. But none of them had very much to go on. Katrina had been secretive in life, and she remained secretive in death. They'd received a letter from the procurator fiscal summarizing his findings after it was all over. Malcolm had wanted as much information as possible, though Heather had said this was foolish—morbid even—and he would only upset himself further. Heather had never even looked at the letter herself. The fiscal had warned Malcolm that it contained "distressing details" (You don't say, Malcolm had wanted to reply), but in the end it hadn't told him much he didn't know already, despite running to five close-typed pages. It contained only the facts of the matter: a summary of the police investigation, with who died, and how, and where, and in what order. There was also a brief discussion of John's debts.

Malcolm had gone to see the fiscal in person over in Oban, and the man had taken him through the findings, answering all his questions. He had been very kind. Malcolm went home on the ferry, still clutching his letter, still having learned nothing new. But why would the police or the fiscal have been able to unearth the truth about his brother when Malcolm himself could not? He had put the letter away in the bottom drawer of his desk and never looked at it again. "Why keep it at all?" Heather had said, and Malcolm hadn't had an answer for her except that he felt he had to.

There was one thing he came back to from time to time. It was a conversation he'd had with Katrina's sister Jill after the funeral for Katrina, Nicky and Beth. They'd all gathered in Malcolm and Heather's cottage for the wake, though the place had been much too small really; people had spilled out into the garden, but thankfully the rain held off. Malcolm found himself standing in the narrow hallway with Jill, who looked as exhausted by the day's events as he was. She was rather difficult to talk to, a reserved woman, not unlike Katrina in that respect, but without the warmth that softened Katrina's shyness. After some awkward small talk about the turnout, Jill had said abruptly, "You know, she rang me, a few weeks ago. Hadn't heard from her for two years by then."

Malcolm had nodded. He knew that people always regretted not having spent enough time with the dead person before they passed; he had felt this briefly about his own father, and he'd hated the man.

"She asked if she and the children could come and stay for a while," Jill went on. "A holiday, she said. I was about to tell her there wasn't room. We weren't close anymore. But there was something in her voice."

This was the part that had stayed with Malcolm over the years: something in her voice.

It probably meant nothing. People invented all kinds of things to torment themselves after a death. Katrina didn't seem to have pursued the idea, anyway. The next Jill had heard of her sister was a distraught phone call from Heather several weeks later, and then the lurid media reports. (Malcolm and Heather had kept Tommy away from all that, at least. That was one thing they had done right.)

"You never spoke to Heather like that," Tommy said now, breaking into his thoughts. "The way my father spoke to my mother. Unkindly, I mean."

"No." God, he hoped not.

"So why did my father treat his wife like that and you didn't?"

"We weren't the same person," Malcolm said, hearing how defensive he sounded.

"I just don't understand," Tommy said, "how he ended up one way and you ended up another. He can't have been born bad. Can he?"

Malcolm shook his head. "I don't know." It wasn't as though he hadn't thought about it. It didn't sound likely, though. Babies were babies, weren't they? Children were children.

"What was *your* father like?" Tommy said.

Malcolm sighed. He thought carefully and said, "He was unhappy. He didn't like our mother, and I'm not sure he liked us much either. Me and John." He hesitated. "He was a bit of a bastard, truth be told."

Tommy said, "So you see, then. It gets passed on."

"Aye, maybe."

Malcolm caught Tommy's stricken expression for just a moment before Tommy could hide it, and realized, belatedly, what his nephew had been attempting to ask him. Why was he so slow today? Trying to match Tommy's indirectness with his own, he said, "I don't believe I am like my father. That's not always the way it goes. I don't believe we're doomed to become our parents."

"No?"

"It's not genetic," Malcolm said, "the kind of –" he paused, searching for a suitably vague word—"*attitude* your father had, the attitude my father had. Maybe you learn it. Maybe John learned it. But it isn't inevitable."

Tommy didn't speak for a few moments. Then he shrugged, and drained his mug. "Yeah, maybe. Anyway, I think I'll go up." He produced what might have been an attempt at a smile. "All that chamomile. Making me tired."

"O.K.," Malcolm said. To fill the slight pause that followed, he added, "Sleep well. I'll be out with Robert in the morning, but back in the afternoon."

"Right. Night, Malcolm."

Then Tommy was gone from the kitchen and Malcolm breathed out slowly.

When it came to John, Malcolm could see as well as Tommy that the bare facts of the matter didn't add up to much. Their father had been hard on them. Their mother had favoured Malcolm. Neither explained why John would take it into his head to murder his wife and children.

Of course, Malcolm knew it would be easy to claim now, to let himself think now, that he and John had never been close, that he had never really known his brother. It wouldn't be true. Or at least, it would be both true and not true, which seemed to Malcolm to be the case with so many things, especially as he grew older.

He and John had played together as young children. They had always been together. As teenagers, they had begun to go their separate ways, even while they lived in the same house and worked side by side on the croft, but as young boys they had been comrades. They had roamed across the cliffs and the beaches together, just as Tommy and Nicky had done. They climbed over the rocks in the north to watch the seals and in summer they swam in the sea, playing football on the beach to dry off. When they helped their father, it would usually be together too, feeding the sheep or getting them down from the common grazing and, when they were older and stronger, cutting the peat and helping with lambing. They were united in this, the hard work and the shocking cold of the early mornings, trying to warm your hands and shield your face from the wind as the sun came up over the cliffs and turned the machair gold.

Most of Malcolm's memories were outside, and when he pictured himself as a teenager, holding a sheep while his father sheared it or battling the wind on the hillside or driving the harvester across the low-lying fields, he always saw John there too, even if he knew he'd more likely been alone at the time.

And John had disliked the croft. Had he always, or had this come later? Malcolm thought John had wanted different things even as a child. He had a memory of his brother and the satchel, a leather school satchel John had been desperate for and had finally received one Christmas. Malcolm wasn't sure how old his brother had been then—perhaps seven or eight? He remembered the satchel because he had found it so incomprehensible at the time, how passionately John had his heart set on it, when neither of them had any use for a smart leather book-bag like that; they had very little to carry to school, and their old rucksacks did the job fine. Malcolm couldn't get his head around craving something that had no real use. Maybe he had teased John about it. He felt certain his father had, saying something like, "You'll be carrying the feed in that, will you?"

But Malcolm recalled John's excitement when he'd opened the satchel that Christmas, how John had leapt up to hug his mother and she had laughed and hugged him back, and

Malcolm had felt pleased to see this, and surprised. John had carried the satchel about with him everywhere for a time, Malcolm recalled, and it had looked funny with his old thick jersey with holes in the elbows and his muddy boots.

Then later, another memory: he and John coming into the kitchen when their mother had a friend round (he could not remember who it had been), and the woman saying, "That's a smart satchel, John. What have you got in there?"

Then, before John could answer, their mother saying, "Oh, it's empty. He has nothing in there at all. He just carries it around for show."

She'd said it lightly, with a laugh in her voice, and Malcolm was sure she hadn't meant to be cruel. But he had felt his brother's humiliation. He didn't know if he was misremembering, but he thought John had stopped carrying the satchel around after that.

Malcolm could see it was silly to dwell on something like this. In any case, he knew as well as anyone what a strange darkness the past was, how we plucked pieces from it and refitted them to our own purposes. The past was a story we told ourselves.

"We could move, you know," Heather had said to him in the months after it happened. "Take Tommy away and take ourselves away too. Go somewhere where nobody knows us."

This was in the days when Malcolm was most painfully aware of the questions people were asking themselves. Did violence run in families? Did whatever rage had been in John live on in his son, and maybe even in Malcolm?

Whatever people were thinking, Malcolm had always known it would be impossible for them to move. He thought Heather knew it too. When he had told her, "This is our home," she hadn't pursued the subject further.

But they should have taken Tommy and run, Malcolm thought now, sitting alone in his kitchen with his cooling chamomile tea. He had been selfish to insist they stay, even after it became clear that Tommy would never cope on the island. Malcolm had talked of the croft, and of the house, and of their roots, and Heather hadn't argued. But those hadn't been the real reasons, and he wondered if Heather had known this too.

She had believed it would be better for them to go somewhere new, where they wouldn't always be known as the family of the man who murdered his wife and children. But the idea had terrified Malcolm. Away from the island, away from its tethers, *he* would know, *he* would know he was the brother of the man who killed his family, and what else was there but that once he was off the island? Here, everyone knew him well, and everyone had known him long before it happened. However much they might talk about him behind his back, however much they might have to say about the killings, he would always be Malcolm to them, and Heather would be Heather, and they worked a croft to the west of the island, and they had always belonged here. Malcolm desperately needed the islanders to give him a context beyond his brother's crimes, because he no longer believed he could do that for himself. Off the island, he would exist only in the orbit of the murders. So this was the selfishness he had never admitted to, not even to Heather; even after it became clear Tommy could not stay here, Malcolm could never have contemplated leaving, because however afraid he had been for Tommy, he had always been more afraid for himself.

I'm sorry, he wanted to say to Tommy now. I let you down.

And in how many ways? He had failed to protect him before—and Nicky, and Beth—and he had failed to protect him afterwards. On both charges, there were arguments he could make that would sound convincing to others. He could defend himself if he cared to. But he did not care to.

14

Tom lay upstairs in bed, as usual not sleeping. The agitation seemed worse tonight, and he couldn't say why except that his father felt close at hand. But it was not as though he was ever far away. He had come with Tom to Nottingham where he'd lived with Jill, to Manchester, to Edinburgh, to Lisbon, followed him to London, had finally taken up residence in the flat Tom shared with Caroline. Tom had hoped for a while that Caroline might be the one to chase him away, though in the end he realized that was too much to ask of anyone.

He had met Caroline when he was at a particularly low ebb, but this was something he'd never told her; it wasn't right to make someone feel you were dependent on them, that you needed them more than was really acceptable. He sometimes wondered why she was with him—she was amazing, she could have been with anyone—but he wasn't sure he understood relationships anyway. Why was anyone ever with anybody else? She had said she enjoyed his company. She said she loved him. They had been happy together for a while.

But of course, he was still his father's son.

"You were very quiet this evening," Caroline had told him a few months ago. They were walking to the Tube after dinner with friends, and Tom had not been in a good mood. He had felt, obscurely, that it was her fault.

He had said, "Didn't have much choice, did I? You wouldn't let anyone get a word in edgeways."

He had seen the shock on her face and then the hurt, and

had felt briefly pleased to have wounded her, while observing himself feeling this. Hating himself.

He remembered how his father had commented on his mother's clothes, sending her back upstairs to change before church. He had said the colours were too bright, or that her outfit was ugly (or even "frumpy', that silly word Tommy and Nicky had laughed about afterwards, because they thought it sounded like a pudding). Tommy had felt angry at the time on his mother's behalf, but he had known too that it was her fault for not dressing the right way. She made things difficult when she didn't need to. And Tommy had thought all fathers were like this, that behind closed doors this was how all men treated their wives.

As an adult, Tom had had to train himself to blame his father, not his mother. He considered himself enlightened now. He had worked hard and had learned to challenge every automatic thought he had. Still, though. Still. His father's views lurked somewhere within him, coiled up in his guts like a tapeworm. It was his father's voice Tom heard when he told Caroline she talked too much.

Later that night, back in their flat, he had said, "Sorry. I'm sorry, I don't know why I said that. It wasn't true."

"You said it to upset me," Caroline replied.

"Yes. I'm sorry."

She'd forgiven him the next day, because she trusted him, even though she shouldn't (did he blame her for that, too?). Part of Tom had watched the whole scene play out from a distance, observing his own remorse—which was genuine—while wondering when the next time would be.

And there was always a next time. Tom would grow cold, would become withdrawn, would snap at Caroline over nothing. Would be critical of her when she was eating too loudly, or scattering crumbs over the carpet, leaving all her make-up out in the bathroom, or her clothes on the floor. She had been messy; that much was true. Mostly he managed to keep these criticisms to himself, silent, savage ripples that he felt in his chest as he watched her. Sometimes they would escape in a sharp remark that he would later regret. It was one thing to be like his father, another thing to let everyone know it.

Caroline was usually patient with him when he was like this, when the depression came and everything around him seemed to constrict and darken. Perhaps he resented her even more for that, because in her quiet watchfulness during these times she reminded him of his mother.

He'd gone through Caroline's phone once while she was out on a run, convinced (for no reason that made sense) that she was cheating on him, panic bursting in his chest as he scrolled through her texts. He'd found nothing, of course, beyond some messages to a colleague that were slightly too friendly in tone—but that was Caroline's tone with everyone. Anyway, that wasn't the point, Tom thought afterwards. The point was that he'd done it. He never mentioned it to Caroline.

But he grew resentful if she stayed out late at work drinks, or even if she didn't stay out late; even if she went at all. *He* would be there, the man she'd been messaging, and if not him, then someone else. But Caroline worked in publishing; she needed to go to these drinks things. Tom allowed her to go (yes, allowed her, he heard it too), then punished her with his distance when she came home. When this happened, she might cry or she might react with anger of her own. Always, when the blackness had lifted the next day, Tom would feel ashamed. But he'd known exactly what he was doing at the time, and he knew he'd do it again.

He had been amazed, over and over, that she did not leave him. Of course, he was not monstrous all the time, or even most of the time. They laughed a lot together. But it was always there. He was terrified of her leaving him, while judging her harshly for not doing it. It was a strange form of cognitive dissonance, being able to recognize his father's attitudes as hideous while finding them living within himself. But he would not pass this sickness on to his child. And wouldn't it be better if he avoided relationships completely? He would not inflict himself on women. He thought that if he could do nothing else for his mother, perhaps he could do that for her.

Sometimes he wondered if Caroline had been frightened of him. He didn't believe she had, but perhaps that was because he couldn't bear to believe it. He knew she'd been happy with him, knew because she'd frequently told him. The early days, especially, had been wonderful, and for a while Tom really had thought this time might be all right.

But it was no good. To be a man was to be angry. To be a man was to be afraid.

15

It took Malcolm some time to locate the source of his unease regarding the meal at Fiona's. He knew it would be awkward for Tommy—was that it? He thought it might be awkward for him too. Someone, at some point, would say the wrong thing, and then there would be one of those silences that Heather had always claimed not to notice. But that wasn't it either. At root, Malcolm thought it had to do with how little he knew Tommy. His nephew seemed unpredictable.

Fiona had rung up again that morning to confirm, as though it was likely Malcolm could either have forgotten, or received a more glamorous offer in the meantime.

"Of course, Fiona, we'll be there," he said. "We're looking forward to it."

"Seven still O.K.?"

"Aye, that's great."

"You'll drive, won't you, Malcolm? It's a long walk in this weather and darkness."

"That's right."

"I think even the Dougdales will drive."

"We will too."

He felt tired simply from the phone call.

Malcolm worked with Robert as usual in the morning, and then after lunch he walked with Tommy halfway to Craigmore. Although November was creeping closer, the sky was blue and the sun shone on them with watery persistence. The hills looked brighter than usual, even the dark patches of bracken spotlit with gold.

"It's beautiful here," Tommy said, as they climbed up on to the cliffs and looked down at the beach. "Sometimes I forget."

"It's more hospitable in summer," Malcolm said. "I'll grant you that."

"I never think of it in summer." Tommy put his hands in the pockets of his coat and continued to stare ahead. "I always picture it in the rain or the mist. I always see it in greys and browns."

"There are plenty of those."

"But other colours, too."

Back at the house, Tommy went upstairs and didn't reappear for some time. When he finally came down, Malcolm saw that he'd changed into the shirt he'd first arrived in. He wondered if he himself should put on a smarter shirt, a less holey jersey, since Tommy seemed to have made an effort, but decided against it. It never would have occurred to him usually. He'd picked up a bottle of red wine in the shop on his way back from Robert's farm that morning, and now he brandished it awkwardly at Tommy and said, "Well, I suppose we'd best be off."

Tommy was silent in the car. It was dark outside, so the scenery provided little opportunity for conversation. Malcolm realized suddenly that they would have to pass Tommy's old house to get to the McKenzies', which lay further along the same track. He wondered why this fact hadn't occurred to him sooner, and had no idea whether he should comment on it or keep quiet. It was the Dougdales' house now, of course. Malcolm supposed that sitting down to eat with them would be strange for Tommy; he hoped no one would bring up the connection.

As they neared the eastern side of the island, he felt he had to say something. All he could manage was, "You all right with this, Tommy?"

"What?" his nephew said, turning towards him; he had been staring out of the window into the darkness. "Yeah, course."

"We don't have to stay long."

"It's fine."

A few minutes later, they turned off the main road on to the lane where Tommy used to live.

"Almost there," Malcolm said unnecessarily.

Neither of them commented as they drove past Tommy's old house. No lights were on inside, and the porch light was off too, so it was difficult to make out the house beyond its dark outline, set a little way back from the road. The Dougdales must have left already.

Five minutes later, they reached the McKenzies' house, right at the end of the track. Two cars were in the driveway, and Malcolm recognized the red Volvo as the Dougdales' and the blue Toyota as the McKenzies' own. The MacDonalds, it seemed, had not yet arrived.

Malcolm pulled up on the verge. The silence that followed felt unusually thick and still without the sound of the engine.

"I'm not very good at small talk," Tommy said after a moment.

"Me neither."

They didn't have time to ring the doorbell before Fiona opened the door, presumably having heard the car.

"Malcolm," she said. "Tommy. It's so nice that you could come. Oh, a claret, how lovely." She took the bottle from Malcolm and ushered them through to the small, bright living room where Chris and Mary Dougdale were on their feet, drinks in hand, talking to Gavin.

"Malcolm! Tommy!" Gavin said, with a cheeriness that seemed overdone to Malcolm. "Good to see you again." He came over and shook Tommy's hand vigorously, then clapped Malcolm on the shoulder. Malcolm had never seen this mild man act so heartily, and was slightly alarmed; Gavin had been normal with them the other day, but he wondered if he had been primed by Fiona this time. *Make sure you're* jolly, Malcolm imagined her telling him. *Be as jolly as possible, Gavin.* He almost laughed out loud at the idea.

The Dougdales' greeting was more muted. Although they had been on the island for almost twenty years by now, they were still regarded as incomers by most of the islanders, one or two of whom were given to wondering, with more curiosity than malice, when the Dougdales might pack up and go back to Stirling. Furthermore, Chris's work as a graphic designer, running a small company from his study, continued to baffle the islanders, some of whom had not yet adjusted to the arrival of broadband on Litta. Mary was the island's teacher, having taken over from the woman who replaced Aileen Brown, the one who'd only stayed a year, finding the island, she said, impossibly lonely, impossibly remote. (This was still joked about in the bar from time to time: the idea that someone could have gone so far as to get a job on Litta and move their whole family there without noticing beforehand how remote it was. They had all been kind, however, at the time, trying hard to ensure Hilda Grady felt welcome. None of them ever admitted how their feelings had been hurt by her departure, by her declaration of loneliness in the face of all their efforts.) Despite having been on the island so long, Mary still seemed to carry with her a faint air of city glamour; though when Malcolm said something along these lines to Heather once, Heather had snorted and said, "Mal, she's from Stirling, not *Paris*. You just mean she looks a wee bit less windswept than the rest of us."

Tonight, Mary was wearing make-up—not a common sight here—and Malcolm was momentarily taken aback by the insistent dark red of her lipstick. He thought it made her mouth look thin, but that might have been because he wasn't used to it and, as Heather had often said, he didn't like things he was not used to.

They were sensible people with no nonsense about them, but Malcolm thought that they must feel some discomfort all the same at finally meeting the boy whose family was killed in their house.

"It's a pleasure," Chris said, shaking Tommy's hand and nodding at Malcolm.

"We've heard so much about you, Tommy," Mary said, and then seemed to show, by a fractional change in her expression, that she regretted this banality, which carried so much more weight than she'd intended.

Fortunately the short silence that followed was broken by Gavin. "Can I get you both a drink?" he said. "Wine, beer, whisky?"

"Just water for me, please," Tommy said, and Malcolm quickly added, "And I'll have a whisky if it's going, Gavin," to ensure no one had time to query Tommy's request.

Fiona had been hanging up their coats in the hall, and now she came back in. Of course she could never help but make a fuss. When Gavin returned with a glass of water and a whisky, she said, "Gavin, get Tommy some cordial to have in his drink. He can't be drinking plain water like that."

"It's O.K.," Tommy said. "I like it."

"I suppose water can be very refreshing, can't it?" Fiona said, back-pedalling rapidly. "Sometimes nothing else will do, will it?"

Tommy shook his head, smiling politely. Malcolm hoped the whole evening wouldn't be like this.

The doorbell went and Fiona said, "That must be Ed and Kathy," with a slight tone of surprise, as though she hadn't been expecting them. She came back a moment later followed by the MacDonalds—Kathy, large and comfortable, her husband, slender and grey and perpetually frowning a little, even when he appeared otherwise to be in a good mood. The only time he cheered up a bit was when the drink was in him.

"Hi, Malcolm," Kathy said. "Good to see you again, Tommy."

Malcolm was immediately grateful for her easy manner, and wondered again at the mystery of her marriage to Ed, who seemed on edge even with friends as old as these. Malcolm tried to imagine what he was like with strangers, and then realized that seeing Ed meet Tommy again as an adult was probably one of the first times he'd witnessed Ed interacting with a stranger.

Ed overcame this social hurdle by saying nothing, putting his hands in his pockets and looking at his feet.

Gavin bustled round again, taking drink orders and then returning with beers for Ed and Kathy. Malcolm sipped his whisky and wished he'd asked for a beer too. At some point he seemed to have gone off whisky. Heather had liked it; perhaps now she was gone he didn't need to pretend anymore. He found himself standing with Fiona, who was saying, "How is it out on the farm, Malcolm? Tupping must be underway now."

"Almost," Malcolm said. "Robert pushed it back a week. Next week, I think we'll make a start."

"The work never stops, does it?"

"No. That's a fact."

Fiona turned to Tommy, standing silently beside them. "Did you never consider the farming life, Tommy?"

"No."

"I suppose it isn't for everyone."

Malcolm watched Tommy, unsure whether his nephew would reply or if he himself would need to say something to cover the silence. But after a moment, Tommy came out with, "I do like the outdoors. But farming's hard. It wouldn't have suited me."

"And remind me again, what is it you do in London?" Fiona said.

"Grant development manager," Tommy said succinctly, a phrase that meant precisely nothing to Malcolm. "At a research centre."

"Do you enjoy that?" Fiona asked, clearly as much at a loss as Malcolm.

"Not especially," Tommy said.

"Well," Fiona said. "We all have to do something, don't we? To keep the wolf from the door."

"Crofting's never really done that," Malcolm murmured.

"Ah, but that's a way of life, not a job."

"I suppose." Malcolm wondered suddenly, and perhaps for the first time in his life, what else he might have done if there hadn't been the croft. Become an accountant like John? No, he'd never been much good with figures. He'd have worked on the ferries, most probably. Croft or no croft, he'd never have left the island, even in his early twenties with his whole life ahead of him. Perhaps all this time what he'd thought of as love had really been fear.

Fiona excused herself to go and check on the lamb, and Malcolm found himself briefly alone with Tommy. "You O.K.?" he said, and Tommy nodded.

The next moment, Ed sidled up to them, emboldened by his beer. He'd refused the offer of a glass, and Malcolm could see from the way he lifted the can to his mouth that most of it was already gone.

"You on the water, lad?" Ed said to Tommy.

"Yes."

"That's not really the way we do things out here," Ed said.

There was a short, awkward pause, and then Ed laughed. Malcolm wondered if he'd been drinking before he even arrived, perhaps wishing to prepare himself for the ordeal ahead. If so, Malcolm could hardly blame him.

"Water's very refreshing," Tommy said. He met Malcolm's eye, his expression giving nothing away. "Sometimes nothing else will do."

Kathy had been talking to Chris Dougdale and Gavin (Mary was nowhere to be seen, perhaps helping Fiona in the kitchen), but now she came up to join them.

"Ed, are you behaving yourself?" she said to her husband in her good-natured way, but Malcolm thought he detected a note of anxiety in her voice.

"Aye," Ed said. "Just catching up with Malcolm and getting reacquainted with wee Tommy."

"The man's in his thirties, Ed," Kathy said.

"Not in my head," Ed said. "When you've known someone since they were a bairn, you always see them that way. They never grow up."

Involuntarily, Malcolm thought of Nicky and Beth, and hoped Tommy wasn't thinking of them too.

"What's it like, being back here?" Kathy said to Tommy. "Does it look just how you remember?"

"Yes, I think so," Tommy said. "The landscape doesn't change much, does it?" He paused. "New generation of sheep, though."

There was a moment's hesitation before everyone realized he was making a joke, and Kathy and Ed laughed heartily. Malcolm smiled and Tommy looked ruefully down at the floor, as if embarrassed by his own weak attempt at humour.

Fiona and Mary reappeared at that point, coming to join the small circle. "What's all this hilarity about?" Fiona said, and Malcolm winced for Tommy as his joke was repeated by Kathy, and then Fiona and Mary laughed too, in a slightly forced manner.

"What we need," Mary said, "is a new generation of people to join the sheep."

"Aye, Tommy," Kathy said. "That must be one thing you've

noticed. All of us are old now. You've come to an island full of the elderly and the decrepit."

"Speak for yourself," Ed said. More forced laughter.

"I don't think that's entirely fair," Fiona began. "What about the Logans? Lovely young couple, Tommy, about your age, in their thirties—'

"Forties, hen," Gavin put in from across the room, where he was standing with Chris by the fireplace.

"Well, young, anyway," Fiona said, with a brief reproachful glance at her husband. "They came here two years back, with their two girls, who are filling places in the school, aren't they, Mary?"

"That's right," Mary said. "Nice children, too. Mia and Suzie."

"And they seem settled and here to stay," Fiona concluded. "So there's still a bit of young blood coming in."

"They're not here to stay," Gavin said, coming over now, followed by Chris. "They're taking a career break from their hectic life in Edinburgh, and as soon as Mia's ready to start secondary school, they'll up sticks and move back to the mainland. She's ten now, isn't she? We've got them for another year at the most."

"Gavin, you're being pessimistic," Fiona told him.

"James Logan as good as told me that was their plan," Gavin said. "We have to face facts. People don't move here to stay. Not now."

"Well, Chris and Mary did, didn't they?" Fiona said triumphantly, taking in both Dougdales in her appeal. "They're still here, nearly twenty years later, when nobody thought they'd stay. You don't mind me saying that now, Chris and Mary? You're proof that there's hope yet."

"It's true," Mary said. "We're going nowhere."

"Well, that's a relief," Gavin said gallantly. "I can't think of better neighbours."

This comment seemed to hang in the air for a few moments as its unfortunate implications struck everyone at once, carrying as it did the glancing suggestion that it was nice to have some neighbours who weren't going to self-destruct in a horrific murder-suicide.

Malcolm wracked his brains for something to say, something to change the subject, but while he was still thinking, Tommy broke the silence.

"But even if new people aren't arriving," he said, "it says something for the island that none of you have ever left. The people who are born here usually stay."

Malcolm glanced at his nephew, thinking that this was generous of him.

Fiona smiled warmly at Tommy and said, "Maybe it's not too late to win you back, Tommy."

"Yes, maybe you'll enjoy your visit so much," Kathy added, "you'll never want to leave again."

Tommy gave that smile of his, the one that committed him to nothing. "Maybe."

The meal was lamb shanks with mashed potato and cabbage. It was very good. Malcolm thought Fiona had probably agonized over this meal, a suspicion that was borne out by Gavin's comment as the others praised the food: "I'm glad you like it. Fiona's been in a state about it, haven't you?"

He hadn't meant to embarrass her, Malcolm was sure, but he could see that Fiona minded. "I haven't," she said, a red flush coming into her cheeks.

"Yes, I bet you've heard about nothing else all day but lamb shanks," Ed said, taking it up. "Kathy's the same when she's having people over. Frets and frets about the cooking."

Well, maybe you should help her, Malcolm thought, though he knew he'd never assisted Heather much while she was alive. He'd believed it wasn't his place, but he saw all the ways now in which he could have done more. Not that Heather would have had it, probably. *You stick to your sheep,* he imagined, or perhaps even remembered, her telling him.

"Gavin, Kathy's glass is empty, and so is Chris's," Fiona said, rather sharply, Malcolm thought. "Could you sort out more drinks, please?"

Gavin went out to get a fresh bottle of wine. Ed, seated to Malcolm's right and across the table from Tommy, said, "Still on the water, Tommy? Can't we tempt you to have a proper drink?"

"Ed, leave him alone," Kathy said.

Ed was definitely drunk, Malcolm thought. He wished, once again, that he could think of something to say to turn the conversation, but he'd never been good at this; he'd always relied too much on Heather to keep the conversation going. He tried to imagine what she might say, and came up with, "Winter's coming," which sounded more ominous than he'd intended.

He saw Tommy choke slightly on his water and quickly hide his mouth. Well, it is, Malcolm wanted to tell him.

"Yes, the weather's closing in," Mary said, as Gavin returned with the wine and went round refilling everyone's glasses (Tommy covered his empty wine glass with his hand and gave a polite shake of the head which fortunately didn't set Ed off again). "It's getting darker earlier and earlier. Bit depressing, isn't it?"

"I don't know," Kathy said. "I always quite enjoy the winter, getting the fire going in the evenings and huddling up inside. And you have to have the winter, don't you," she added, "in order to appreciate the spring."

The pause that followed lent this comment an unexpected profundity.

"That's very deep," Ed said after a moment. "Very deep, Kathy."

"In the midst of life, we are in death," Gavin said, rather surprisingly, as he resumed his seat. Malcolm wondered if he was drunk too.

Catching his wife's exasperated glance, Gavin said, "I mean, you need death in order to appreciate life. Don't you?"

"Can we please stop talking about death?" Kathy said.

Malcolm managed not to look at Tommy.

"You started it," Ed said.

"Ed, I did not."

"You did. You were talking about winter and spring."

"It wasn't a metaphor."

Chris and Mary Dougdale started laughing, and the atmosphere eased. Malcolm was pleased that another small crisis had passed, but he felt that it was turning into a difficult evening. No one seemed relaxed, and no one was being themselves. The ghost of John Baird was among them.

"Have you caught up with any other old friends, Tommy?" Kathy asked.

"Not really," Tommy said. "Malcolm told me Angus MacIntyre left. From school. And the Wilson twins, gone too."

"The youngsters, all gone," Fiona said, and Malcolm was concerned that the old lament would start up again.

"We ran into Ken," he said quickly, "out by Alban Bay."

"And you met Ross on the ferry of course," Fiona said to Tommy. "Did you remember them, the people you've met again?"

"Some of them," Tommy said, adding, almost apologetically, "I was young when I left."

"Of course," Mary said. "I find it hard enough to remember the people right in front of me these days, let alone from years ago."

"Senility," Chris said, in his first contribution to the conversation for some time.

"I'd like to remind you that I'm three years *younger* than

you," Mary said, turning to him, "so there'll be no more of your 'senility' comments."

Gavin looked round the table. "Who's ready for seconds? More mash, Malcolm? What about you, John?"

He was looking straight at Tommy. Malcolm felt his whole body turn cold. He saw the moment Gavin realized what he'd said, the way his smile froze.

"Tommy," Gavin corrected himself quickly. Then, apparently feeling it would be useless to try to brush over it, he added, "Sorry."

"It's fine," Tommy said.

Malcolm looked desperately for a way to save the situation, but came up with nothing.

"It's lovely mash," Kathy said to Fiona loudly. "Very buttery."

Tommy, perhaps taking pity on them, said to Mary across the table, "Malcolm said you're from Stirling originally?"

"That's right," Mary said, and Malcolm felt the gratitude of the others as strongly as his own. "Or at least, I grew up in the countryside nearby, but Chris was born in Stirling. We met at the FE college there."

"Many, *many* years ago," Chris said.

"Enough of that."

"My mother was from Stirling," Tommy said.

Kathy said gamely, "Yes, she was. I remember now. Have you ever visited?"

"No," Tommy said. "I've never been." He hesitated. "Seems strange now. My mother didn't have a good relationship with *her* mother, I think. We never went to see her when I was a child."

"It's a lovely place," Kathy said.

"So I've heard."

"The countryside around there is really beautiful," Mary added. "Lots of farms, too."

Tommy nodded.

"And plenty of historical interest," Fiona said. "The castle, of course."

Malcolm didn't think she had ever been. He hadn't himself, and now he wondered why. So many places he'd never seen. He'd only been to Edinburgh once, and never to London. Sixty-two years old, and he'd never been to London.

By the time dessert was served, everyone seemed more relaxed (or else had simply drunk more, Malcolm thought; he had drunk more than he was accustomed to himself, although he was only on his second or third glass of wine. Better stop soon, he thought—he still had to drive himself and Tommy home. Though perhaps Tommy could do it. He realized he had no idea whether or not Tommy knew how to drive).

Fiona brought out a large tiramisu in a glass bowl and everyone applauded. Gavin fetched a dessert wine for them all to sample. It was so sweet it made Malcolm shudder.

He had thought Tommy would refuse the dessert wine as he had refused all other drinks offers, but Tommy accepted a small measure in his glass, sipped it, gave his polite smile and said, "Very nice."

Gavin seemed pleased by this and said, "Aye, it is. I got it in Oban. Been waiting for the right time to try it."

"We're very touched," Ed said. "You make us feel special." His face had taken on that bleary look it got sometimes and Malcolm felt a passing flicker of distaste. This wasn't the idea of the island he wanted Tommy to take away.

"It's not for you, Ed," Gavin said. "It's Tommy here who's guest of honour."

Tommy swallowed the rest of his wine down. Gavin topped up his glass again and something about the quick way Tommy raised it to his lips made Malcolm feel uneasy.

Some time after that, Fiona brought out cheese (Christ, Malcolm thought, they never usually had this much food) and

Gavin served yet more drinks. There was a loose, hazy atmosphere in the room now. The talk turned inevitably, for a while, to farming, and then briefly to politics (a subject in which nobody was much interested except Mary, who kept herself abreast of current affairs far more eagerly than anybody else on the island. Probably came, Ross had said once, from being an incomer).

Across the table from him, Malcolm saw Tommy accepting a glass of red wine from Gavin. His nephew was sitting back in his chair now, almost lounging, more at ease—or so it seemed—than Malcolm had seen him since he arrived on the island.

"Let's have a toast," Ed said suddenly. He looked eagerly around the table. "A toast to Tommy's homecoming."

There was a general murmur of agreement, and everyone obediently raised their glasses.

"Welcome back, Tommy," Ed said. "We should have killed the fatted calf, shouldn't we? Instead of having lamb. It's a crying shame you've been away so long."

"Ed," Kathy said, a warning note in her voice, as if she could anticipate where her husband might be going with this.

"Well, it is," Ed said. "He mustn't let what happened keep him away. He's an island man, a Baird man, just like Malcolm. Just like John. It was madness, pure and simple. Nobody blames him, Tommy—he wasn't himself."

All the air seemed to go out of the room. Malcolm's eyes met Fiona's for a second, before she quickly glanced away; she looked horror struck.

For a few moments, Tommy didn't speak. Malcolm began to think the moment would pass on its own and they could just change the subject—why couldn't he think of anything to say?—but then Tommy said, "He wasn't mad."

"No, of course not," Ed said. "Just at the very end."

"I think that's enough now, Ed," Malcolm managed to say.

"Yes, love," Kathy added. "Tommy doesn't want to talk about this."

Ed nodded and appeared ready to hold his peace. But after taking a sip of wine, he leaned towards Tommy. He seemed about to lay his hand on his arm, before thinking better of it and letting it rest between them on the table. He said, "We all knew your dad, Tommy. He wasn't a bad man. He did a terrible thing. A terrible, terrible thing," he went on, seeming to have got momentarily stuck on the word. "But he didn't know what he was doing. Can't have."

And somehow Malcolm knew this was the worst thing Ed could have said.

He watched as Tommy turned to Ed and said, his voice quiet and cold, "He knew exactly what he was doing."

Silence. Nobody at this point knew how to intervene, and instead Malcolm felt they were all watching Tommy with nervous fascination to see what he would do next.

"You're not being honest about who he was," Tommy said. He'd taken his eyes off Ed and was staring down at his empty cheese plate, so it wasn't clear if he was addressing Ed or all of them. He seemed to Malcolm to be utterly sober now, unlike everyone around him. "A good man *does not murder his family*. He wasn't ever a good man. Don't pretend it was a moment of madness just to make yourselves feel better."

There was a long, helpless silence, into which Ed nodded drunkenly once or twice, though he couldn't seem to look at Tommy. It was Mary who finally spoke, perhaps because she and Chris hadn't even been here and so were surely exempt from the blame attached to the rest of them. She said, "I'm so sorry, Tommy. It must have been so hard."

And this simple comment seemed to be as close to the right thing to say as was possible when clearly there was no right thing to say. Tommy sighed, rolled back his shoulders, and gave a small nod.

"Coffee?" Fiona said suddenly. "Who'd like some coffee? Or a nice cup of tea?"

"Aye, that'd be lovely," Kathy said, at the same time as Gavin said, "Good idea, Fi. That's just what we need."

Looking at Tommy, Malcolm felt it was up to him to end this ordeal, not just for Tommy and himself, but for all of them. Nonetheless, he knew they couldn't leave immediately, not with Tommy's words still hanging in the air. That would make the thing seem worse, not better. No, they would have to get through coffee—half an hour maximum, he calculated—and then, finally, it would be over.

And somehow they all muddled through the next twenty minutes, sticking to neutral topics as they sipped their coffee (Malcolm gulped his down quickly), Kathy and Mary making heroic efforts to get the conversation back on track by speaking of their children, of who would be home to visit and when. At last Malcolm judged enough time had passed that he and Tommy could make their escape.

He said, "I think we'd better be off, Fiona. It's getting late."

"Come on now, Malcolm," she said. "There's no rush. Tommy hasn't even finished his coffee."

"It's O.K.," Tommy said, taking a final sip from his cup. "I'm done."

Malcolm added, "I have to be up early tomorrow for Robert. And Tommy's had a long day too." Why had he added that? Tommy wasn't a child.

But then Tommy said, "Thank you for having us," in a low, polite voice, for all the world as though he was still eight years old and his life had never gone off track.

"It's been so good to see you," Fiona said faintly, and there were general murmurs of agreement. Malcolm said his good-byes and tried to disentangle himself and Tommy as swiftly as possible, though Ed seemed particularly eager to shake both of their hands at quite some length, as if to say, *No hard feelings,* and then finally Malcolm and Tommy were outside in the freezing darkness and the door had closed behind them.

Tommy walked without a word round to the passenger side of the car and got in. Malcolm allowed himself a couple of seconds to breathe the night air deeply, to be alone in the safety of the darkness, before he opened the driver's door.

He took the drive slowly, afraid of his own disorientation, the blackness of the night, the roughness of the track. He was thankful for the darkness as they passed Tommy's old house—that, at least, was one sight they could do without at this particular moment. He gripped the steering wheel and stared ahead at the small patch of road lit up by his headlights. It was highly unlikely that they'd meet another car, but even once they were on the tarmacked main road there was the danger of going into a ditch, or into the rocks where the road cut through the hills.

Malcolm didn't feel they could complete the whole drive in silence, but it was difficult to know what to say to Tommy. He wanted to say something—anything—to dispel this terrible feeling that had come over him, that Tommy had brought over everyone in Fiona's small dining room.

"The food was good," he said at last.

"Yes."

"Fiona's a good cook."

"Yeah."

There was a long silence, then Malcolm finally said, "I'm sorry about Ed."

"I know."

"He was drunk. And he's a bit of an idiot even when he's sober."

"It's not just him," Tommy said. "It's all of them."

"They mean well."

"Most people do," Tommy said. Then, "Meaning well isn't enough."

"It's not fair to blame them," Malcolm said, knowing what he really meant was, *It's not fair to blame me.* But of course it was.

"Why not?" Tommy said, his voice savage. "They were there, weren't they? You all were. It didn't come out of nowhere."

"Tommy, it wasn't like that. Nobody could have imagined—"

"Perhaps you've convinced yourselves it was none of your business. But it was your business."

Malcolm had no answer to this.

When they pulled up outside his house, he turned off the engine and they sat in silence for a couple of moments. Finally Malcolm said, because he knew he had to, "Did he hurt you, Tommy?"

"No. Not in the way you mean."

"I'm sorry." The car light went off, so he could no longer see Tommy's face.

Tommy said levelly, "I hate this fucking island. If I could, I'd wipe it off the face of the earth."

He opened the car door abruptly and got out. By the time Malcolm had followed him into the house, Tommy had already disappeared upstairs to his bed. Malcolm remained alone in the kitchen for several hours, knowing there would be no possibility of sleep.

16

So not an unmitigated success, Malcolm thought the following morning.

He was relieved to be going out early to work with Robert. No sign of Tommy when he set off at seven A.M. Malcolm left him a note saying he'd be gone a while.

The weather was bad, even by their usual standards. After the calm of the day before, it had turned, and the wind had been hurling itself against the side of the cottage since Malcolm woke at six, bringing with it harsh, freezing rain. Malcolm zipped his coat up to his chin, pulled on a woolly hat and set off into the cold and wet.

A hard morning. He and Robert spent an hour and a half taking the feed supplements out to the ewes on the rough grazing, heaving the bags from the truck and pouring the mixture into the block containers, watched impassively by the sheep through a haze of rain. It was impossible to talk much as they worked; all their energy was taken up with carrying the bags and withstanding the onslaught of the weather. But Malcolm was glad to lose himself in the heft of physical labour. It was difficult to think about anything else with your back and shoulders aching and the wind tumbling around your ears.

"What now?" he said to Robert when they'd finished and were leaning against the side of the truck. The rain had stopped, but the wind was still fierce and although they were half sheltered here, Malcolm still had to raise his voice to be heard.

"It's all right, I can manage today."

"I don't mind," Malcolm said.

He could feel Robert looking at him. "I thought you'd want to be home, spending time with Tommy."

"Not," Malcolm said, "when there's work that needs doing."

"Well, in that case, it's about time I trimmed their hooves. We could do the ones in the pasture."

On the in-bye land by the farmhouse, they herded the ewes into pens and then caught them one by one, pulling them on to their backs and holding them still between their legs while they dug compacted mud from their hooves and trimmed the ends with hoof cutters. It was a docile flock, but no sheep especially enjoyed having its hooves trimmed. Malcolm kept a firm grip and did the job as quickly as he could, releasing each sheep back into the pasture in turn with a "Good girl" and "There you go". It took a long time, even with two of them.

"No sign of rot," Malcolm said when they paused.

"Not so far," Robert said. "Touch wood. It's good to have your help, Malcolm. You keep them calm."

"I'm well practised," Malcolm said.

"Gordon's well practised," Robert said, referring to his eldest son, "but he still spooks them whenever he does it. You have a way with sheep."

Malcolm snorted. "Thanks, Robert."

"I'm serious."

"Well, it's more than anyone would say about me and people." He imagined, briefly, relating this exchange to Tommy. Then he decided he didn't want to think about Tommy just now.

At noon, Martha, Robert's wife, fed them soup in the farmhouse kitchen. They ate quickly, both wanting to get back to work, but Malcolm enjoyed the brief respite from the cold.

"How are things up there?" Robert said, sitting across the

table from him and making no effort to drink his soup without slurping, however many disapproving faces Martha made at him.

"Fine," Malcolm said. Then he added, to make it seem normal, to convince himself it *had* been normal, "We went to eat at Fiona and Gavin's last night."

"Oh, aye?"

"Kathy and Ed were there. Chris and Mary, too."

"Nice evening?"

"Aye. She's a good cook."

Thinking back over the night before, he supposed it could have been worse. It had been nothing much at all, really. Just a couple of sharp comments from Tommy, some awkwardness for everyone, a slightly abrupt end to the evening. Beyond that, what? A sense of barely suppressed rage just glancing out at them in the moments when Tommy let it. Nothing that could be easily put into words, and it was this, coupled with their own embarrassment, that Malcolm thought would prevent the others discussing the evening much among themselves afterwards.

He would have to ring Fiona to say thank you, of course. Probably, he thought, neither of them would mention the awkward part, but would gloss over it with general platitudes about the evening. He began to see that Tommy might be right in his suggestion that they didn't confront things here. But wasn't that the safest way in the end? Nothing that had happened could be undone.

The rain had started up again, pattering against the window.

"Shall we get back to work?" Malcolm said.

By the time he returned home in the late afternoon, he was exhausted and soaked, smelling strongly of sheep, all his muscles aching. He found Tommy sitting on the sofa in the living room, wearing Malcolm's clothes and reading *Tess of the D'Urbervilles*.

Malcolm hovered in the doorway and, when Tommy looked up, gestured at the book. "Any good?"

"He likes the colour red," Tommy said. "Blood. Fate. You know."

Malcolm didn't know. He wasn't sure even Heather would have known what to do with this comment. She always said she just liked the plots.

"What did you study at university?" he asked Tommy suddenly. "Was it English?"

Tommy smiled. "No. History."

"Oh." There seemed nowhere left to go with this conversation. "Did you enjoy it?"

"It was all right."

If Malcolm had thought their exchange the previous evening might have shaken something loose between him and Tommy, at least stripped away one layer of reserve, he appeared to have been wrong. He felt more paralysed with awkwardness than ever.

"I'm going to change," he said, and left the room.

When he finally came back downstairs, having taken rather longer than he needed (he was ready to acknowledge now that he might possibly be avoiding Tommy), he found Tommy in the kitchen, frying onions. The smell made Malcolm's eyes sting.

"I went to the shop earlier," Tommy said, turning as he entered.

"Really? Long walk on a day like this." Malcolm hovered in the doorway for a moment, then, seeing no escape, went to sit at the table.

"I wanted the exercise. I picked up some things. Thought I'd make tea."

"Right," Malcolm said. Then, rallying, "That's nice. Thanks."

"Pasta with a mushroom sauce. Hope that's O.K. I don't have a very wide repertoire."

"Did Kathy serve you?"

"No. It was Fiona."

Malcolm was silent, wondering what it had cost Tommy to make that visit, to endure that interaction. Tommy's face gave nothing away.

"I told her thanks for last night," Tommy said, turning back to the pan.

"Good. That's good."

So they were mentioning it then.

"Told her they were the best lamb shanks I'd ever had."

Malcolm found it difficult to imagine Tommy making this comment. "They were certainly good," he said. He felt a sudden and uncharacteristic need for a drink, and went to get the old bottle of whisky down from the cupboard. It would do, in the absence of anything else.

"I'm going to have a wee dram," he said. "You don't mind?"

"Of course not," Tommy said. He added mushrooms to the onions in the pan.

Malcolm sat down at the table and sipped his whisky. He'd forgotten how steadying drink could be sometimes.

Tommy said, his back to Malcolm, "Look, I'm sorry about last night."

Caught off guard, Malcolm didn't immediately reply. After a moment, he said, "Nothing to be sorry for."

Tommy nodded and continued to stir the mushrooms. Malcolm thought this signalled the end of the exchange—conversations seemed to stop and start abruptly with Tommy, frightening topics looming up out of nowhere and then vanishing almost as quickly as they came—but then Tommy said, "I've thought this whole time that it was my father I wanted to ask you about. But now I think that isn't true. Maybe it's my mother."

Carefully, Malcolm said, "What do you want to know?"

Tommy was stirring more vigorously now. He said, "What she was *like*, I suppose. I mean, I remember what she was like to me. Most of the time, I remember. But how did she seem to other people?"

Malcolm would not have found this an easy question to answer about anyone, but least of all, perhaps, about Katrina.

"She was . . ."

And there was Katrina before him.

"She seems nice," Heather had said after they first met her. "And very beautiful, of course. But is she a bit . . . ?"

"What?" Malcolm had said.

"I don't know. Bland?"

Malcolm was surprised at this; it wasn't like Heather to be hard on people. He didn't remember how he'd replied. He'd found Katrina reserved, but not bland. He thought there was plenty going on beneath the surface. And later, of course, Heather and Katrina became friends. He'd hear them laughing together in the next room, or talking in low voices.

"What do you talk about?" he'd ask Heather.

"Oh, nothing really," she'd say. "Just nonsense."

Malcolm never reminded Heather of her earlier comment about Katrina, though he was curious to know at what point his wife's opinion had changed, and how she judged Katrina's character now. But perhaps, he thought, Heather wouldn't have been able to answer, would not really have understood the question. She liked people, but she didn't tend to think much about them when they weren't in front of her; she didn't go in for "plumbing their depths" as she said Malcolm did, making this comment with both fondness and bemusement. Heather had no use for their depths.

Like the rest of them, Heather had known little about Katrina's marriage. Malcolm had seen from her shock after the murders that Heather had been no more aware of what might have gone on than anybody else. And how Heather had blamed herself.

But perhaps Katrina had a hardness in her, too. No good making her out to be a saint, because nobody was. She had absorbed so much from other people, who poured out their secrets to her ("Thank you for listening to me," Malcolm would hear them say to her down by the harbour, or on the road outside the school); but Katrina offered so little of herself in return. Was this selflessness, as you might assume, or was it miserliness? Later, Malcolm thought it might have been self-preservation.

How much of this could he say to Tommy, who was still waiting patiently for an answer?

"Your mother," Malcolm began, "was very kind. She had time for everyone." Poor Katrina, he thought, reduced to these colourless phrases, as though she'd been as bland as Heather had once believed. Malcolm knew he had to do better. He said, "I know she must have been unhappy, but she never showed it. We knew so little." Here he was again, trying to defend himself. He changed tack. "She adored you children. She . . ." He'd been about to say, *She would have died for you,* and stopped himself just in time. "She would have done anything for you," he amended. "You three were her whole life."

Tommy had turned to face him and was listening closely, his head slightly on one side. When Malcolm stopped, he said, "That's how she made it feel to us, too. I suppose that's what good parents do—make you feel like you really matter."

Malcolm was quiet, thinking of his own mother.

"My father didn't like her to talk to other people too much," Tommy said.

Malcolm considered this. Another thing he should have seen at the time. *Had seen*, but hadn't acknowledged properly, hadn't seen in the right way. He remembered John hurrying Katrina away after church, saying they had to be getting the lunch on. He remembered the closed look on Katrina's face when her husband was beside her, how much quieter her voice and her laugh became. Or maybe he was misremembering.

"I think your father had a lot of problems," he said. "Most people wouldn't have guessed. But I always knew he had . . . anger. A lot of anger. I just didn't realize—'

"No, I know that," Tommy said. "I was upset last night, that's all."

How is it, Malcolm thought, that we can both see and not see what's in front of our faces? He had known something wasn't right in that marriage. He had always felt it, even if he'd never articulated it. He knew John and Katrina were not like him and Heather. But it wasn't as though John had treated Katrina like their own father had treated their mother—no shouting or hitting so far as Malcolm had been aware. He hadn't realized there were other kinds of danger.

While Tommy was boiling the kettle for the pasta, Malcolm slipped out of the room and went upstairs. In his bedroom, he dug through a couple of the old boxes at the bottom of his wardrobe until he found the envelope he was looking for.

He brought it downstairs, took out the top picture and passed it, a little shyly, to Tommy, who was still standing at the hob.

The picture showed Katrina outside the house, hers and John's (the Dougdales' now, Malcolm thought), crouching down with Tommy and Nicky on either side of her, Nicky aged about three or four and Tommy still a toddler. The light looked warm and the boys were in jerseys but no coats. They looked serious in that way small children sometimes do. Nicky was frowning at the camera but Tommy was looking at his mother. His small arm was outstretched, reaching for his mother's hair. Katrina was laughing, turning to catch his hand as the photo was taken.

"She was very pretty, wasn't she?" Tommy said, and Malcolm nodded, feeling the old ache in his heart.

"Do you have any of my father?"

With some reluctance, Malcolm drew out the other picture, a faded photograph of Katrina and John, sitting side by side on the beach. There was a slightly strained quality to their smiles which suggested they had been posing for too long. Heather was there too, at the edge of the photograph, looking away; she'd never liked having her picture taken. Malcolm supposed he must have taken the photo, but he didn't recall the occasion now.

Tommy took it from him and frowned at it in silence for a long time.

Malcolm wondered what was going through his mind, whether Tommy was struck by the resemblance between himself and his father, but all Tommy said when he finally spoke was, "He wasn't as attractive as my mother, was he?"

"I think he could be charming, when he wanted to be," Malcolm said, and then wondered why on earth he'd felt moved to defend his brother. But perhaps it wasn't that. Perhaps it was more that he felt the need to explain Katrina to Tommy, how she might have ended up marrying him. He said, "He would go out of his way to be charming. It was important to him, I think, that people liked him."

Abruptly, Tommy passed the photograph back to him. "Can I keep the other one?" he said. "Of my mother with me and Nicky?"

"Of course. It's yours." Malcolm stepped away from him. "Let me get you a new envelope to put it in, keep it safe." He went quickly into the living room and rummaged through the desk drawers until he unearthed a fresh envelope. He was glad to have a moment alone, and glad as well to have something to occupy his hands, which he discovered now were shaking.

17

H is mother's face was clearer as he lay on his bed later that evening, but Tom wasn't sure if he had stolen her face from the photograph in his hand (he had it out again, couldn't seem to leave it alone) or if the picture had prompted his own memory.

If he could go back.

There were many other wrongs he would have liked to correct. How he had treated Caroline, for instance. But still, if he could go back, and if he wasn't able to change the greatest crime he'd committed, he would choose this one. His mother would turn to him and ask for help with the laundry and he would say, "Yes."

But you were a child, he told himself. *Don't magnify all of your actions.*

Still, though. He had exposed his mother to his father's anger. The argument between his parents had been one that he had provoked, and it had taken place only a few days before the murders. It was possible that he had done real damage. And in any case, regardless of whether the row had contributed to what happened next, it remained true that one of Tom's final acts towards his mother had been to betray her.

He dozed off eventually and when he woke again it was the middle of the night and he was cold from lying on top of the covers. Sitting up stiffly, he found there was one clear question in his head, as though it was being spoken by somebody else.

Where was Nicky?

His mother was once again standing by the sink, and he was saying, No, no, he would not help with the laundry, and then he was going off to play with Angus. But where was Nicky?

This was a loose thread he had always ignored, so dwarfed was it by everything that had happened afterwards. Now, however, he pulled at it. Nicky had not been asked to help put away the laundry. That fact had never played much of a part in the story, although surely it must have fed his own sense of injustice at the time and strengthened his refusal to help. Had Nicky been out of the house? Carefully, as if picking gravel from a wound, Tom tried to take the memory apart. Both his parents were at home, so neither of them had taken Nicky out. Angus was waiting down the road for Tommy, so Nicky was not off somewhere with him.

It was the strangest thing.

Realizing he had to pee, Tom dragged himself up and groped his way along the corridor to the bathroom. How much longer would Malcolm let him stay? he thought. It had been eleven days already. Tom was certain his uncle didn't want him here, however Malcolm might try (not very successfully) to pretend. Nobody wanted him here. The thought came to him without self-pity.

When he'd finished and washed his hands, he stared into the mirror above the sink for a while. He didn't feel much sense of recognition when he looked at his own face, and he wondered if this was normal. Worse than the dissociation were the times when he saw only his father's face looking back at him.

He had to make some kind of plan, he thought. He needed to come up with an idea of where to go next, what he might do. But he was tired. He was afraid there was no next.

There were still traces of shaving foam and tiny dark hairs in the sink from that morning. Tom ran the tap to splash them away. The water drained slowly, so he took the grille out, wiping the black slime off the edge with his finger and tapping it into the darkness of the plughole. Then he bent forward to peer after it. The grime round the edges of the plughole faded almost immediately into black; impossible to tell how deep it went. Tom was distracted for a moment by the idea of the void tunnelling on and on, sliding deeper into black; he imagined being small enough to vanish down it. He turned the tap on harder to see if he could make the water catch up with itself and rise to the surface. It was almost disappointing when he managed it, a faint sheen a long way below, beginning as a glimmer then gradually thickening, ascending, surging over the edges and turning clear and harmless within the safety of the sink.

He rinsed his hands again, and as he turned off the taps the missing piece of his memory came back, sidling quietly to the front of his mind. Where was Nicky? Nicky was in bed that day, reading his comics. Nicky's shoulder was still sore; it was right after he had fallen between the rocks on the beach and he and Tommy had had to walk half the way home. Nicky had to rest for a couple of days, wasn't allowed out to play, and wouldn't be expected to help with any household tasks.

Tom experienced a strange sense of the pieces of the world realigning themselves around him. There was some satisfaction in having solved this puzzle, but mostly he felt thrown off balance. As he went back along the corridor to his room, something else occurred to him. Nicky dislocated his shoulder when he was about eight years old. Tom himself must have been six. This realization took the breath from Tom's lungs: the incident could not have taken place right before the murders.

Was it possible? Tom lay back down on his bed and tried to think. He was almost certain that he wasn't mistaken about Nicky's shoulder still healing that day. That part, as soon as it came to him, *felt* true: not that his mind had invented it now, but that it had always been there, just out of sight. But who knew what the truth was? It was not as though he had anybody to ask.

He got under the covers and tried to warm himself. Although he hadn't bothered closing his curtains before bed, the room was in complete darkness. Nights out here were pitch black if the moon was hidden, not like in cities where the darkness was always diluted. Tom had forgotten the heavy texture of night on the islands.

Once more he tried to focus on the memory, but it wouldn't stay still for long enough. He hated the indistinctness of the past; it frightened him. Above all, it seemed cruel to him how vividly the feelings themselves remained—terror, shame—even when so many of the details were slippery. It meant he suffered all the anguish of the past without it ever being eased by an adult's detachment. Turning on his side, he pulled his knees up and closed his eyes.

When he woke again, it was dawn; the room was half lit by weak morning light. Tom sat up and let everything come back to him. His head felt a little clearer as he went downstairs to make a cup of coffee, relieved to find Malcolm wasn't up yet.

Standing barefoot by the kettle and looking out at the dim moorland, Tom decided the most likely explanation was that his mind had conflated two similar incidents. He thought the row over the laundry probably had taken place years, and not days, before the murders. But perhaps there had also been an argument a couple of days before the killings—just not one he remembered now. Then, later, after everything went so wrong in his head, he had muddled the two together.

Once it had come to him, the idea did not surprise him. His mind was too intent on holding on to another memory: the terrible one that took up his entire core. Tom began to see how this had eventually distorted all his other memories. But it seemed no less than he deserved, that his mind had latched on long ago to that single moment and decided to keep it clear and sharp at the expense of everything else. Over time, his other memories had been twisted around the unbearable one until they all became warped by its ugly shape.

18

I t rained hard that morning, and the wind was furious. Malcolm went out to work with Robert early, leaving Tom on his own. Having prowled around downstairs for a couple of hours, Tom accepted that it wasn't walking weather; he would be blown off his feet. But he didn't know what to do with himself. He didn't feel steady today.

For a while he tried to read, and when he couldn't sit still any longer, he went up to his room and listened to the wind sweeping around the sides of the cottage and the rain beating against the windows. He hoped Malcolm wasn't up on the cliffs today.

If he went outside, Tom knew exactly how the moorland would look under the onslaught of rain, knew how the grasses would be blown flat, how the sea would be turbulent and grey, half hidden by the dense mist. He knew too how the landscape would transform once the weather cleared, the dark clouds swept away with disconcerting suddenness and the sun coming through, everywhere the colour changing, the grassland turning green again and the sea and sky a bright blue. When the weather changed here, it changed fast. But while it was like this, you couldn't imagine it ever being another way. The storm was as much a fact of the landscape as the sea was.

Tom began to feel the weather closing in on him. There were gusts of anxiety moving through his body, but he was only tired, he told himself. His sleep had been fitful. He tried lying down on his bed to rest, but couldn't relax as the wind howled and rumbled outside. It was making the windows rattle in their frames. Even the cottage walls seemed to shake with it, though Tom knew this must be in his head.

Abruptly, he pushed himself up off the bed and went downstairs again. Keep moving, he thought. But there was nowhere to go. In front of the living-room window, he pressed the heels of his hands against his eyes. He wished Malcolm would come back. His thoughts were moving beyond his control. The laundry, the dislocated shoulder, his mother's red hair—he'd lost her face again.

The whole cottage creaked and groaned as the wind surged around its walls. Tom could almost picture the wind itself, bank after bank of taut, violent air rushing against the walls. He had forgotten it could be like this, how you could feel that all the elements were raging against you. He imagined the cottage collapsing on him, Malcolm coming home to a pile of rubble, finding Tom bloodied and broken beneath it.

The danger of this kind of storm: it took you out of time. Tom leaned his forehead against the window to feel the shock of the cold glass. He tried to take careful, deep breaths. Closer and closer the weather came, until he felt the storm around his face, in his ears, in his body and his brain.

And he saw it all again; it was always with him, but sometimes it came over him all at once like a sudden faintness. He had known last night that it was almost on him again. The room through the slats in the wardrobe door looked unusually bright. The memory was in broken pieces, but the fragments were strung together by the feeling of cold that accompanied them, the icy shiver going through him, through him and through him, and the world seeming to slant and go into slow motion as in a nightmare. There was no noise except the throb of blood in his ears and a sound like the rushing of wings.

He saw the bedroom door opening, and he saw Nicky

coming in. Then there was a short gap before the next picture, which was Nicky standing in the middle of the room, looking around him. Tommy felt through the cold that his brother was searching for somewhere to hide, and he knew that Nicky had frozen, just like Tommy himself had, and could not make a decision.

Then the next moment Tommy was whispering, "Nicky, Nicky," and pushing the wardrobe door open a crack. And Nicky came in quickly to join him. They huddled together in the dark and waited. Nicky's hand was in Tommy's. In this version, Nicky was allowed to grow up, and eventually he got married and had children of his own.

Then there was the other version in which Tommy felt nothing but the cold going through him, and he did not speak.

In this version, the next fragment was his father walking into the room, very slow and calm, sliced into neat layers by the slats in the door. And the picture after that was the shotgun. Nothing seemed to move, and so there seemed no interval at all between that moment and the picture that came next of the blood on the wall, in streaks through the slats in the wardrobe. Tommy stayed where he was throughout it all, not even breathing now, trying to control his shivering, and he watched his father turn and seem to stare straight at him, as though he could see through the wardrobe door. And there was nothing else after that, nothing except the icy cold inside him and the knowledge that whatever he did now he would never get warm.

PART 2

1

Katrina's mother said, "We don't have any secrets. People who love each other don't have secrets."

Katrina, although she was only eleven at this point, was starting to wish that they did have some secrets. Her mother had told her recently, for instance, that she found it difficult to orgasm during penetrative sex. Katrina didn't fully understand every element of this information, but she knew she was being told something adult and horrifying, and it brought a twisty feeling to her stomach and a hotness to her face.

Sometimes she was flattered that her mother confided in her. She knew she was her mother's best friend because her mother often said so, and Katrina was moved by the sense of her own importance; she was starting to be aware that her friends' mothers did not rely on their daughters in the way that Katrina's mother relied on her. Katrina's sister Jill was seven years older than she was and had already left home to live with a boyfriend in Edinburgh. Katrina's mother said Jill was "a person it was difficult to be close to'. Katrina felt a guilty swell of pride at this. She knew she herself was not like that.

But it was tiring sometimes. Her mother was often sad, often had low moods, and then Katrina would have to make her feel better. And Katrina was allowed to keep nothing safe or secret in her own head. Everything must be shared. If her mother suspected Katrina was holding something back, she would go on and on at her until Katrina was worn down and would either say something true or manufacture something to please her mother, like, "I had a headache today," upon which her mother would say, "I have the most terrible headache now," and they would have to go and get in bed together and lie in the dark for hours until it passed.

Katrina's mother needed her more after Katrina's father left, but Katrina wasn't really sorry to see him go. She loved him sometimes, when he would sing his special song for her or hold her on his lap as they watched films together. But that stopped when Katrina was seven because her mother said it was "inappropriate", a word she used often, though Katrina remained vague on its meaning given that her mother used it to encompass so many things. She missed her father's warmth though, the cuddles he'd given her, however occasional they'd been, and the song he'd sung her: *My bonnie lies over the ocean, my bonnie lies over the sea.*

After Katrina's mother used the word "inappropriate", that bumpy, cumbersome word that seemed to carry so much power, Katrina's father mostly acted as if Katrina wasn't there, though he would still chat and laugh with Jill sometimes, if he was in the right mood. Occasionally, late at night, he would stumble into furniture. Katrina also knew the word "alcoholic" from a young age because she often heard her mother say it. "Disgusting alcoholic," she would say. "I didn't know when I married him." Then she would lean in close to Katrina, so the scent of her perfume, a sweetness Katrina usually loved, became overpowering and sickly, and her breath smelled sour. And she would say, "Never trust a man. They're liars. Marrying him was the worst mistake of my life."

Katrina was a bright child and was able to follow this statement to its logical conclusion: her own birth, too, was a mistake. She felt guilty for the difficulties they'd all caused her mother.

Katrina's father finally left when she was ten years old, not long after Jill had packed up and gone to Edinburgh. Katrina simply came down to breakfast one day to find him gone. The household had halved in a matter of months. Katrina had been more upset when Jill left, though she would not miss the rows Jill had had with their mother towards the end.

Katrina was surprised at how distraught her mother was at her father's departure, given that Katrina had come to think of him by then as their enemy. She thought the house would be more peaceful without him. Maybe now she would be able to sit quietly and do her homework without being frightened by the sudden sound of yelling or doors slamming downstairs. Still, Katrina would sometimes lie awake at night in the aftermath (in fact, this would go on for years) and think about the fact that her own father hadn't liked her enough to stick around. He had stayed for Jill, it seemed, but not for her.

Her mother took to her bed for three days and refused to get up. "He was my whole life," she said over and over again. Katrina hadn't been to school that week, because her mother said she couldn't bear to be left alone. Katrina sat for hours on end in the dark, stuffy bedroom while her mother cried and talked about betrayal. They were running low on food by the third day, and Katrina had resorted to feeding herself and her mother peanut butter on toast for every meal. She wasn't sure what they would do when the bread from the freezer ran out, and she was starting to feel very anxious about it.

She slept late on the fourth day, exhausted by it all, and when she got up and shuffled into her mother's bedroom in her nightdress, she found her mother gone. Katrina momentarily panicked, believing in that moment that her mother had left as well, but then she heard her mother's voice from downstairs, calling, "Katrina, come and have your breakfast."

In the kitchen, her mother had set out two plates, and next to each one was a glass of orange juice. Katrina could immediately see it was the expensive kind with bits, which she was never usually allowed. Her mother was cooking eggs and bacon in a frying pan and heating up baked beans in a saucepan. There was already toast in the toast rack and a new pat of butter on the table. Katrina, still half asleep, wondered where all this food had come from, and then, with even more confusion, where her mother's good mood had come from.

"We're going to have such a lovely time, now it's just the two of us," her mother said. "Aren't we? It's us girls against the world."

Katrina nodded. She thought of Jill, living her new life in Edinburgh, and wondered when she would come back to visit, already half knowing the answer was never. Still, Katrina was relieved to see her mother up, and she was also absolutely starving, so she squashed down the prickly anxious feeling in her chest and sat at the table to receive her food.

There followed several months of "girls' trips", which involved Katrina being swooped upon suddenly, made to put on a series of new dresses her mother had bought for her (each, Katrina noted with dismay, frillier than the last), and then taken on a day out. Sometimes these were wonderful: they would go into Glasgow and Katrina's mother would visit the shops and then buy Katrina a huge milkshake and take her to the cinema ("the pictures", Katrina's mother said, although Katrina knew only old people called it this, and she thought her mother must know this too). Or they would drive for an hour to get to the beach and then eat fish and chips and ice cream sitting on the sand, however cold the wind was.

"Aren't we having a lovely time?" her mother would say to her, and usually Katrina would agree.

Other times, however, these outings were more bizarre, like when her mother took her to the hairdresser's, had them seated in chairs side by side and said with her high, tinkling laugh, "Make us look like sisters." Perhaps the hairdresser had taken pity on Katrina, because she gave both of them fairly nondescript shoulder-length cuts that weren't striking enough in themselves to make the similarity emphatic. Katrina didn't mind her new cut, but she had preferred having her hair long so she could wear it in two plaits.

Some of these outings would take place on school days, which Katrina didn't like. She enjoyed school and worried about getting behind with her work. The worst occasion was when she was supposed to be presenting her project on the Victorians to the rest of the class. Katrina had been working on it for two weeks and had created a model of a Victorian schoolroom out of two shoeboxes she'd cut and sellotaped to make into one, with desks made of matchboxes, and the dolls from her dollhouse stitched into tiny uniforms she'd sewn herself out of dark blue cloth. A teacher at the front brandished a matchstick cane. When Katrina's mother said on the Wednesday morning Katrina was supposed to present, "I've got a lovely surprise for you today," Katrina's heart sank.

It was unusual for her not to acquiesce immediately with her mother's plans, but in this case, she said, "I've got to present my history project at school today, Mum. I can't miss it. It's my turn."

"Don't be so silly," her mother said. She was smiling, but it was one of those hard-around-the-edges smiles that Katrina had learned to distrust. "It's just a boring school project."

"It's on the Victorians," Katrina said, aware that this comment wasn't really conveying everything she wanted to say.

"Don't be tedious, love," her mother said, and the matter was settled.

They went into Glasgow and had lunch in a restaurant that Katrina could tell was very fancy and that she worried they couldn't afford. Afterwards her mother took her to a bookshop and picked out a book for her on Victorian religion, saying to Katrina as she paid, "There you go. Now you can't claim you're missing out on your education." Smiling at the shop assistant, she added, "My daughter is *extremely* conscientious about her schoolwork." She was doing that accent she sometimes put on—it was posh, almost English.

Katrina could see the book was for adults; it was very thick and the print was tiny. Besides, it was a hardback and the anxious feeling in her chest got even stronger when she saw how much it cost. She did not say any of this to her mother, because she knew if she did her mother's smile would vanish and she would say Katrina was ungrateful.

When Katrina went back to school the next day, she asked her teacher if she would still be able to present her project, but Mrs Christie said, "Sorry, but there's no more time. We have to move on to the solar system." Then, seeing Katrina's dismay, she added, "But I'll look at it very carefully, I promise."

Katrina handed her project over, but Mrs Christie never gave it back, nor even mentioned it again. Katrina didn't get the merit mark she had hoped for. She heard from some of the others that they'd got merit marks the day before at the end of their presentations and she was sure that if she'd been there she would have got one too, and then she would have had ten in her merit book and would have got a bookmark and a badge from the headmaster. As it was, she never made it to ten that term so she never got her bookmark.

For a while, Katrina's father did come back to visit her occasionally. There were rare, strained Saturdays during which he'd take her out for a walk and then to eat a piece of cake in the café round the corner. But Katrina's mother usually insisted on being present too, "to supervise", and these outings would follow a predictable course from her mother's sniping comments to her father's increasingly infuriated replies, and then, if it was a good day, things would resolve into a sullen silence, or, on unluckier days, a row. Either way, Katrina often never received her piece of cake. The visits became rarer and rarer, and eventually stopped altogether. Mostly, Katrina didn't mind.

But as the months went on, she grew more and more concerned about money. Her mother worked part-time as a receptionist at an optician's, and she often complained that Katrina's father didn't send her enough money each month to supplement her income.

"If it wasn't clear before," she said to Katrina, "it's certainly clear now how little he cares about his own daughter. I daresay he's drinking it all away. Perhaps he wants us to starve."

Katrina had never in her life gone without food, but the idea took root and panicked her. Perhaps it was only a matter of time before the money ran out. She began to overeat at mealtimes, only half aware of it, as though cramming down food for the famished months ahead.

"Darling, you'll get fat if you carry on like this," her mother said one day, as Katrina reached for a second helping of mashed potato. She made it sound like getting fat was a worse fate than starvation, but Katrina couldn't stop. She developed a terror of going to her bed hungry, and started to hoard Jacob's cream crackers in her bedroom, which she bought with her pocket money and the birthday money her grandparents sent her. She didn't get fat, but her mother said no one would ever marry her if she went around wearing that anxious expression the whole time. "Which in some ways," her mother added, "might be a blessing. Better a spinster than married to a man like your father."

Katrina found out some years later that Jill had continued to see their father, right up until his death from a heart attack at the age of fifty-one, when Katrina was in her early twenties and newly engaged. It was Jill who delivered the news to her. Katrina felt a pang of sadness, but no more than that; it was difficult to feel much for someone who had essentially been a stranger.

"He was a good man," Jill had said through her tears. "He had his troubles, but he was kind."

Katrina had been ashamed at how little she felt herself. She missed her father, though, on her wedding day. Unexpectedly, the tears came as she walked down the aisle on her mother's arm—tears everyone else interpreted as those of a happy bride, not of a young woman crying for the father who had left her, or had perhaps been driven away.

It was almost a relief, given the increasing frequency of their "girls' trips", when Katrina's mother turned her attention away from her daughter and back on to men. It had never even crossed Katrina's mind, considering how often her mother expressed her relief at her husband's absence and how much she seemed to hate him during his occasional visits, that her mother was interested in auditioning potential replacements. Nevertheless, six months after her separation, Katrina's mother brought the first of her boyfriends home. He was called Michael, and Katrina's mother claimed she had met him on the bus to work. "It was meant to be," she said. Michael was kind to Katrina; when he came round in the evenings, he would sometimes bring her a packet of flying saucers and ask her what she was learning at school. But Katrina had scarcely begun to hope he would marry her mother and provide for them when he vanished and was replaced by Joe, who never spoke to Katrina or even looked at her, and then Alan, who had a beard and smelled of cigarettes and sweat, and then Callum, who did speak to Katrina but in a sly, jokey way she didn't understand.

The days out stopped as soon as the boyfriends began, or rather they continued, but usually without Katrina. Instead her mother went to the beach or to the cinema or to restaurants with her boyfriends. Sometimes Katrina would be brought grudgingly along, but more often she was left with a neighbour, or at home by herself.

Not that her mother would allow Katrina to feel left out.

Katrina was always kept up to date with the intimate details of her mother's latest relationship. She knew, for instance, that her mother felt "safer" with Joe than she had done with a man for many years, but also that Joe was a feeble lover ("You know, between the sheets," Katrina's mother added for extra clarification. "*Sexually.*"), whereas Callum knew how to please a woman ("*sexually*") but couldn't, Katrina's mother said, be trusted.

"And because I don't orgasm easily from penetrative sex," Katrina's mother said, "I need a man to do a bit of extra work. Not all of them are willing." She looked at Katrina with a small smile. "You'll understand one day. Men can be very selfish." Then, after a short pause, "I'm talking about the stimulation of the *clitoris.*"

Katrina fled at this point, saying she had to do her homework. Her mother always saw through this excuse.

"How did I raise such a prude?" she called after Katrina. "You should be grateful I'm trying to educate you. Most mothers prefer to keep their daughters in the dark."

Katrina found it difficult to look at her mother's partners after that. Sometimes, too, she heard the noises coming from her mother's room, even in the middle of the afternoon. She stayed out of the house as much as possible, visiting friends (she had few) or going on long, solitary walks around town, or reading in her bedroom. She was so awkward and tongue-tied around her mother's boyfriends that her mother accused her of being sullen and ungrateful.

"I gave up a lot to have you," she would remind Katrina. "I had my own life in Glasgow, dates every night, hundreds of friends and a lovely wee flat I lived in all by myself. I threw a lot of parties in those days, before you came along." (Katrina could see that her mother had got her confused with Jill, that first unexpected pregnancy before she had "got the hang of the sponge". Katrina herself had been the second blip. In any case, she had heard her mother complain in other moods about how she'd had to slum it in a filthy, rat-infested bedsit when she lived in Glasgow because her parents never gave her any help.) "I don't hold it against you, of course," Katrina's mother would add. "But it hurts me when you're so moody and spoilt, after all the sacrifices I've made for you. Do you know how difficult it's been, bringing up two daughters all on my own? Your father never helped. And now I'm left alone with you. It's been desperately lonely." Here, she would often start crying, and Katrina would have to comfort her.

One of the positives of her mother's boyfriends was that it gave Katrina the opportunity to do her schoolwork in peace without her mother calling her a bluestocking, or complaining that Katrina was neglecting her. Katrina was fourteen now, and had begun to see, with some gentle encouragement from her teachers, that she was passably clever and had a chance of doing well in her Highers when the time came. Though she struggled with maths, she was good at English and history, could express herself neatly and concisely, and had an intuitive understanding of grammar. Her English teacher suggested she might consider teaching or journalism, and since the idea of standing up in front of a class terrified her, Katrina settled on journalism.

She knew better than to voice this idea to her mother, who would tell her, Katrina knew, not to be so silly, that she wasn't cut out for journalism, that you had to be much tougher and quicker than Katrina to make it as a journalist. She would say it in a kindly, smiling way, of course, as though all she wanted was to help Katrina. But Katrina was starting to distrust her mother's help. For so many years she had felt as though she could hardly breathe, that there was no space left over for her; her mother took it all. She wasn't yet able to view her mother with any level of detachment, but nevertheless she began to feel a fierce impulse to get away.

After Callum finally left, following many months of shouting and door slamming (Katrina had come to regard these
things wearily as a fact of life), Katrina's mother retired to her
bed, just as she had done after Katrina's father walked out.
Katrina—sixteen, by now—took it in her stride. She worked
on Saturdays and Sundays at the local newsagent's, so at least
they would have enough money for vegetables to make soup if
her mother lost her job. They would not starve. Over the next
week, she brought her mother cups of tea and slices of toast
with jam, and encouraged her to wash from time to time. This
storm, she knew, would pass, just as all the others had.

And naturally it did. Katrina's mother rose up from her bed
like Lazarus, washed and set her hair, applied her bright lipstick and declared that all she needed in life was her daughter,
and that as long as they had each other, no man could hurt
them. She did not know, of course, that Katrina was already
starting to harden her heart against her.

The following year, Katrina sat her Highers and did well.
She left school not long before she turned eighteen and, much
to her own and her mother's surprise, secured her first job at
the *Stirling Reporter* without too much effort, writing the death
notices.

"They just want someone to make the tea," her mother said.
"You watch out, hen. You're only there so they can take advantage of you. They hired you for your looks."

This comment came as a surprise to Katrina; her mother
had never before suggested that Katrina was pretty. It was true
that in her last two years at school, boys had started paying her
attention, but this had only disconcerted her, and she had
ignored them until they lost heart. Katrina had always known,
of course, that her mother was beautiful. She knew, too, that
she herself looked nothing like her. It was dark-eyed Jill who
took after their mother in appearance. In fact, there had been
times in the past when Katrina's mother had looked her up and

down critically and said, "You got your looks from your father, unfortunately." Her mother had suggested once or twice that it would be especially important for Katrina to show herself to be very sweet and biddable around men, because not everyone was lucky enough to be able to rely on their appearance.

Katrina was aware that she had reached adulthood with no clear sense of her own personality, no real idea of her likes and dislikes, or even where her own edges were. It was difficult to feel where her mother stopped and she began, and almost impossible to patrol those borders.

What she did have was a strong instinct for movement. It was the deepest, truest thing she knew. She had to get away, although she didn't know how this could be achieved or whether her mother would let her go, or indeed if Katrina herself could even exist outside of her mother's sphere (perhaps she would simply fade away as she moved clear of it, having no definition beyond those boundaries). Nevertheless, it had to be attempted. Katrina put her head down and focused on her work, even while her mother commented that she was wasting her time, that Katrina didn't have the right temperament for reporting.

Jill, mostly absent from their lives over the past few years, proved an unexpected ally in this. She invited Katrina to stay with her in Edinburgh for a weekend, and they climbed in the rain to the top of Arthur's Seat and ate cake on Princes Street, and then Jill made curry for tea in the tiny flat she shared with her boyfriend (a different one, Katrina was surprised to note, from the one she'd originally left to live with, or "eloped with", as their mother liked to put it). Katrina had never had curry before, nor spent the night away from home. She was nervous around the boyfriend Chris, though he was very polite to her. Jill had cut her hair short and bleached it, and she was wearing bright red lipstick like Debbie Harry. In the evening, Jill and Chris smoked cigarettes that Chris rolled for them (Katrina refused one), and the three of them sipped red wine out of beakers as Jill cooked. Katrina thought her sister was the most glamorous person she'd ever met.

"Of course you have to get away," Jill said in that cool voice of hers, turning from the saucepan to look at Katrina. "You can't stay at home with her any longer. You'll lose your mind."

Katrina already knew this was true, but still something— perhaps some long-buried feeling of reproach towards Jill— made her say, "If I leave, she'll have no one."

Then Jill said something surprising. "Our mother," she began, and here she paused and gave the curry a vicious stir, "is incapable of love. It's not her fault, but it's true. She has no sense of other people's feelings, no interest in them or even awareness. I suppose it's a mental disorder of some kind, but I can't feel sorry for her. She lives alone in her world—the people around her are just moving, coloured shapes. So Katrina, it doesn't really matter whether you stay or go. You're no one to her—or rather the role you play could be filled by anyone. Do you understand that? That's why it's so important that you leave."

Chris had his arm around Jill's shoulders now, but Katrina could see her sister's back stayed tense, and after a moment she shrugged Chris off. Katrina herself was quiet, absorbing this sudden rush of words. While she felt her sister was overstating the case, Jill's outburst brought with it a sudden sense of freedom, almost vertiginous in its unfamiliarity. She said, as Jill continued to stir the curry as though nothing had happened, "I want to apply for a job at the *Glasgow Herald*. Then I'd be earning enough, just about, to move to Glasgow. Only I don't think they'd take me."

Jill turned to face her. "You know, I bet they would."

Chris added, "At least there's no harm in asking, is there?" and for some reason it was this more than anything that clinched it for Katrina. She did apply the following week, and was interviewed and taken on as a junior reporter, writing articles for the business section. She found a room to rent, and arranged it all without consulting her mother.

"You're moving *out*?" her mother said, when the subject was finally broached. "But you can't!"

"I have to, Mum," Katrina said, almost shaking from the stress of it. "I need to be close to work."

"Nonsense. It's only a forty-minute drive into Glasgow. I'll get you a second-hand car."

Katrina held firm. She didn't want to drive, she said.

"Don't be so selfish," her mother said. "It's always been just the two of us. You can't leave me on my own."

This was the mode of attack Katrina had feared the most. She suspected that she *was* being selfish, perhaps monstrously so. But she knew, too, that she had to go forwards, that she had to get away as Jill said. She was glad she had had the foresight to find a room in advance, to pay the landlady a small deposit from her savings and arrange to move in the following week. Otherwise, faced with this, she didn't think she'd ever have been able to go through with it.

"You'll be O.K., Mum," she said, attempting to sound cheerful and bracing. "I'll be back every weekend, and I can come round for tea some evenings in the week, too."

"You won't be able to get here. You must be mad if you think I'll pick you up, drive all that way."

"I'll get the bus," Katrina said.

"I won't pick you up from the stop."

"I'll walk. Honestly, Mum, you'll hardly notice I'm gone."

Her mother began to cry loudly, but when Katrina tried to comfort her, she batted her away, talking inarticulately about how selfish Katrina was, how Katrina wouldn't be capable of living alone in the city, that she wouldn't cope, that she would probably be raped and murdered within the first week.

"You can't even cook," she said, and Katrina, who had been cooking for both of them since she was eleven, let this pass.

"I'll manage," she said.

"But what will happen to me?"

"You'll be fine."

"How can you do this to me?"

"I'll be back to visit all the time," Katrina said again. She felt as though she were committing a terrible crime, and the excitement of her new job—it had felt like the first genuine achievement of her life—was spoiled utterly. But still she was determined to go through with it. Perhaps this was the first real indication she'd had of her own personality: that she was irredeemably selfish, deep down. She could hardly regret it, though; she had begun to see how she might survive.

Her new room was a little back bedroom in the house of a middle-aged widow in west Glasgow, not too far from the offices of the *Herald*. Katrina only had to take a fifteen-minute bus ride each morning, and it felt like luxury to get ready in the quiet of her own room, putting on a new pink lipstick without her mother ridiculing it, and eating breakfast undisturbed. Her landlady was stern and imperious, but mostly left Katrina alone once she'd satisfied herself that Katrina wasn't the kind to try to bring men back, or to break the rules about when she was allowed to use the kitchen or take a bath.

At twenty years old, Katrina found herself really happy for the first time in her life. She liked her job, and she enjoyed being in the office, the general atmosphere of industriousness, the jokes she shared with the others. Her older male colleagues were mostly kind to her, if a little patronizing; one or two would ask her to make them tea, as though she was a secretary (Katrina usually did it, because it seemed too awkward to go and ask one of the real secretaries to do it on her behalf). Katrina also discovered during this time that she could make people laugh. She became more animated in the way she relayed anecdotes, dryer and more self-deprecating, often find-ing herself exaggerating her stories. Some of her colleagues became friends, and from time to time they would go to the pub together after work.

She didn't see her sister much after moving to Glasgow. Jill and Chris had had a baby, so Jill was occupied with her new son, and Katrina with her new life. Her visits to her mother went from every weekend to every other weekend, and though Katrina had thought her mother would make a huge fuss, instead she seemed quietly resigned, as though already aware the battle was lost.

So at the age of twenty-two and finally having escaped her mother, Katrina walked into a pub in Glasgow's West End and met John.

2

Perhaps it was true what John said later, that she was looking for marriage, although she was hardly aware of it. Though she loved the small, neat life she had made for herself, she still carried a sense of being in flight. She craved the kind of stability that was borne on deep foundations, the reassuring concrete of a husband and children lying thickly beneath the surface of her life.

It was a Thursday night, leaving drinks for one of Katrina's colleagues in a pub they'd never visited before. ("A special occasion calls for a different venue," someone had said, and the plan was made.)

John, at twenty-five, was not exactly handsome, but he had a nice face. He had dark brown eyes which Katrina liked, and though he wasn't especially tall, though his mouth was wide and his front teeth a bit too large, Katrina found his appearance appealing. Several of her male colleagues had made passes at her since she'd started at the *Herald*, but Katrina had become adept at brushing these off, politely and shyly, careful never to offend. She'd scanned their ranks discreetly and decided none of them would do for a boyfriend. In any case, most of them were married.

John would later tell her she was the most beautiful woman he'd ever seen in real life, and Katrina would be embarrassed, but grateful.

There was no opportunity for John to approach her on her own in the pub that night, because Katrina wasn't the kind of girl confident enough to go up to the bar to get a round in like the men, and tended to rely on others to fetch her drinks. John waited instead until she was on the edge of the group of her colleagues, only five of them left by that point, and then he simply walked up to her.

"Do you mind me asking," he began, "if that's your natural hair colour?"

Katrina did mind him asking, although the rudeness of the question was partly allayed by the warmth of his manner.

"It is," she said, not committing to a smile, but ready to be charmed, if he turned out to be charming.

"I've never seen such lovely dark-red hair," he said. "It's very striking."

Mae, Katrina's colleague, whom she had been chatting to up to this point, snorted and turned away to talk to the rest of the group, clearly deciding to leave them to it. Katrina wished she hadn't, because she immediately felt awkward.

John, however, seemed pleased. He asked her about herself, and, upon eliciting that she worked at the *Herald*, said, "So I'd better watch what I say, hadn't I? Else I might make it into print."

"Hardly," Katrina said. "I work for the business section."

"A real career girl," John said, smiling.

"Hardly," Katrina said again, and then wondered if she'd forgotten all her other words.

"But a girl as pretty as you won't be doing that for long," John said. "Someone will come along and marry you. Or are you one of those modern women who don't believe in marriage?"

"No," Katrina said.

John was an accountant and had been living in Glasgow since he was eighteen and started his training. But he'd grown up on Litta, he said, in the southern Hebrides. The island was remote and beautiful, with fewer than a hundred residents.

And now he had Katrina's attention. "That must have been amazing," she said. She tried to picture it.

"It was," John said. "A wonderful place to be a child—though as a teenager all I wanted was to get away. It was too isolated for me then. I feel differently now. I'd like to go back eventually. Bring up my own children there."

"I've never been. Not to anywhere in the Hebrides."

"You must," he said with a new intensity. "There's nowhere better."

Somehow it was this that started it, the passion with which he began to describe his home and his childhood, this that won Katrina over more than anything else. She wanted to see it too: those empty windswept beaches, the sea crashing against the black rocks, the cliffs and moorland and hills, the gannets and seals and sheep.

She started spending her evenings with John, going to the cinema, or to pubs and restaurants all around the city. She liked how he took care of her, and how solicitous he was, asking her what she'd like to do, what film she wanted to see or what food she'd like to eat, and then arranging it all for them. He would order for her in restaurants, choose the wine for both of them, and Katrina enjoyed the peace of not having to make decisions, the feeling of security she had with John. The attention, too. Extraordinary to discover someone could find her so interesting. He didn't make her laugh, that was true—not like some of her colleagues. And Katrina found that she became a more serious version of herself when she was with him, more thoughtful perhaps, less frivolous. But there were other things besides laughter.

He'd be there waiting for her most evenings outside her office, and would then escort her to whatever destination he had planned, even when it was close to his own office in the East End, so that he had to travel out of his way to pick her up. Katrina would point out that it would make much more sense for them to meet in the middle, but John would shrug and smile and say he liked to collect her, that he didn't want to miss a moment with her. Sometimes he'd even get the *Herald*'s receptionist to let him in, and would simply appear at her desk at five thirty, greeting her colleagues and asking if she was ready to go. Katrina was always pleased to see him, but occasionally these sudden appearances threw her off guard, as though he might catch her in the middle of something (but what, she wasn't sure).

Later—much later—it would occur to her that she'd fallen in love simply because she wanted to be in love. It could have been anyone. That was the pity of it.

It was a long time before she introduced him to her mother. There was an evening with Jill and Chris first, a strained meal in a small Italian restaurant in Edinburgh, during which nobody seemed to be behaving like themselves. Katrina was disappointed afterwards when she asked John if he liked them and he only said, "They seemed fine." But she reminded herself that John could be shy sometimes, and even she didn't know Jill very well anymore.

Introducing John to her mother proved similarly anticlimactic, though for different reasons. Katrina had steeled herself for some kind of scene, for her mother weeping and telling John how Katrina had abandoned her, or else her taking an immediate dislike to John and treating him to her speech on how all men were bastards. Katrina imagined John's face, white and set, as he endured these indignities, and she could hardly bear it.

In the event, her mother was civil, though seemingly detached. She offered John sherry and asked him about his work, even listening politely to his answer without turning the subject to herself. She provided a very reasonable tea of sandwiches, scones, and seed cake, and was quick to offer

John seconds. All in all, she behaved for the entire afternoon like somebody else's mother. Katrina was suspicious and perplexed.

"You were very quiet," John said as they drove back to Glasgow. "But your mum was nice. I thought you said she was difficult?"

Katrina felt a momentary prickle of irritation. It occurred to her then that this uncharacteristic, undermining civility might be her mother's revenge on her.

She and John had sex for the first time a few months into their relationship. John said it meant a lot to him that it was Katrina's first time, that she'd saved herself for him. She was worried about getting pregnant, but John said it wouldn't happen, and even if it did, it wouldn't matter because they'd be married soon anyway.

"Unless you're planning on marrying somebody else?" he added with a smile.

"No."

"Well then."

It was better than she'd expected. John was skinny and pale beneath his clothes, and Katrina felt oddly protective of him. She didn't feel much excitement—she had a suspicion her mother had ruined sex for her anyway—and the act itself was a bit like being poked with a sharp object over and over again. But there was something touching and primal about being naked and wrapped around each other. It felt a bit like being born.

"I love you," John told her afterwards, his arm under her head. He said it often, but Katrina still felt delight when the words came. This, she thought, was finally "it". Now her life could begin properly, and she would be safe forever.

There was just one unsettling incident, about six months after they'd met. Katrina was attending leaving drinks for Mae, who was moving down to London, and told John she couldn't see him that evening. She didn't like doing this; she already knew it hurt his feelings when she said she was busy, and she'd started to miss more and more evenings with her colleagues as a result. But Mae was her best friend at work, and Katrina had promised to attend.

John didn't seem to mind at first. He told her to go and have a lovely time, and Katrina felt relieved he didn't ask if he could come too, because her colleagues already teased her about how much time she spent with him. She said she'd only stay a couple of hours and would meet him afterwards, but as it was she'd been in the pub for less than an hour when John appeared at her elbow saying he'd come to collect her.

"But it's too early to leave yet," Katrina said. Then, thinking she could still save the evening, she added, "Stay and have a drink with us."

Mae was nearby and added her voice to Katrina's, putting her arm around her friend's shoulders. "Don't you know I might never see her again after tonight? You're not going to drag her away already, are you?"

Katrina could see from John's face that he wasn't in the mood to joke with Mae, or to humour any of them for that matter. Instinctively she felt the need to mediate, and above all to get John away from there before he became even more displeased with her.

He was silent as they walked to the car, brushing off all Katrina's attempts at conversation. Once they'd got in, she said, "What's wrong, John? Why are you being so . . ." and then she didn't know which words to use, and settled in the end for, "unlike yourself."

"I don't know what you're talking about," he said with a short laugh. But he wouldn't speak to her on the drive back to his flat.

"Have I done something?" she said at last, when they were nearly home. "I can see you're upset—"

"I'm not upset," he said. "You're imagining things again."

Again? she thought.

His strange, silent mood persisted once they were back in his flat, even though he initiated sex with her. Katrina hoped this meant things would return to normal between them, but John wasn't loving like he usually was. He was distant and perfunctory, manoeuvring her into different positions in a way that seemed strangely impersonal, and not once looking into her eyes or kissing her. It made Katrina want to cry, but she managed not to.

Finally, as they lay next to each other, John said, "I can see why you were so keen to shake me off."

"Shake you off?" Katrina said. "What do you mean?" She turned on her side to look at him, but he continued to stare up at the ceiling. She hated this most of all, she realized, the way he wouldn't look at her, wouldn't seem to acknowledge her presence, even while speaking to her.

He said in the same quiet voice, "So you could go tarting around with all those men."

"All those—? John, there were only two men there!" Katrina said, too baffled even to be angry.

"Yes, I'm sure you do know the exact number," he said. "And when did you change into that miniskirt, or have you been showing your legs off like that all day?"

"It was hardly a miniskirt," Katrina said, trying to keep her voice reasonable. "And anyway, I don't think the merest glimpse of my knees will have driven anyone into a wild passion." She spoke lightly, thinking that now the mood would change and they could laugh about it together.

But John snapped, "You don't know what you're talking about."

At the venom of his voice, Katrina felt the tears starting up in her eyes. "Why are you being like this?" she said. He was behaving like someone else entirely. Katrina wondered how she had driven him to it, and how she could make him go back to how he was before.

Her tears, it seemed, made a difference. Finally, John turned towards her. "Oh, love," he said. "There's no need to get upset. I just don't want you making yourself look silly. I care so much about you. Perhaps it would be easier if I cared less."

"I didn't look silly," Katrina said, crying properly now. "I didn't."

"I know you believe that," he said. "But you have to understand, men see things very differently from women. All those men you work with, they will have been looking at you and thinking you're a slut, dressed like that and flirting with them in the pub."

"No they won't," Katrina said. She rubbed her hands across her face. She felt unmoored. "They're not like that."

"Darling, they are. All men are. Almost all, anyway. Look, stop crying." He took a handkerchief from his bedside drawer and gently reached out to dry her tears. "You've been a wee bit naïve, that's all. This is just a misunderstanding."

And afterwards that was how Katrina tried to think of it, if she allowed herself to think of it at all. She tried to exercise better judgment, avoided wearing short skirts or anything too tight, and made such an effort not to behave in any way that might be construed as flirtatious with her male colleagues that Ronald, the one she liked best, asked one of the secretaries to find out if he'd done something to upset her. Katrina was mortified, and realized she'd got the balance wrong again. She was friendlier from then on, without, she hoped, being too friendly. At least Ronald never asked her to make him tea again.

Katrina and John married the week after Katrina's twenty-third birthday. When Katrina told Jill about the engagement on the telephone, Jill didn't sound happy about it. She said, "Are you sure? You're very young."

"I'm sure," Katrina said.

"But have you really thought it through?"

"Aye, of course."

At the end of the call, Katrina felt put out, but Jill and Chris came to the wedding two months later, at Glasgow City Chambers, and made a show of being cheerful. They even presented Katrina and John with a case of champagne, and Katrina was worried about how they'd afforded it. But John said it was a cheap kind of champagne, not really champagne at all, and wouldn't have cost them much.

The other guests at the wedding were Katrina's mother, who cried during the toasts afterwards at the George Hotel and said she didn't feel like she was losing a daughter so much as gaining a son; Katrina's friend Mae who had come all the way up from London for the occasion; Katrina's school friend Beth whom she hardly saw by then, but felt she ought to invite; and John's brother Malcolm with his wife Heather—a quiet, gentle couple who appeared rather out of their depth throughout the day. John's mother, apparently, was not well enough to make the crossing over to the mainland, and John's father was dead. The guest list looked a bit sparse to Katrina in the run-up to the wedding, and she had asked John if there were any friends he'd like to invite. He'd shaken his head and said, "The only person I need is you," and Katrina had been satisfied with this, because she felt the same.

She had agreed with John that they'd move to Litta to have a family, but she had thought this would be a few years into the future. She'd envisaged spending a while longer in Glasgow, living in the flat he rented, cooking for him, going out to the pub some evenings, reading together by their gas heater, spending long, lazy weekends in bed, luxuriating in their love for one another.

However, far more quickly than Katrina had anticipated—within a month of the wedding, in fact—she was pregnant. She'd wanted for some time to go on the pill, but John had never liked the idea; he said it was dangerous, and anyway, it encouraged promiscuity.

"*Promiscuity?*" she said. "Are you serious?"

"I meant in general. I didn't mean you in particular."

"Oh, thanks," Katrina said.

He laughed and put out his hand to her. "The side effects, my love. It can be really dangerous. Won't you trust me with this? I'll take care of it, I promise."

Katrina decided to concede. And it was true that usually John would withdraw before he came, though not always. Katrina had given up trying to remind him. He said it ruined the moment, and sometimes it made him angry. A woman shouldn't be telling a man what to do at a moment like *that*. Katrina had realized by now how sensitive John could be about certain things. If anything, this only made her love him more, this vulnerability at his core. His mother, from what little John had said about her, had a lot to answer for. Katrina made a silent decision to protect John's feelings wherever possible. He wasn't alone anymore; she would look after him.

Anyway, Katrina couldn't feel too dismayed at the pregnancy, not when it made John so happy. What kind of woman isn't delighted to find out she's carrying her husband's child?

John said they could stay on the mainland until she had the baby, but after that it would be time to move. He had already secured a house on Litta and was looking for a job as an accountant in Oban. He intended to work there a few days a week, commuting by ferry when the weather permitted and staying in rented accommodation on the mainland when necessary. He had it all planned out. Aware of her own disloyalty,

Katrina secretly hoped he wouldn't find a job in Oban just yet, and that they would have to wait a while longer. But as John said himself, he was successful in all his ventures—Katrina had almost come to see it as part of his character, like a vein of gold running through rock—and he was taken on by a firm in Oban just a week before Katrina's due date.

So six weeks after Nicky was born, they moved out to the island, Katrina still lost in a fog of exhaustion and shock.

"Are you sure?" Jill said again on the telephone.

"Of course," Katrina replied. "It's what we've always planned."

"It's very far," Jill said. "Two and a half hours on the ferry, is that right?"

"Just under," Katrina said, wondering why she suddenly felt so defensive.

"Well," Jill said, "good luck to you," and for the first time in her life Katrina felt as though she disliked her sister.

3

Katrina knew no one on the island, and the isolation of her new setting, the bleakness of its dark hills and the endless expanse of sea, appalled her. She was cold all the time during that first winter. The cottage John had taken was draughty and there was no central heating. There was an old storage heater, but it used so much electricity that they couldn't afford to put it on very often. Katrina felt the dampness of the salt air even inside the cottage, even inside her clothes, even inside her bones.

She worried about Nicky being cold, and kept him wrapped in so many layers he sometimes looked almost spherical. There was a fireplace in the living room, and Katrina grew proficient at building a fire and keeping it going all day, remaining huddled in front of it with Nicky for hours at a time when the weather was particularly cold and wet.

On better days, she would put Nicky in his sling and go out exploring her new home, tramping across the moorland and through the hills along the island's single road. It brought her little pleasure. Everything was a variation of grey, even the sheep who watched her balefully as she passed them.

Katrina had thought of herself as fairly self-reliant before coming to the island but in those first few months she was desperately lonely, especially as John often stayed overnight on the mainland and left her on her own. When he was home, he was preoccupied, different to the man she remembered, but in no clear way she could put her finger on. Nicky didn't seem to sleep much and Katrina found herself unable to keep up with the shopping and cooking and laundry. John was mostly patient, but she knew he minded if he came home to find the house a mess and no meal prepared. And these were all basic tasks, she knew. The baby, too, made her angry with his constant crying and she felt guilty for how much she resented him. It had never occurred to her that she would be a failure as a mother, but she began to see how it had always been impossible that she would be anything else. She remembered Jill saying that their own mother had no feelings for other people, and Katrina could see that she herself had never stood a chance at something she had never been shown how to do. She began to wish she had never met John. It wasn't fair on either of them. She began to wish she had never been born.

With such a small population, she couldn't have kept to herself for long, even if she'd wanted to. Malcolm and Heather lived a twenty-minute drive away on the other side of the island, and Heather would drop round from time to time to see Katrina. She seemed surprised at how often John was absent, and Katrina found she resented Heather's surprise, wishing she would keep away. It made her angry to be caught out like this, with the house a state and Katrina herself a state too, her hair not washed for days, her face haggard with exhaustion, the baby crying as always and refusing to be comforted. She imagined what Heather might be saying afterwards to Malcolm, who would probably pass it on to John: "Of course, she's trying her best, the poor lass, but anyone can see she's not really cut out for it."

She did her best to be polite to Heather, while wanting her gone.

"It must be tough," Heather said to her once, sipping coffee awkwardly in the living room. "Having a new baby, especially so far from home in a place like this."

Katrina was surprised at the rage she felt. Heather had no children herself. She had no right to judge Katrina.

"Is there anything I can do to help?" Heather added.

Katrina raised her chin. "No thank you. We're fine."

It wasn't normal, though, to cry this much. Even before she got out of bed in the mornings, Katrina would feel the tears starting to roll down her face as though she'd lost all control of herself. It was pathetic. If John was around, she'd have to wipe them away quickly while he wasn't looking. Once he'd left for work, or retreated to his study if he was working from home (Katrina would be under strict instructions not to disturb him), she would be able to let the tears fall freely. She almost laughed sometimes at the ridiculousness of it, herself crying as she held the crying Nicky, two babies instead of one.

This was how her nearest neighbour Fiona found her one day when John was away: crying in the living room as she held her distraught baby. Katrina ignored the doorbell because she was in no state to see anyone like this, and didn't want to in any case, but she hadn't reckoned on the woman's persistence. Moments later, Fiona had loomed up at the living-room window and was tapping on it gently.

Katrina had no choice but to let her in. Stupid, nosy woman.

"You poor dear, look at the state of you," Fiona said.

Katrina tried to wipe her tears and give Fiona a smile that would show she was fine, but Fiona was having none of it. She took the crying baby off Katrina and bustled into the kitchen to make tea.

Katrina was still crying when Fiona came back into the living room.

"Come on now, it's all right," Fiona said. Nicky, unbelievably, seemed to have gone to sleep, and Fiona laid him down gently in his cot without him stirring. "I'll just get the tea," she said, and returned a moment later with two mugs. How she'd managed to make it while lulling Nicky to sleep, Katrina could not fathom. She felt even more useless by comparison.

"Well, of *course* you're overwhelmed," Fiona said as she settled into an armchair. "All the way out here on your own with a new baby."

Katrina wished people would stop saying she was on her own.

Then Fiona said something unexpected. "You know, I think I cried every day during Stuart's first year. He's five now, thank God. It does get better."

At these words, Katrina felt the first glimmer of hope she'd experienced in months.

She said, "I don't feel like I'm coping well."

"My dear," Fiona said, "nobody does. If you're managing to keep yourself and the baby alive, I'd say you're doing just fine."

After that, Fiona took to bringing meals round a couple of times a week: a lasagne or casserole or pie that could easily be heated up.

"It's no trouble," she said when Katrina protested. "I'm making the food anyway. It's no bother to make a few extra helpings."

She was a kind woman, Katrina thought. Sometimes, tearfully swallowing down Fiona's food (which she sometimes simply ate cold, straight from the dish) during a short respite as Nicky slept, she felt she'd never loved anyone more than she loved Fiona.

And it did get better, though very slowly. Spring came and although the weather was still cold, the sun was bright and made the sea sparkle. Everywhere, colour returned. Katrina started spending more time with Heather, and felt herself beginning to relax in her presence. She got to know the other islanders—she didn't have much choice in the matter, so determined were they to include her—and as Katrina grew happier,

John seemed warmer towards her again, telling her sometimes how pretty she looked.

When Nicky was just over a year old, Katrina discovered she was pregnant again, and she wasn't as frightened as she might have predicted. She found she was actually looking forward to having another baby, or if not to the day-to-day reality of it, then at least to the idea of having two children instead of one. She hoped they would love each other and play together. At the thought of this, she felt a pang for Jill, whom she was barely in touch with now. Their phone conversations had become increasingly stilted over the past year, as Katrina found she had less and less she wanted to say to Jill about her life on the island; she couldn't tell Jill she was unhappy because Jill had predicted it all along. When Chris had left Jill some months before, Katrina had been too exhausted and overwhelmed herself to know what to say, or to offer anything much in the way of comfort. She thought relations had been even more distant between them since then, but nevertheless, when Jill called her up after a couple of months of silence to say she'd taken Henry and moved down to England with him, Katrina was hurt not to have been told about this plan in advance.

"It's natural that you've grown apart," John said. "You're very different, and you live very different lives. Besides, I think she's always been jealous of you."

"Me?" Katrina said. "No she hasn't."

"Jill can be quite difficult sometimes," John said.

"She's my only family, really." Her mother, Katrina had decided, didn't count. Katrina almost never rang her now—she'd had no energy left for another dependent after Nicky was born—but she did send her occasional postcards, to which her mother did not reply.

"I'm your family now," John said. "You don't need anyone else."

And feeling the truth of this, settled in her own house with her husband and son and another baby on the way, finally believing she had got the hang of it all, Katrina experienced something close to contentment.

But a ghost of unease remained. Katrina felt, alongside her new calm, that the world was contracting and narrowing until it consisted only of the desire for her husband to be happy and her two babies, born and unborn, to be healthy. She didn't know if this just meant she had everything she wanted already, or if it was true for everyone that after you became a proper adult you stopped looking forward the way you once had.

4

She never did work out what went wrong between her and John after Tommy's birth, why he suddenly seemed to lose all patience with her after that second baby. It had been a difficult labour, and Tommy was eventually delivered by C-section (thank God Katrina had held out for a hospital birth on the mainland, not a home birth, as John had wanted). Katrina was weak for a long time afterwards and couldn't do much around the house, though she tried her best. She managed, just about, to care for Nicky and the new baby, but she had to let many other things go. Fiona helped for a while, but John, when he realized how much Fiona was doing, didn't like it. He said it made it look like he wasn't caring for his own wife. Katrina had to withdraw from Fiona, to tell her that she was managing fine now and that John was around more.

But maybe it wasn't this weakness that irritated him. Maybe he had been waiting all along to see which way she would fall, and up until that point he had still believed she could suit him; maybe he had even believed she could save him. Whatever his dream had been, he was thoroughly disillusioned by the time their second son was six months old.

"You've put on so much weight," he said to her. "I know some women let themselves go after they have children, but I didn't think you'd be one of them. You didn't seem lazy when I met you."

Katrina wondered if she had deceived him in this. She

hadn't intentionally, she thought. But she was starting to feel that she was lazy. Everything was such a struggle.

When she cried, which was often again now, John said she was unstable, and perhaps she was. "You're hard work," he'd tell her, and sometimes he'd seem to say it fondly, but it always made her ashamed.

Katrina tried to change herself to fit with John's idea of how she should be. She ate very little so she could lose the baby weight as soon as possible, and tried to be bright and cheerful when he came back from Oban, or out of his study in the evenings, tried not to burst into tears when he made the mildest of criticisms. "You're so sensitive," he'd say. Katrina wasn't sure where all the love and joy of their early relationship had gone, but she thought that if she'd only tried harder, paid better attention, it wouldn't have slipped away like this without her noticing.

Despite her best efforts, they often argued now, and Katrina knew John was right when he said she was to blame. She lost her temper with him in ways she never had in her life before, and then he would stand back, watching her with that rueful half-smile on his face, as though he'd known all along she would end up shouting like this, but had still hoped to be wrong. How regularly she disappointed him. When she was angry like this, Katrina couldn't even remember how it had happened, except that John seemed so cruel sometimes in the things he said, and the more she tried to defend herself, the worse she came to seem to herself and to him. She, who had always been so calm and self-contained as a child, discovered what it meant now to be "beside yourself".

She couldn't believe how she shouted at him. He never raised his voice to her.

"You're from a broken home," John told her. "You don't know how to have a normal relationship. It's not your fault really. But it's hard for me. Your mother warped you."

Was she warped? Katrina thought about this word, this ugly word with its too-long vowel sound, as though it too were twisted out of shape. She carried it in her head as she went about her daily tasks. Perhaps that was what caused her to make silly mistakes, burning food and shrinking John's favourite shirt (she had not even known he had a favourite shirt until she shrank it).

"I told you not to put it in with the others," John told her, holding it up with a frown. The sleeves were too short now and the body looked oddly slim.

"I didn't know it was hand wash," Katrina said. "I'm sorry. I thought it was the same as the others." What kind of shirt was hand wash only?

He shook his head, doing that smile again. "Darling, I told you."

"You didn't." She was certain of this, knew that he was mistaken. This time, she told herself, she would hold her ground.

"Yes I did. You never remember. Your head's like a sieve."

Katrina steeled herself. "John, you didn't tell me. I'm sorry I shrank it. But you honestly didn't tell me."

His smile vanished. "Surely it isn't worth lying about, Katrina."

And reality tilted. She didn't think she was lying. But she was so tired and he was always so certain. She said, less confident now, "I don't remember you telling me."

"All right, darling, I believe you."

She was relieved at this.

Then he said, "But why didn't you check the label?"

He pushed her too far.

"I don't check the label of every item I wash, John! There's so much laundry to do every day."

"There's no need to lose your temper."

"I *haven't* lost my temper," she said, keeping her voice deliberately level.

"Yes you have. You're practically shouting at me. It's only a shirt, for Christ's sake."

"Only a shirt! You were the one making a . . . a huge fuss about it." And now what always happened was happening: her voice was rising and her words were tripping over each other.

"No I wasn't," he said calmly. "I simply noticed that my shirt had shrunk. I'm not sure why I'm the one who's suddenly under attack. Anyone would think I'd shrunk *your* shirt, not the other way around."

He maddened her. She really thought she was going mad. She tried to calm down, but the tears were already starting and her thoughts were incoherent, not ranged neatly like his. "I wasn't attacking you," she said, and her voice sounded high like a child's. Of course he couldn't take her seriously.

"Well, I'm sure you didn't mean to," he said. "But I've had a long day at work and the last thing I need is to come home and be shouted at."

"I'm sorry."

He put out his hand to her. "That's all right, my love. I know you're tired. And it really doesn't matter. It's only a shirt."

He was so patient, even when she lost his things.

"Where are my car keys?" he'd call to her from the living room.

"I don't know," Katrina would call back. "I haven't seen them."

"I put them on the side table like always," John said, coming into the kitchen. "You must have moved them."

"I haven't, love. I haven't touched them."

"Are you suggesting," John said, speaking slowly as though addressing an imbecile, "that they've got up and walked off of their own accord?"

"No. But perhaps you misremembered where you put them."

"Do you think that's the most likely explanation, Katrina?"

She wasn't sure. "I haven't moved them," she said.

But later he found them on the coffee table, underneath one of Katrina's books. She was certain she hadn't put them there—almost certain.

"It doesn't matter," John said, when she protested. He held out his hands wearily. "At least we've found them now. But you're getting so scatty, love."

This was true—she was often tired, often forgetful. And yet sometimes after one of these incidents the idea would come to her that he might be misplacing his things deliberately: moving them himself and then accusing her. Whenever this thought occurred to her, even if only fleetingly, she knew she must really be losing her grip.

It wasn't until years later, when she was pregnant with Beth, that Katrina saw, or perhaps allowed herself to see, the full cold sweep of her husband's nature. She had realized not long after Tommy's birth that she was afraid of him. But now she saw it all. Although he never shouted, was never physically aggressive, she began to see that his contempt was a violence in itself. Katrina felt it wind around her and constrict her breath. And his scorn wasn't reserved for Katrina alone. It stretched wide and encompassed almost every other person he knew, from his colleagues at the accountancy firm to his own brother (Malcolm, John said, was slow and unimaginative; a bore; good with his hands but not good at much else). Everything with him became a fierce struggle to prove his superiority, the loathsome deficiency of others.

Katrina tried to sneer with him at the people and things he despised. He made fun of Fiona, who he said was a pathetic busybody, and Katrina could see his point, though it pained her when Fiona had been so kind. She thought Malcolm was kind too, and she liked his gentleness, though she knew he wasn't quick and clever like John. She tried to appreciate the distinction between them. John said she wasn't sharp herself, not discerning enough about people, and it was true, certainly, that she was more easily pleased than him. It seemed a comfort at first when his scorn was directed outwards, not at her. But before long, Katrina felt its polluting effects within herself. Everywhere she looked she began to see inadequacy and weakness as he did.

And it was Katrina herself he hated most of all. He had believed once that he could be happy with her, she thought. That was at the root of it. When he finally realized he could not, he quietly began to despise her. In one sense, she could hardly blame him. She had presented a hope to him, even though she had not known it, and then she had failed him, again without knowing it, just as everyone else had. There had been a few times in his life, she perceived, that had seemed to offer a glimmer of something else: something that might help him, might make him like everyone else. All had proved to be illusions, and all had to be punished for the deceit.

Outwardly he was very different, with everyone except for her. He turned a smooth, smiling face to the world, and it troubled Katrina how charming she could see other people finding him; it made her feel again as though she was going mad, as though all the coldness in him, if not imagined by her, was at least caused by her. Of course he wanted people to like him; everybody did. But it worried Katrina that he seemed to care so little for her opinion, that she was the only one allowed to see him as he truly was. Perhaps he saw nothing wrong in the way he behaved towards her, his coldness and his criticisms. He appeared to believe she deserved it. Sometimes she agreed with him.

But she would not bring her children up with this kind of rage. Not sensible Nicky and sweet, anxious Tommy. Not darling Beth, who was already starting to show a more lively personality than her brothers, and who might, if she were allowed to continue like this, grow up to be far more sociable and cheerful than the rest of them. Although her daughter was so young, it was her sons whom Katrina feared for the most. They were both sensitive, both thoughtful and so considerate of one another that Katrina sometimes felt a lump in her throat when she watched them together. They were not made for conflict, and Katrina knew instinctively that they could never be the kind of sons John wanted. As they grew older, this would become more and more apparent, and then nothing would protect them from his disappointment. Katrina knew the chilling quality of this disappointment only too well. Somehow, she thought, she would have to save them. But she knew, hopelessly, that there was no defence against John. Not so long as you were near him.

PART 3

1

It was raining again. Fiona sat upstairs on her bed and watched the rain against the window and tried not to think of Tommy. She had this bedroom to herself, Gavin having slept in Stuart's old room for more than ten years now, since Fiona had reached a point where she couldn't cope with his snoring any longer. When Stuart came to visit, Gavin moved back in with Fiona and neither of them mentioned their customary sleeping arrangements (it would upset Stuart, Fiona felt. She was certain, anyway, that he would have something to say about it).

Fiona loved this space, with its crisp white sheets and pink quilt folded neatly across the bed, all her things arranged precisely on the dresser, no clutter, no dust, everything clean of her husband's earthy, cumbersome presence. She resented ever having to share the room with Gavin, even if it was only once a year when Stuart came home. It smelled different with Gavin in it, and took on, Fiona felt, a crumpled, soiled feel. It made her almost glad when Stuart left again, and she could throw the window open and clean the room top to bottom, change the sheets, take possession of it again. If Gavin came upstairs wanting something from her, she knew he wouldn't come straight into the room, even though it had been his bedroom too for almost thirty years, but would knock and wait politely outside the door, and instead of calling, "Come in," Fiona would meet him at the door, blocking his way. She had noticed this in herself, and in him.

Fiona put out her hand and stroked the quilt, absent-mindedly smoothing any wrinkles; she always liked making the bed in the morning, pulling the quilt taut. She took a moment to enjoy the feel of the material beneath her hand. Focus on the present moment—that was all the rage these days, wasn't it? Mindfulness. Fiona had read an article about it the other day and it had sounded appealing. There were many things in the past she would rather not think about. She assumed this was the same for most people by the time they were her age.

But it wasn't so easy to stay focused on the present when the past rose up before you so insistently, when it wandered about the island and bumped into you unexpectedly, when it came round to your house to eat. And it was unfortunate, Fiona thought, how much Tommy looked like his father. Nobody would be able to forget the connection while looking at him, not even for a second. But it was true too that there were touches of his mother in him. Fiona hadn't noticed it at first, but it was there when she pictured him now. It might be the shape of his eyes, or it might be his mouth. It might just be something in his expression. Fiona had never been very good at faces.

She had done her best by Tommy, for Katrina's sake, but he had made things awkward. He had actually come close, Fiona thought, to making a scene. She had tried to discuss it with Gavin afterwards, but Gavin had said, "It wasn't that bad, Fi. Of course he's going to be touchy about John, and you know how Ed is when he's drunk." Then, when Fiona didn't reply, he'd added, "The lamb was delicious, hen. Very tender." She managed, just about, not to reproach him with his own wretched error: calling the man John, for God's sake.

Fiona had been forced to come upstairs today because Gavin was downstairs, stomping about and verbalizing every thought that came into his head—*Just looking for a stamp—God, what a day it is, all this rain—I pity Malcolm if he's out with Robert today, he's earned his rest, poor man—Aye, the wind's getting up now, isn't it?*—and Fiona thought if she had to listen to him any longer she might actually kill him.

She had told him she was going to sort the laundry, but here she was, sitting on the bed and staring blankly out at the rain. Sometimes she felt there was little else in her life except water. The grey sea surrounding them, always seeming to creep closer, however much they tried to ignore it; the rain coming down hour after hour, the moorland sodden, the sheep's wool glistening. Fiona had grown up on Mull, was an island girl through and through, hadn't even hesitated when Gavin suggested they settle here, his home. But Litta was not like Mull. Mull was a large island: nearly three thousand people, several schools, shops, hotels and easy access to the mainland. Out here was another matter. It was cold and it was wild. It wasn't civilized like Mull; Litta was all drenched land and sea. It felt like living on the edge of the world, at the point where other people had dropped away and there were just a few ragged survivors left, huddled together on this dark hunk of rock, braced against the wind and the endless rain.

She did not know sometimes how the others could bear it, but if she ever voiced these feelings to Gavin, he would laugh and say, "Aye, it's not for everyone." It was impossible to get him to take things seriously. Nobody else on the island ever seemed to mind its terrible isolation. They took pride in it, in fact, so that Fiona could never express any contrary opinion without revealing some weakness in herself, some shameful unfitness that she had always known it was her duty to hide.

But she coped well. She knew this was true. She put on a good show, made the best of things, and she expected her husband, who had brought her here after all, to do the same, so that if Gavin ever expressed any minor complaint—the ferries were irregular, or the service had been temporarily halted due to staff shortages—Fiona would snap at him, "We're lucky to have them," when really this was not what she thought at all.

When Katrina had first come to the island, Fiona had recognized the bewilderment in her as though it had been her own. In someone else it might have made her angry, but Fiona saw how Katrina guarded her weakness just as she herself did, and perhaps it was this that had made Fiona unbend to her. They had been close for a while, when Katrina had first arrived and was still struggling. Fiona believed they had been close, at any rate. She sometimes thought she had never been happier than during that first year, when she saw Katrina almost every day. She hadn't had a close friend before, not since she was a young girl at least. Fiona had often wondered why, and had even wept over it in secret a few times, when she was much younger. She had watched other women in the past, noticing how easily they seemed to form friendships with one another. With her, there was always, it appeared, some invisible barrier that could not be surmounted, some simple trick that eluded her. People never gave her quite what she wanted, and she sometimes thought she caught them turning discreetly away from her, turning towards others instead, so that she wanted to clutch at them and say, "What is it I'm not giving you? Tell me, and I'll give it." She tried so hard, and other people were not grateful.

Katrina had been, though. Fiona had thought that whatever the trick was, she had finally mastered it. For once, it had felt easy. But it was natural, of course, that it had not lasted. Katrina had a young family and a husband to look after, and once she was coping better it was only to be expected that her focus would turn inwards again. The raising of the drawbridge had been so slow and gentle that Fiona hardly noticed until Katrina was completely walled off. Fiona's visits to Katrina grew shorter and less frequent—often Katrina wouldn't be in, or even if she was, Fiona did not feel welcome—and Katrina rarely returned them. They remained friends (Fiona thought so, at any rate), but they were no longer close, especially by the time Katrina's boys were in school. Fiona had not resented it, of course; she had understood. Katrina was not the type to have close friends, and her first priority had to be her husband and children. She was the kind of person who didn't need to look outside the home for her fulfilment. Nevertheless, Fiona could not help it if sometimes she felt she had been . . . well, *used* was the word. She felt a little used.

All the same, they had been good neighbours, Katrina and John. Pleasant people to spend an evening with. John especially had gone out of his way to be helpful and kind. Nothing was ever too much trouble for him (how thoughtful he had been when the car broke down). In truth, by the end, Fiona would have said she was fonder of John than of Katrina.

"Fi, are you all right up there?" Gavin called.

"Yes," she called back. Soon she would have to reappear with an armful of laundry or else he would come up to check on her, and she felt she could not bear that.

In a moment, she would go. For now, she continued to watch the water against the windows. The weather was pressing in too close, as it always did. Tommy looked like his father, but if there was coldness in him, as Fiona thought she had detected, then perhaps that came from his mother.

2

Malcolm was out of the house when Tom woke the next morning, perhaps his thirteenth or fourteenth day on the island; he was starting to lose track. While he ate his cereal, he read a book he'd found on Malcolm's shelf about the Vikings. It was A4, with colour illustrations, and Tom spent a long time looking at the section about Viking raids on Iona, the brutal slaying of the monks and the loss of so many treasures. He would like to go to Iona again, he thought. He'd been taken to visit the abbey as a child.

Later, he went upstairs and switched on his phone. The anxiety was giving him a stomach ache, but he couldn't put it off any longer. Couldn't always be such a coward.

Caroline answered on the third ring.

"Tom, where are you?" she said.

"Still on the island."

"With your uncle?"

"Yeah." There was a long pause as Tom realized he should have planned this conversation in advance. He said, "How have you been?"

"Not great, obviously."

"I'm sorry," he said. "I messed everything up."

"Yes."

A silence, then Caroline added, "You're not coming back, are you? Not back here. To me."

"No."

"Not sure why I asked." Her voice sounded faint. "I already knew that. You were quite clear."

"I'm sorry," he said again. "You didn't deserve this." What a pointless, empty statement.

Apparently Caroline thought so too. She burst out, "What do you think it's been like for me? A fortnight of wondering if you're O.K."

"Sorry."

"Stop saying that. It's useless to me."

There was another silence. Besides apologizing, Tom wasn't sure what else to say.

"So that's it then?" Caroline said at last. "All over."

"Yes."

"I wish I'd never met you. I wish I could go back and make it not happen." Her voice broke.

"I wish you could too," Tom said. They'd met at a party. The room had been packed. It would have been so easy to turn away from her, not towards her.

"The worst part," Caroline said, "is that I will always worry about you. Even on the days I'm furious with you, I still worry about you. I think I'll worry about you forever."

"You don't need to," Tom said. "Please don't." He intended it apologetically, but now he thought he sounded churlish.

"I'd rather not as well," Caroline said. "But there it is."

Tom could offer nothing but a statement of fact. "I should have behaved better. I treated you so badly. Like I—'

"What? Hated me?" Caroline stopped and sniffed. Then she said, "No. It's yourself you've always hated."

Tom was silent.

"I'll move on, I know," Caroline said. "Eventually."

He recognized her courage, and was moved by it. "You'll get married. To someone much better."

"Hope so." Then she said, suddenly brisk, "I'll box up your stuff. Where should I send it?"

"I . . . I'm not sure yet. I'll let you know."

"Right."

Tom hesitated, remembering the warmth of her in his arms. How funny she was, and how kind. He said, "Do you know, Caz . . ." and couldn't go on.

"What?"

Tom looked for the right words, but they weren't there.

There was a long pause, then Caroline said deliberately, "You take care, Tom."

"And you. Just . . . take care."

Then it was done. Tom turned the phone off and laid it carefully down on his bedside table. How exhausted you could feel just from staying alive, day after day, year after year. At least Caroline was free now.

He went downstairs to make a sandwich for his lunch, but found he couldn't eat. Then it came over him again, the restlessness that felt like rage. Feeling the need to be in motion, he put on his jacket and boots and went outside.

The air was fresh and the wind was cold. Tom found his steps taking him north along the road, as though he was going to look for seals with Nicky. The rough moorland stretched out on either side, sloping and uneven, broken with rocky outcrops and patched with bracken the colour of dried blood. In the distance, rugged hills loomed up, blocking the horizon like a mountain range.

Tom walked for some time without any thoughts in his head at all. It was a kind of release, for a while, to focus only on the tramp of his footsteps and the cold on his face, carrying with it the damp of sea air even when the sea was nowhere in sight. He would tire himself out, and later he would sleep. But though he walked fiercely and fast, the restlessness didn't leave him completely. The island, being so unpeopled, gave the illusion of freedom and space, made you think you could walk for hours and hours until you had exhausted yourself, and still be left with great tracts of ground to cover. But this wasn't the case. In reality, it was a small rock, bounded by the sea on every side. It was little more than a large pen and you were no less confined for being outside than if you'd been locked in a room with no windows. Tom thought you could probably go mad here, trying to walk yourself free but seeing no escape beyond the endless sea and sky. He thought of the Vikings, those ruthless warriors for whom the sea had been no barrier but rather a rousing challenge, a call to arms. It troubled him that he couldn't say now whether he'd admired them as a child for their courage or for their violence.

He'd been walking for about half an hour when he saw in the distance, before the road curved out of sight, a figure in a pink waterproof. No, he thought. He would not talk to any of these islanders today, and he would certainly not talk to Fiona McKenzie. Not caring if the distant figure had seen him or not, he turned and left the road, walking down the slope to his right where the road was slightly raised, and out on to the moorland. The terrain was so uneven, the rocky hummocks and ridges so numerous, that he was soon hidden from the sight of the road.

And now, away from the road, he felt the strange scale of the place more keenly than before. It was not that of a small island. Surrounded by jagged outcrops and the expanse of moorland, you felt yourself lost in a vast, mountainous wilderness.

It had rained heavily again overnight and the ground was boggy beneath his feet. Tom tried to step on the thicker clumps of yellow grass and avoid the bright green patches where the ground was at its marshiest, but his boots were soon soaked from straying into small pools, and it wasn't long before the water had seeped through to his socks. He decided, once he was a safe distance from the road, to aim for higher ground, and began to make his way towards one of the small hills before him. He was now heading inland, and he thought that if he curved left again shortly, he would be walking north-west across the moorland and would eventually reach the machair on the north-west coast, which he could cross to join the road again.

But he couldn't continue in the direction he wanted; he came to a stream that must have risen up during the night's rain, or at least thickened, and it barred his way. It was too wide to jump and too deep to walk through without soaking his jeans up to the calves as well as his already-wet boots. Tom turned again and followed the stream for some time, hoping for a suitable crossing point, but although he followed its winding path for twenty minutes, at no point did it become narrow enough for him to jump. Not wanting to retrace his steps, he changed direction instead, and made for one of the outcrops behind him. A small band of wild goats was eating the grass near the top of the mound, and watched Tom sullenly as he climbed it, scattering with startling grace when he neared them. The hill wasn't high enough to afford a useful view of the ground below that might guide him back to the road. None of them were, he thought. The terrain was too much of a patch-work, with one mound hiding the next from view. Tom saw only the occasional sheep; there wasn't much here for them to graze on.

Still, he liked knowing he wouldn't meet anyone else walk-ing out here, and since he was in no hurry anyway, he didn't particularly mind taking a more circuitous route back than he'd planned. He continued to scramble up and down differ-ent outcrops, and found that the concentration required in order not to slip on the damp rocks or miss his footing meant that he was free for the time being from other anxieties. Eventually, having walked for a long time without seeming to make any progress, he began to think he'd better focus on get-ting back to the road or he would not be home before dark. He wasn't exactly sure which direction to go in anymore, but he thought he probably needed to bend to the right, which he had an idea was west.

It took him longer than it should have done to accept that he was lost, because it seemed so impossible that he *could* be lost, right here on this island he'd known so well once and on what was, after all, such a small stretch of land: there were only a few miles of hills and moorland to get lost *on* and somehow he had managed it. The northern-central part of the island lacked the clear landmarks of the coastal areas. It was easy to go round in circles without realizing it, as Tom came to believe he had been doing. Even easier once the light was fading, as it was now.

He needed to rest and decide what to do next. He found a thick gorse bush halfway down one of the mounds, which afforded him some shelter from the wind—growing stronger now—while avoiding the damp of the lower ground. His feet were very cold in the wet boots. Tom huddled down in the shelter of the gorse and thought, This is a predicament.

He had no real fear. It wasn't cold enough yet that a man would freeze to death out in the open air at night, and there were no deep bogs he was likely to stray into. Still, if he really couldn't find his way home, it looked to be a very uncomfortable night. There was no hope, even, of someone coming out to look for him in a car; he was too far from the road for that to be helpful at all.

Never mind.

He rested his arms on his knees and let his mind clear for a few moments. He would gather his energy and then make a plan.

But the stillness in his mind was dangerous. It was in these moments that other things found their way in. Tom had felt it coming closer and closer over the past few days, the memory of how his survival had come at the cost of Nicky's. Now he felt his older brother, forever a child, standing beside him. He had never known why his father had spared him and not Nicky, who was his favourite after all. It was possible, Tom thought sometimes, that his father simply couldn't be bothered to search for him. Perhaps if it had been Nicky, he would have searched.

Abruptly, Tom forced himself to his feet. He would not sit still. He would continue to walk, and not change direction. Even if he was going the wrong way, he would reach some part of the road eventually; he could hardly avoid it, given that it ran in a loop.

And he did eventually reach it, having stumbled in and out of pools in the darkness, his boots soaked and his ankle painfully twisted from where he'd stepped into a dip in the ground. Then he saw lights in the distance, and from the number of them he realized he must have come to the loop of the road on the eastern side of the island, where houses clustered around the port.

This was not good news. It would take him hours to walk home from here along the road, but it would be madness to go back on to the moorland. Tom felt very tired and foolish. He began to follow the road home.

To keep his thoughts at bay, he focused again on the steady trudge of his feet, but still he felt a rising panic in his chest that grew stronger every minute. It was because he was so tired, he thought. And he had been on the island too long. Of course he should have known better than to come back here, should have known better than to think it would solve anything. All it had done was make things worse.

As the panic seemed to be reaching its pitch, he realized where it came from: his feet were taking him closer and closer to the track leading to his old house. He would have to pass it soon. Then he was upon it.

Without making a conscious decision to do so, Tom broke into a run, but even the pain in his ankle and the sound of his own broken breaths in his ears were not enough to push out the other things in his head. Only when the house was long behind him did he allow himself to stop, bent double with his hands on his knees, his harsh breaths vocalized like sobs. He would never outrun this.

Tom walked for almost two hours without knowing what he was doing. He was unsure if the shaking was due to exhaustion or cold or fear. Eventually he was so tired and his ankle hurt so much that the pieces of Nicky grew hazy around the edges and then, finally, faded away.

At some point later he heard the sweep of a car approaching in the distance, the smooth rumble growing louder before the car appeared from around the bend up ahead, drenching Tom in the white of its headlights. Squinting, Tom moved closer to the edge of the road to ensure he wasn't in its path. But instead of gliding past him, the car slowed and then pulled up a few feet ahead of him. As Tom limped towards it, the driver opened their door, and Tom saw it was Gavin McKenzie, with Fiona next to him in the car. Was there no escape from the woman?

"Tommy, it's a wee bit late for a walk," Gavin said as Tom drew level. "You going home? We'll give you a lift."

It was an agony to be caught like this. Tom tried to compose his face, to remember how to talk to others. He said, "No. I'm O.K." Then, almost too late, "Thank you."

"Nonsense," Fiona said, leaning across from the passenger seat. "We'll take you home."

"It's out of your way," Tom managed. "The wrong direction."

"It'll only take us twenty minutes to drop you off, but it's a long walk for you at this time of night," Fiona said.

"No," Tom said. He tried to give them a smile that he hoped looked casual and conclusive all at once. "It's O.K., I'm happy to walk." He made to move past the car.

"Don't be silly, Tommy," Fiona persisted. "Get in."

Tom stopped again. "I don't want a lift," he said finally. He made sure to keep his voice very polite; he felt for a moment as though his mother was watching him.

"You can't walk all that way in the dark," Fiona said.

"Leave me alone," Tom said. Being forced to have this conversation felt like having sandpaper scraped across his skin.

"We're only trying to help." Fiona sounded affronted now.

"It's not help if people don't want it."

Gavin said softly, "It's O.K., hen. He doesn't want a lift." He added, "Goodnight, Tommy."

But Fiona said, "You should recognize when people are trying to help you, Tommy. Don't be stubborn, now." There was a note of self-righteousness in her voice that enraged Tom.

"Look," he said, "will you just fuck off?"

A short, shocked pause, then Fiona began, "Now you listen—" but Tom ignored her and limped on past the car, grateful when the darkness became total again. He wasn't sure, after a time, where the night ended and he began. He just needed to sleep, he told himself. He'd lived through worse than this.

He saw Malcolm's house long before he was anywhere near it; all the lights were on. It floated brightly in the darkness.

When he finally reached it and limped through the front door, Malcolm came and met him in the hallway. Tom realized his uncle had waited up for him, and for some reason the idea made him angry.

Malcolm rubbed his hand across his face. "You're back."

"I got lost," Tom said, wondering if he was about to get in trouble. He didn't care.

"Are you O.K.?"

Tom shrugged. "Yeah." His ankle hurt. He was too tired to think.

"You're shivering," Malcolm said. "Come and have a hot

drink. There's cocoa. I'll make a hot-water bottle and get a blanket."

"No," Tom said, the word coming out more harshly than he'd intended. "I'm fine. I just want to go to bed."

Malcolm put out his hand to touch Tom's arm. His voice was quiet and insistent. "I was worried."

"No need," Tom said, stepping back, out of reach.

He looked at Malcolm, and heavy in the air between them was what Tom thought but did not say: What am I to you anyway?

He turned from Malcolm and went up the stairs.

3

Returning from Robert's farm at six to find Tommy absent had not concerned Malcolm at first. It was almost dark outside, but Tommy knew the island well, and in any case it was easy enough to navigate the road in the darkness. Malcolm made himself a cup of tea and settled down to wait.

But by the time it had got to seven thirty, he was uneasy. Tommy had never stayed out beyond dusk before, and if he'd known he'd be gone, why hadn't he left a note? He might have his phone with him, Malcolm supposed, but it didn't seem likely Tommy would call; Malcolm was quite sure Tommy didn't have his number, just as Malcolm didn't have Tommy's. He made another cup of tea and tried to read the paper.

Eventually it occurred to him that it was a ferry day; Tommy might have gone for good. Perhaps it was always going to be this way, that Tommy would disappear as suddenly as he'd arrived, without even saying goodbye. Malcolm experienced the sense of relief he might have anticipated at this realization, but it was faint. Overlaying it, and far stronger, was his dismay. He was surprised, in fact, at how hurt he felt. And it was too soon for Tommy to have left. Malcolm was afraid. He knew too little about Tommy to be confident he would be O.K., and now Tommy was gone, Malcolm had no way of contacting him. He cursed himself for not having asked for a phone number or an address while he had the chance, for letting Tommy slip through his fingers again. What would Heather have said?

The house felt very empty to him this evening, even though he'd lived alone in it for nearly six years now. He felt he couldn't bear to go upstairs and check Tommy's room, but he made himself do it in the end. And there, to his surprise, he found Tommy's rucksack, as well as his canvas trainers, placed neatly at the end of the bed. Tommy's phone was on the bedside table.

Malcolm's relief at this didn't last long. It was almost nine o' clock by then. Perhaps, he thought, Tommy was simply out on a long walk, needed to clear his head, something like that. But he couldn't push away the visions of Tommy lying hurt, or in trouble. And beneath it all was a bigger fear that he hadn't known he carried: he believed there was a chance that Tommy might be a risk to himself. He believed Tommy might be looking for a way out; he believed—but why all these euphemisms? What good were euphemisms to a man who'd seen what Malcolm had seen? He believed that Tommy might kill himself.

So what now? There were no police on the island, and besides, Tommy had only been missing for a few hours. Malcolm did not even know that Tommy *was* missing. He could ring up his neighbours, ask them to help him search, but where would they search now in all this darkness? He knew what Ross would say, and Davey: *Wait till morning. We'll find him then.* They could do nothing before dawn. At night the darkness here was total: dense and heavy, an almost solid thing.

So Malcolm sat in his small kitchen and waited. And as the time wore on, it seemed inevitable that his brother would come to him. There was no escaping John. To be related so closely to someone who had committed such a crime—it was difficult to get your head around.

Sometimes it made things easier if Malcolm pretended there had been a sudden change in his brother: that the man who murdered his wife and children was not the one Malcolm had grown up with. He tried to think of it as the other islanders did, as a bolt from the blue, a moment of madness, all those neat phrases that packaged up what had happened into a more manageable form. But Malcolm knew that not having seen it coming was not the same as being amazed by it.

He had always noticed, for instance, that the boys were unusually quiet around John. They were different, sillier and more childlike, when their father was not around, but in front of John they took on a curious frozen quality, almost as though they were holding their breath. Malcolm had said as much to Heather once, and Heather had replied that John was a strict father, but that wasn't a bad thing. And anyway, it wasn't as though he hit them. But Katrina always had her eye on John too, Malcolm thought. Even when she was talking to someone else, her gaze would slip sideways to her husband. It surely wasn't normal for a woman to be so watchful around her own husband, though Malcolm could never have put this part into words to share with Heather. John watched Katrina too, but his watching had a different quality to it. Malcolm had seen that as well. He had seen enough. The brutal paradox was that the warning only appeared after the event; it was only revealed *by* the event. The worst needed to happen before Malcolm could make sense of the signs that had been there all along. But a warning that came afterwards was no warning at all.

Malcolm hadn't even known his brother owned a shotgun. What use did an accountant have for a gun? But John had had it for years, they discovered afterwards, since not long after he moved back to the island. There was a gun cabinet bolted to the wall of John's study. Malcolm had never seen it, had never been in there until afterwards. He couldn't imagine why John had gone to the trouble of acquiring the shotgun certificate in the first place, and then the trouble of renewing it. Their father had taught them to shoot years before, out on the croft, but John had never been much good: he could no more hit a tin can than a rabbit. He needed his targets closer, Malcolm thought.

At last, not long after ten, the sound of the door came and a moment later there was Tommy in the hallway, pale and shivering. Malcolm's relief made him take refuge in practicalities. He heard himself offering Tommy a blanket, offering him cocoa, a hot water bottle. None of this was what he really wanted to say. In any case, Tommy would accept nothing from him.

Early the next morning, Malcolm called up Robert and said he couldn't come out to work on the farm that day. He wasn't well, he said, the lie feeling strange in his mouth. Then he made a cup of tea—interminable tea—and sat down once more to wait.

When Tommy finally came into the kitchen, Malcolm said, "Morning. You get some sleep?" and Tommy said, "Yeah," and went over to put the kettle on.

He didn't look like he'd got much sleep.

"Feeling O.K.?" Malcolm said.

"Yeah."

Tommy waited in silence for the kettle to boil, made his tea and brought it over to the table. He sipped it but did not speak.

Malcolm wasn't sure how to overcome this impasse. He'd never known how to bridge the gap between himself and others, and now there was no Heather to help him. He imagined her watching this scene now. *You men,* she would have scolded. *You men never talk to each other.*

No, they had not been taught how. And yet Malcolm had never really felt like a man. He had always carried a guilty feeling of subterfuge, as though he might be found out any moment. His outside was right; his father had always approved of him in this way—of his height, his strength, his hardiness and his facility with the croft. But beneath the skin, Malcolm had never been sure what was expected of him. He was sensitive, Heather had said to him once; he thought about things deeply. She had said it fondly (perhaps with the faintest hint of exasperation too), but it had stung Malcolm. He had felt almost embarrassed, as though he'd been caught out doing something illicit. Heather had been more masculine than Malcolm in many ways, in her bluntness and her pragmatism, her ability to brush things off, to *just get on with things.* (She could still speak honestly, though, when she needed to. She could still say, *This hurt my feelings,* or, *This made me happy.* She could still say, *I love you.*)

Malcolm knew he had plenty of animal courage, the kind of physical strength his father admired. He would battle on through a storm or work through the freezing night without complaint, but he was certain, after more than sixty years on this earth, that he lacked moral courage. He had often thought he recognized in his brother a manliness that he himself lacked: John had determination and purpose where Malcolm was weak and wavering. But John had been smaller and skinnier, and their father said he was soft. Malcolm had always known this wasn't true, that their father had them the wrong way round. He could never have said any of this out loud. It probably wouldn't have made a difference.

Malcolm had only half learned the lessons of his father and of the world, and where did that leave him? As a kind of piecemeal man, a Frankenstein's monster, his masculinity patched and tattered. Nonetheless, he wanted to ask now—but ask who?—whether being a man always required you to have power over somebody else. Did it have to? Were there not other ways?

Christ, Malcolm thought, looking across at Tommy. This couldn't go on forever. He tried to hold his nerve as he said,

"Tommy, you know you're welcome here. As long as you like. But what do you want to do? What's your plan?" He couldn't believe how long it had taken him to ask this.

Tommy looked up at him. "Plan?" he said. "Malcolm, I've never had one of those."

"I don't mean to sound like . . ."

Tommy shrugged. "I promise I won't stay much longer. A few more days, that's all."

"I'm not trying to get rid of you," Malcolm said. "I just wondered what . . ." He stopped.

"What was going on in my head," Tommy finished for him.

"Something like that."

"Most days," Tommy said, "I don't even know myself."

Tommy was upstairs in his room when the doorbell went that afternoon. Malcolm wasn't especially surprised to see Fiona standing there; of all the people he knew, she was the most likely to drop round unexpectedly. This didn't mean he was pleased to see her. He had enough on his plate, he felt, without having to make conversation with Fiona today.

"Fiona!" he said, aiming for heartiness and stumbling closer to hysteria. "This is a nice surprise."

She said, hovering on the doorstep with uncharacteristic hesitancy, "Is Tommy in?"

"He's upstairs. Asleep, I think. I'd probably best not wake him." He thought of the dark circles under Tommy's eyes.

"No," Fiona said. "Don't wake him." Appearing more decided now, she stepped across the threshold.

"Can I get you a cup of tea?"

"Yes, thank you." She followed him into the kitchen and for a while they made stilted conversation about the weather and Gavin's bad back, which had apparently flared up again.

Malcolm started to feel that Fiona had something particular she wanted to say. There was something strange in her manner, something a little more forced and awkward than usual. He couldn't for the life of him work out what was up.

Still she did not get to the point, even when he'd handed her a mug of tea and shepherded her through to the living room.

"Are you warm enough?" he said. There was a definite chill in the air. It was the first day of November, he realized. "Shall I light the fire?"

"No, don't trouble yourself on my account." She pulled her thick woollen cardigan more closely around her, and the slight theatricality of the gesture irritated Malcolm.

"I'll light the fire," he said. "It'll be nicer for Tommy, too, when he comes down."

This, at least, gave him something to do with his hands, and allowed him to turn his back to her for a while as he laid the logs and got the kindling in the centre going.

Finally, as Malcolm sat back on his heels surveying his handiwork, the small orange flames licking the edges of the larger logs now, Fiona said, "Actually, Malcolm, there's something I wanted to speak to you about."

It had been the fact that his back was to her, Malcolm thought. This was what had allowed her, at last, to get it out.

Cautiously, he turned. "Oh yes?"

"It's about Tommy."

And now Malcolm found himself on the defensive. His reaction surprised him. His instinct, immediately, was to close this conversation down. He could not, of course. And he had no idea what Fiona might say, so why the urgent need to shield Tommy? For all he knew, she was about to invite Tommy to work in the shop with her.

He got stiffly to his feet and went to sit in his usual chair, opposite the sofa where Fiona was sitting. "What's up, Fiona?"

She grew awkward again under his gaze. "It's rather a difficult thing to express to you. I wouldn't say anything if I didn't feel I had to. You understand that, Malcolm?"

Get it out, he thought. He refused to help her.

Faced with his silence, Fiona turned her mug anxiously in her hands. She said, "You know I'm saying this only as your friend, Malcolm. We've known each other a long time."

"Aye."

"Well . . . it's this, really. There's been some concern among some of us."

"Concern?" Malcolm said, keeping his voice neutral.

"About Tommy. About his visit here. About his . . . *behaviour*."

"What behaviour?" Malcolm said.

"No one's denying he's had a terrible time," Fiona said, her words coming more eagerly now. "No one should have to go through what he went through. And it's not surprising, really, after everything, if he's a wee bit . . ."

Malcolm felt a strong urge to speak, but forced himself not to.

"Unstable," Fiona finished at last.

"Unstable in what way?" Malcolm said coldly. "I've seen no evidence of it."

"You saw how he was the other night. At our house. You saw how angry he was, Malcolm. You can't pretend you didn't see it."

"No, I saw it," Malcolm said. "And I wasn't surprised. Of course he's angry." He was surprised at how angry he felt himself. "He'll be angry his whole life. That's something he has to live with."

"And then there was his behaviour last night," Fiona said.

This threw Malcolm off balance. "What do you mean?"

"You know he was out walking, very late?"

"I don't think there's anything particularly alarming in that, Fiona," Malcolm said, attempting to lighten his tone. "I sometimes do it myself."

"We met him, Gavin and I," Fiona said. "He was very aggressive. We only offered him a lift."

"Maybe he didn't want a lift."

"Well, yes, he made that quite clear. He *swore* at me, Malcolm!"

"O.K.," Malcolm said. "Well, O.K. I'm very sorry, Fiona. That's not on. Of course it isn't. I apologize for his bad manners. I'll speak to him. It won't happen again."

"It was more than bad manners," Fiona said. "He frightened me." When Malcolm didn't reply, she added, "There's something not right about him. I'm sorry to say this to you, Malcolm, I really am. But you know it's true. He's come back here for no other reason than to punish us."

"Fiona, come on now," Malcolm said. "That's surely a bit far-fetched."

"It isn't!" she said, her voice rising in indignation. "Gavin agrees with me."

Does he now? Malcolm thought. He doubted it.

"We're afraid of what Tommy might do," Fiona said. "And honestly, Malcolm, the most important thing is that it isn't good for him, being here. It surely isn't. We all want what's best for him. That's the main thing. And here he is, drifting about, remembering things, upsetting himself—"

"Upsetting *you*," Malcolm said.

"I can see you don't like hearing this," Fiona said. "And I do understand. Truly I do. He's your nephew, after all. But we think it would be best for everyone if Tommy's visit came to an end soon. I'm sure you want what's best for him, just like the rest of us."

"I do want what's best for him," Malcolm said. He was silent for a few moments. Then he got to his feet. "Thank you for your visit, Fiona. Tommy will stay with me for as long as he likes. He's going nowhere."

"I was speaking as your friend," Fiona said, standing up uncertainly. She put her half-drunk tea down on the side table. "I hope you know that I only want to help."

"Tommy will stay here as long as he likes," Malcolm repeated. "This is his home."

"Well, I've said my piece," Fiona said, going past him into the hall. "I spoke out of concern for you, and for Tommy. I hope you'll remember that, Malcolm."

"Aye." He opened the front door for her. "Take care, Fiona."

She looked at him for a moment more, then gave a small shake of her head and stepped outside. Malcolm closed the door behind her. He waited a minute or so until he heard the sound of her car engine starting up, then went through to the kitchen, frowning to himself.

He found Tommy sitting at the table, his hands clasped in front of him. It gave Malcolm quite a start.

"How long have you been down here?" he said.

"A while," Tommy said, looking at his hands where they lay on the tabletop.

"How much did you hear?"

"All of it, I think. All the parts that concerned me, anyway."

Malcolm sighed and took a seat opposite him. "I wish you hadn't."

"Are you going to tell me she means well?"

"No."

"I'll go," Tommy said. "Tomorrow's Saturday, isn't it? The ferry will be here again. I'll be gone first thing. I was going to go anyway."

"No you weren't," Malcolm said. "And I don't want you to."

"Yeah, you said that," Tommy said. "I heard. But you don't mean it."

"I do. You'll always have a home here."

He was astonished when Tommy put his head in his hands and started to cry.

4

Fiona managed to hold back the tears until she'd got the car going, and even then she only let a few escape her eyes and trickle down her cheeks. She'd always had a lot of self-control and she didn't allow any noise to escape her, didn't allow her face to crumple up pathetically, until she turned the bend in the road and Malcolm's cottage was out of sight. She was embarrassed at herself, at the high-pitched sounds coming from her mouth, but at least there was nobody to witness it.

She was crying because she was so angry, she thought. Malcolm had no right. Anyone could see Tommy's presence was doing no good here, just causing everyone—most of all himself—a lot of upset. All Fiona wanted was to help. But people never wanted her help. They threw it back in her face.

And what had Katrina been asking for except to be helped, except to be saved from herself? Why else would she have confided in Fiona of all people, not in Heather, to whom she was so much closer by then?

Fiona sped up, taking the narrow road much faster than usual, anxious to put space between herself and Malcolm's cottage. But in driving home, she was also driving back to the track she'd once shared with Katrina and John, the house in which they had died. They had tainted everything. "Blood all over the walls," Greg Brown had said, shaking in Fiona's living room that day. Fiona hadn't really believed it, not then. Thought there must have been some terrible mistake.

But even now, could you really say, *really say with certainty*, that Fiona had been wrong? What do any of us do in the end except what we believe is right at the time, without having all of the information, without knowing how things will turn out? We leap into the darkness with our only protection our idea of what is right, and who can ask more of us than that? We do our best, Fiona thought. I have always done my best.

And Katrina had put her in an impossible position.

Fiona took the bend sharply, turning west along the northern loop of the road. No one coming the other way, fortunately; she wasn't sure she could have stopped in time.

There had been that strange moment of ecstasy when Katrina had first begun to speak, the sense of their old intimacy restored, and Fiona had leaned forward and said, "You know, you can tell me anything." It was only when she thought about it properly afterwards that Fiona had begun to feel the first stirrings of dismay. Wasn't it odd for Katrina to have cut her off for years and then to suddenly waltz into her house and sit there sipping tea and dropping bombshells? Fiona had thought Katrina would come by again, but she did not. If she had, if she had come by just one more time to confide in Fiona, then perhaps things might have been different.

I am being used, Fiona had thought—just as she always had been. Picked up and put down and picked up and put down again. It was not fair. Katrina had always done what was best for herself, never with any concern for others, and now here she was again, her selfishness directed towards her own husband this time, and her own children whom she planned on taking so far away. "He can't know," Katrina had said. She had said, "I'm afraid of him."

A man like John!

"I need your help," Katrina had said. "Just to get on to the ferry."

Fiona, unutterably shocked, had said, "O.K."

Reaching the track to her house, she turned the car abruptly. Then she was speeding past that awful place—how could the Dougdales manage to live there?—and towards the safety of her own driveway. She pulled up, but remained where she was, unwilling to unbuckle her seatbelt and go inside until she was sure she was composed.

She had thought about Katrina's request endlessly, painfully, for a week afterwards. But Katrina acted as if nothing had happened between them, speaking so casually, so distantly, to Fiona in the shop a few days later. She did not come by again. And, "Forget about what I said before," she had told Fiona quickly, when they were alone for a moment outside church the following week. Fiona hadn't even had a chance to reply before Heather came up and Katrina turned away to greet her, leaving Fiona standing by herself.

She did not like to feel she had been used.

In the gathering darkness, Fiona took a packet of tissues from her bag to wipe her face. It was lucky she wore no make-up—there was no mascara to run. You'd have to look closely at her to know she'd been crying, and Gavin never looked closely. Finally, she undid her seatbelt and reached out to open the door.

Gavin glanced up only briefly from his crossword book when she came into the living room. As Fiona had expected, he did not notice her red eyes. She had thought herself completely calm now, but when Gavin asked, "Nice afternoon?" she found, to her consternation, that the tears started up again.

"It was fine," she said.

And of course even Gavin could hardly miss the quake in her voice. He looked up properly and said, "Are you all right, hen?"

Fiona burst into tears. She could only stand there and cry like a distraught child and when the words came, they were in a jumble.

"He shouldn't have come back here," she said. "It isn't fair on any of us. Haven't we been through enough, having that horrible thing happen right here, right on our doorstep?"

She was surprised when Gavin got up and put his arms around her clumsily. "There now, Fi," he said, patting her back. "It's all right." But after a pause, he ruined it by adding, "You must remember that however hard it is for us, it's much harder for Tommy."

"So why is he *here* then?" she almost screamed, her voice muffled against his chest. "He's doing nobody any good, just making us all remember." She was aware of the tears all over her face, smearing Gavin's shirt, and wondered if she was having some kind of breakdown.

"Calm down, hen," Gavin said.

"But it isn't fair to blame us!" she said. "You remember what he was like when he came round. And last night! He blames us, but it isn't fair. Nobody could have known what John was going to do. He seemed so *normal*. And three weeks—it was three weeks after!"

She felt Gavin's breath catch, and then he pulled slowly away from her and held her at arms' length, looking into her face. "What do you mean, three weeks?" He was silent for a few moments, then spoke again. "Fiona," he said, and she would wonder later what unerring instinct made him say it. "What did you do?"

"Nothing!" she said. "I did nothing. Why would you ask me that?"

He looked at her steadily. "I don't know."

"What would *I* have done?" she said. "I did nothing."

He shook his head and stepped away from her. "You're not yourself."

"How could I be, with all this upset going on? The sooner Tommy Baird leaves us in peace, the better."

She watched as her husband sighed and turned from her,

picked up his crossword book and sat back down in the armchair. He said, "Go and have a rest, Fi. I think you're overtired."

The nerve of the man. But she knew she would get nothing more from him now.

Anyway, she thought, going into the kitchen to put the kettle on, it had been nothing. A cup of tea would see her right. There had been a gap of three weeks—that said it all, really. What kind of man would wait *three weeks*? And after all, she thought, pouring the boiling water into the mug, he had been so calm, had thanked her politely and told her she'd done the right thing. If the rest of it had been because of Fiona, it would have happened immediately, not three weeks later. She had done what she believed was right, she reminded herself. She had tried to act in everyone's best interests. Children needed stability. And John had deserved to know what Katrina was planning. A man had a right to his wife. A man had a right to his children.

Fiona caught her reflection in the silver kettle. Her face was puffy and red, and she turned quickly away. It wasn't as though there was anyone around to notice, but all the same, she didn't like seeing herself so ugly.

5

D ifficult to say which of them was more embarrassed by Tommy's crying. Malcolm had sat rigidly where he was for a few moments while Tommy wept, before getting awkwardly to his feet and going to stand beside him.

"There now," he said, tentatively touching his shoulder. "It's all right." Emboldened when Tommy didn't shake him off, he left his hand where it was and said again, "It's all right."

Tommy soon wiped his face and tried to get his breath under control. "Sorry," he said.

"Don't be."

"My dad was always furious if me or Nicky cried," Tommy said after a while.

"Mine was the same." The old bastard, he thought. He went back to his seat and waited to see if Tommy would say anything else.

Tommy rubbed his eyes and breathed out slowly. He said, "It's been a rough few days."

"I know."

Tommy wiped his hand over his face again. He said, "I've been meaning to say I'm sorry." He didn't look at Malcolm. "I shouldn't have kept away all those years."

"It doesn't matter now."

"It does. It wasn't fair on you and Heather."

"Fairness doesn't come into it."

Tommy shook his head. Eventually, he said, "I'm not sure what to do."

Malcolm knew the feeling. "Don't do anything," he said. "Just get some rest. Shall we cook something later? We could make a pie." *We could make a pie?* What was wrong with him?

But Tommy didn't seem to think it was a stupid suggestion. He nodded slowly. "O.K."

The next day, they walked together towards Craigmore. Malcolm's idea was to keep Tommy moving, keep his distress at bay, tire him out so he might at least get some proper sleep. Tommy had come downstairs that morning looking as if he hadn't so much as closed his eyes all night. Malcolm was worried he would make himself ill.

"Come on," he said after they'd finished breakfast. "Let's get some fresh air. We'll go north and look for seals."

Tommy didn't argue. Like a child, he went obediently to put on his boots and waterproof.

Malcolm had thought that once he was outside whatever was weighing so heavily on Tommy might ease a little, but still Tommy seemed preoccupied and miserable as they tramped along the northern loop of the road. Tommy kept his hands in his pockets and his head down, looking only at the pot-holed tarmac in front of him and scarcely replying to Malcolm's comments on the landscape. Malcolm didn't know how to help him.

It was not until an hour later when they were finally up on the cliffs and passing the ruined chapel that Tommy said, "There's something I want to tell you."

Malcolm made to pause, but Tommy didn't slow his pace, and didn't look round. Malcolm realized then that Tommy needed this walk, needed the weather and the wide expanse of sea before them, needed to be side by side and not facing Malcolm, in order to get these words out, whatever they were. So he merely said, "Oh?" and didn't look at Tommy.

"It's something about the night it happened," Tommy said.

His words had a slightly flat, mechanical sound to them, as though he was forcing them out one by one, at some cost to himself.

"Right," Malcolm said. "O.K."

When Tommy sped up to walk a few paces ahead, Malcolm didn't try to catch him up, just increased his own pace enough that Tommy wouldn't have to raise his voice to be heard above the wind on the cliffs.

"I've never told anyone," Tommy said. "Not told anyone my whole life."

Christ, Malcolm thought. But all he wanted now was to lessen Tommy's burden, so if he could take part of it himself he would gladly do it. Hand it over, he thought.

But Tommy walked on for some time without speaking, and Malcolm started to fear he wouldn't be able to bring himself to say it after all. He wondered if Tommy had been mulling this confession over, whatever it was, all night.

"What is it, Tommy?" he said at last.

Tommy said quickly, as though he'd been waiting to be prompted, "It's about Nicky." He was walking faster and faster, and Malcolm had to increase his own pace again to keep up.

"O.K."

"It was my fault he died," Tommy said in a rush.

"No it wasn't," Malcolm said reflexively.

"No, Malcolm, *listen*," Tommy said, and now he did pause and turn to look at Malcolm. Malcolm stopped beside him, out of breath. Tommy said, "I know it was my dad, I know he did it and I know I couldn't have stopped him. I know I was just a child. I *know* all that, even if I don't always believe it. But there's something else."

"All right," Malcolm said. "Tell me."

Tommy finally met his eye. "I don't know how."

"Just try to say the words."

"It's something terrible." He played with the sleeve of his jacket.

"I've heard terrible things before," Malcolm said. "I think I'm unshockable now."

"You'll hate me," Tommy said, looking up again. There was something pleading in his expression.

"I doubt it," Malcolm said. "Just tell me, Tommy."

"All right," Tommy said. "All right." He took a long, shuddering breath and began. "You know the night it happened, how I survived."

As if by mutual agreement, they began to walk again, side by side. Malcolm knew better than to interrupt Tommy now he'd started.

"I hid in the wardrobe in my parents' bedroom," Tommy said. "While my father was killing everyone. And he came into the room, but he didn't look in the wardrobe."

Malcolm was aware of this already, but he sensed that Tommy needed to say the words, to say it all. Malcolm waited.

"I hid," Tommy said, "and stayed there the whole time, all through the night and the next day until the police came in and got me."

When he didn't immediately speak again, Malcolm said gently, "That's right."

"There's something else," Tommy said. "Another part I never told."

Once more he tailed off, and didn't speak for so long that at last Malcolm had to prompt him again. "What is it, Tommy?"

"It's the worst thing I ever did. I still don't understand how I could have done it. Except that I was so frightened. That's not an excuse."

Again Malcolm waited.

And at last, Tommy brought it out. "Nicky came in," he said. "Nicky came into the room. But I suppose you know that part too. The part you don't know is that there was a pause before my father came in. He didn't chase Nicky in there and kill him. Nicky came in alone. And he was looking around for somewhere to hide. And he was obviously in a panic and couldn't think of anywhere. He wasn't thinking straight. He must have seen my mother and Beth killed. And I was hiding in the wardrobe and I could see him through the slats and I didn't say anything." Now he'd started, the words were coming fast, almost running together. "I watched him looking for a place to hide and I kept quiet because I was so afraid, and then a moment later my father came in and shot Nicky dead. I watched him die. And if I'd said something, Nicky could have hidden with me in the wardrobe, and either we'd both have lived or we'd have died together."

At some point during Tommy's speech they had stopped walking, and now they stood motionless on the cliffs, looking out to sea. Malcolm opened his mouth to speak, but Tommy interrupted him. "I know what you'll say. I know it all already. You'll say that he would have found us both, that he wouldn't have let us both live, he would have searched and found us. You'll say Nicky would have died anyway, and the only difference would have been that I'd have died too. But I'd rather that. I always thought I was glad I survived, but now I'm certain it would have been better to have died with Nicky than to have survived all alone, knowing that I let him die, that I let him die to save my own life."

Tommy came at last to a shaky stop. He rubbed his hands across his face and turned to look at Malcolm, as if readying himself for his uncle's fury.

Malcolm waited a moment to make sure there was nothing else Tommy wanted to add, then he said softly, "It's understandable, the way you acted, if that is what you did. You were a terrified child." Pity swelled up so strongly in his chest and his throat that he found it difficult to speak. He put out his hand and took hold of Tommy's arm. "It's understandable," he repeated. "But Tommy, I don't think that can be right. Not exactly the way you remember it. Nicky didn't die in the bedroom. He died on the landing. You couldn't have seen it happen."

He watched as his nephew frowned.

"No, Malcolm," Tommy said. "I know what I saw."

"I think you must be mistaken." Malcolm forced himself to speak calmly and clearly. "Your mum and Beth died in the kitchen. Nicky died on the landing, at the top of the stairs. Your dad's body was there too, next to Nicky's."

"You're wrong. I *saw* it."

Malcolm shook his head. "It's all there in the fiscal's report. It's in the letter I had off him, too. It summarizes everything the police found."

"Well, even if it's true that Nicky was *found* on the landing, all that means is that my dad must have carried him there afterwards."

"Do you remember that part?" Malcolm said.

He watched as uncertainty creased his nephew's face. "No. But . . . I was in shock. Things are hazy."

"I think your mind's been playing tricks on you," Malcolm said. "The police, the forensics team—they can tell where someone was killed. There are things like—" he made himself say it—"blood spatter. Blood patterning. There was hardly any blood in the bedroom. Hardly any at all. Just . . . footprints. From where your father had walked."

Tommy was shaking his head, over and over. "So . . . I couldn't have seen him die."

"No."

"But then . . . the rest of it? The rest of it, Malcolm. He must have come into the bedroom and then run out again."

"I don't know. Maybe. But it was at the other end of the landing, your parents' room. Wasn't it? Not right at the top of the stairs. Would he have run along the corridor and then back again?"

"He must have," Tommy said. "I remember seeing him looking around the room. I remember watching him through the slats. He *must* have come into the room."

"Maybe he did," Malcolm said. "He might have done."

"I *must* have seen him," Tommy said. He balled his hands into fists and pressed them to his forehead. "But everything is just so . . . I don't know what's real and what isn't."

Malcolm was silent, unsure what comfort he could give.

Tommy turned suddenly on his heel and began to walk back in the direction they'd come. Malcolm struggled to catch up with him. Out of breath, he drew level with Tommy at last.

"It *feels* true." Tommy spoke without looking round. Malcolm could see there were tears in his eyes. "Whatever happened, it feels true that I betrayed him."

"I know." Malcolm understood this better than he wished: that the truth was what we felt, not what we knew. He forced himself to look it in the face, the mistake he and Heather had made. They had tried to distract Tommy in the aftermath, tried to take his mind off it, to help him move on. How ill equipped they had been to deal with a traumatized child. They had got everything wrong. If they had only talked about it properly, if they had only made space for Tommy to say the words, he wouldn't have been forced to carry this guilt alone for twenty-three years. Malcolm would never forgive himself.

"But whether Nicky came into the room or not, you didn't betray him," he said to Tommy. "Whatever happened, you were just a child. Eight years old. Think of that."

Tommy shook his head. He came to a stop again and furiously wiped the tears from his face. "He died while I hid. They all died while I hid. That part will always be true."

"You didn't do anything wrong," Malcolm said. "You didn't do anything *wrong*, Tommy. You only survived."

Tommy didn't answer. At last they turned together and made for home.

Back at the cottage, Tommy went straight up to his room. Malcolm heard the door close and decided to leave him be. There was no further reassurance he could give that Tommy would accept. Malcolm couldn't tell him exactly what had happened that appalling night. But whatever the truth was, nobody on earth would blame Tommy—nobody except Tommy himself.

Malcolm was sitting at the kitchen table reading the paper when Tommy reappeared a few hours later. He heard him on the stairs and just had time to ready himself before Tommy came into the room.

"Hi," Tommy said briefly, then went straight to the kettle and busied himself making tea. "Would you like some?" he said.

"Yes please."

"Wind's up again."

"Aye."

Malcolm wondered if they were really going to revert to small talk, then he thought, No. Not now. He wouldn't allow it. He said, "How are you feeling?"

"O.K.," Tommy said. He glanced over his shoulder at Malcolm, then added, "Well. Not great."

"No."

Tommy returned to his task, fetching the box of tea bags and two mugs from the cupboard.

Malcolm looked for the right thing to say. There didn't seem to be a right thing. "I'm glad you told me," he said.

Tommy paused on his way to the fridge. "Yeah. Me too. But . . . "

"But what?"

"I wish I knew what *happened*. How can I bear not knowing?

I've been going over and over it in my head, and I just can't get the facts straight. I don't trust myself."

"What happened was that your father killed the others, and you lived. It doesn't matter how."

"It does."

"But no way of surviving would feel all right to you, Tommy," Malcolm said gently. "Isn't that where the problem is?"

Tommy didn't reply. He finished making the tea and brought their mugs over to the table. Neither of them spoke for a while. Malcolm sipped his tea and looked across at Tommy, who was staring out of the window at the darkening sky.

"I wish we could have told you when you were eight that it wasn't your fault," he said.

Tommy shrugged. "I wouldn't have listened."

"We should have moved. After it happened. Heather suggested it, and I said no. But I was wrong. We should have taken you away from here."

"It would have come with us," Tommy said.

Malcolm again searched for the words he needed to help Tommy and couldn't find them. No apology for the past would be sufficient now. At last he said, "I do know what guilt feels like, Tommy."

"You've no reason to feel guilty."

"I should have protected you," Malcolm said. "He was my brother."

"You didn't know."

"Because I never tried to." He stopped, trying to arrange his thoughts. "There was something . . . *off* there. I should have seen it. It was there to see."

Tommy shook his head. "You need to let that go."

"Maybe. But it's hard, isn't it?"

Tommy rubbed his eyes wearily. "Yeah." After a pause, he said, "Did you read all of the fiscal's report?"

"He took me through it, over in Oban," Malcolm said. "And I still have the letter that summarizes it all. If you'd like to see it."

"No. I don't think so." Tommy waited a moment. "What does it say?"

"Just the facts of it. How they were killed and where. The results of the post-mortems. What the police concluded, and so on. That your father killed your mum and Beth and Nicky, and then himself. It doesn't say why, though it does talk a bit about the money problems."

"That's not a reason," Tommy said.

"I know."

Tommy pushed his cooling tea away from him. "There is no reason really. Except for him. *He* was the reason."

"Yes."

"I keep thinking of how calm he was, that whole evening. Before it happened. We had chicken for tea." Tommy stopped. "But who knows if even that memory's real? Only I'm sure I remember him being calm. There was no warning, or none that seemed obvious at the time. I think he must have planned it all out very carefully. Way in advance."

Malcolm nodded. That was the kind of man John was.

Neither of them spoke for a while.

"I hid," Tommy repeated at last. "I hid while they were killed."

"Aye," Malcolm said. "And thank God you did."

6

When John came into the kitchen with the shotgun, Katrina was surprised at her own reaction: she was not shocked. Perhaps for some time she had known, without knowing, that it would come to this. Of course he would kill her.

"You bitch," he was saying, and his voice was very quiet to be saying such savage words. But Katrina was grateful he wasn't shouting. Beth was in her arms, Nicky was watching television in the living room and Tommy was upstairs. She didn't want them to be frightened.

"You fucking bitch," her husband said. "You think you can just leave? You whore. Take my kids away? You bitch."

Oh, Katrina thought, feeling oddly calm. I should have been more careful. She wondered how long he had known. Days, perhaps, or even weeks. He'd given nothing away, not even at tea half an hour before. That was so like him.

She said, "Let me go and give Beth to Nicky."

"Stay where you are, you fucking whore."

All right then. Katrina placed Beth down very gently on the floor. "There you go, my love," she said. "Sit there for now."

She had thought Beth would protest, but she did not. She did not even use the cupboard doors to pull herself to her feet, but sat where she was, eyes wide, only reaching out gently to touch her mother's leg.

John did not look crazed as she might have imagined he would. He looked like himself. His hands, holding the gun up in front of him, were steady. Katrina knew that her own strange composure was the product of extreme terror. As soon as she had seen the gun, she had moved beyond ordinary fear into a half-world she had never experienced before; it was like an out-of-body experience.

She said, "John, please will you put the gun down? Whatever I've done, I'm sorry. I'd never leave you. You're my husband."

"Liar! You won't leave because I won't give you the chance, you fucking bitch."

It was no good. Katrina knew that. She saw the whole course of their relationship in an instant, how she had been deceived about him, but how she was to blame too; she had wanted something from him, and had seen only what fitted her idea of him, an idea she had plucked out of thin air. She had wanted strength and so she had seen it in him, where in fact there was only terrible weakness. The man she had married had been a figment of her desperate imagination. But most of all it had been John's doing. He had lured her in carefully, and she believed there had been real calculation in this. He had seen her, and he had seen what he could make her; he had seen so much further than Katrina herself. But if she had been deceived, it was only because she had wanted to be deceived.

He would kill her and still believe he was a decent man. He would kill her because he believed he had a right to.

If I could go back, she thought. If I could live my life again.

But there was no going back, and in any case there were her children. My darlings, she thought. She would not unwind time and make them vanish even if she could. Or perhaps she would. She did not want to die. She loved how the light moved over the heather in the late afternoons. The sea was shockingly cold even in summer, but so refreshing it made your blood sing. There was a novel by her bed she hadn't finished. She wanted to see Glasgow again.

She did not want to leave all of this.

John was still pointing the shotgun at her and now he had raised his voice to a shout. Katrina wasn't sure she'd heard him shout before. She thought that perhaps, at this last moment, his courage had failed him and so now he needed to work himself up to it. She didn't bother to listen to what he was saying. It didn't matter now. What mattered was the glimmer of what else she thought he might do.

She would not plead for them, because she knew him too well for that. So she said, composed in the face of his yelling, "I'm bad, John. I know that. But the children aren't. They're your children. They take after you."

He would not hurt the children, she thought. She was almost certain.

She said for good measure, "They look like you. Especially Tommy." She had always known Tommy was his least loved child. "But the others too. Everybody says so."

She hoped Malcolm and Heather would take them when it was all over. If not, there was Jill. She trusted Jill not to let them near her mother. Whatever happened, at least they'd have each other.

She looked down at Beth, at the soft wisps of hair on her head. It was golden now, but Katrina wondered if it would darken as Beth got older, if it would be unruly like Nicky's or lie flat like Tommy's. She thought, I would so much have liked to live.

Tom woke feeling shattered. He'd slept more deeply than he had in years, but it didn't feel like there was enough sleep in the world to take the edge off this kind of exhaustion.

When he finally stumbled downstairs, he found Malcolm in the kitchen, cleaning the surfaces.

"Did you sleep O.K.?" Malcolm said.

"Yeah. But I still feel tired." He poured cereal clumsily into a bowl, spilling some in the process.

"I'm not surprised."

Malcolm took his rubber gloves off and returned the cleaning things to the cupboard. "I've got some shopping to do today," he said. "And Kathy called to say a shelf has come down, so I'll fix that for her while I'm there."

"Need any help?"

"No, it's fine."

Tom nodded and took his bowl to the table. He'd already swallowed a couple of mouthfuls before Malcolm added, "But company would be nice."

They set off half an hour later. Tom stared out of the car window at the scenery and asked himself what he was feeling, but came up with nothing; he was numb, as though he'd used up all the energy he'd ever have making his confession to Malcolm. He found he didn't mind the feeling. It was not peace, but the effect was similar.

When they reached the east side of the island, it began to drizzle.

"You remember how Nicky liked the rain?" Malcolm said unexpectedly.

Tom was relieved to find he did remember. "He'd try to get me to run outside with him as soon as it started raining. Strange kid."

"You preferred the sun."

"Of course. I was normal."

"Nicky would come back in sopping wet, and your mother would despair."

Tom looked out of the window again, at the grey sea stretching alongside them through a haze of rain. Beth had liked water too. She'd loved paddling in the sea while he or Nicky held her up. Tom felt sensation returning to him; his chest was hurting now, a slow, dull ache.

He said, "I've never understood why he let me live. Why he didn't search for me. Nicky was his favourite and Beth was only a baby. Why let me live and not them?"

"I don't know," Malcolm said. "But I doubt it was mercy."

"It's never felt like it." Out of the window, he watched the landscape change as they approached Orsaig, the hills subsiding and houses starting to appear. He said, "I don't know how to live with it."

Beside him, Malcolm was silent for a time. Eventually, as the harbour came into view, he said, "Me neither. Never did work it out."

In the shop, Kathy greeted them cheerfully and then popped next door to the post office, leaving Tom to man the till—which he did not know how to use—while Malcolm set about fixing the shelf. Tom leaned on the counter and watched his uncle bend the warped bracket back into shape.

"I think I should go soon," he said finally. "Back to the mainland."

Malcolm paused fractionally in his work. "There's no rush."

"I know. But I can't stay here forever."

"I don't see why not."

Tom smiled. "I wouldn't make much of a farmer, Malcolm. And anyway, I need to sort myself out. Can't keep putting it off."

Malcolm nodded. Carefully, he refitted the bracket into the frame. "What's your plan?"

"I think I'll try Glasgow," Tom said. "It shouldn't be too hard to find a job there. I'm not fussy."

"Aye. O.K. But like I said, there's no rush, is there? Mull it over for a couple of days."

"Yeah." But he knew he had to go. He said, "Shall we have pasta tonight? I could do the mushroom thing again."

"Good idea." Malcolm picked up the shelf. "Could you get the other end now?"

Tom came forward and together they lifted the shelf up to lay it back across the restored brackets.

"Tommy, you're holding your end up too high," Malcolm said after a minute of ineffective manoeuvring. "It won't go on like that."

"You're holding *your* end too low," Tom said, eliciting a huff of amusement from his uncle.

"Bring it down a bit, will you?" Malcolm said. "No, not that much." Then, finally, with mild exasperation: "Just stand back and let me do it. You're more of a hindrance than a help."

Tom obediently let go and stepped back, and, a moment later, Malcolm had fitted the shelf in place.

Returning at this point, Kathy inspected the shelf and beamed at them. "Good as new. You men have your uses after all. Thanks so much, both of you."

"Aye," Malcolm said dryly. "Tommy was a great help."

As Malcolm chatted to Kathy and began to fill a basket with shopping, Tom glanced out of the window and saw a car pulling up by the post office. Watching Fiona McKenzie climb out, he hesitated, then said to Malcolm, "Just nipping outside for a moment. Back soon."

He caught up with Fiona at the bottom of the post office steps.

"Fiona," he said, raising his voice to catch her attention, and inadvertently making her jump. "Sorry. I just . . . wanted to say hi."

"Hello," Fiona said, somewhat coldly, meeting his eye briefly then glancing back to the post office door.

Seeing she was about to walk on, Tom said quickly, "Look, I wanted to say that I'm sorry about the other night. Sorry I was so rude. It was uncalled for."

He thought Fiona wasn't going to reply, but after a moment she nodded and said, "We all have off days."

Tom tried to smile at her. "I seem to have a lot of them."

Fiona faltered. She half turned back to the steps, but then stopped and looked at him again. "You must understand that it's nothing personal," she said.

"No."

"It's just difficult for people to see you back here."

Tom controlled himself, managed to nod and say in a measured voice, "It can't be easy having it all stirred up again. What my father did—I know it affected everyone."

"We all have our burdens to carry," Fiona said. She frowned, then added, "It's true that we were deceived in him."

"Yes."

"And it's true," she said stiffly, "that there were things that could have been done differently."

"Yes," Tom said again. He weighed his words carefully. "But it's also true that nobody's responsible except for him."

As soon as he'd spoken, he wished he could take his words back, because Fiona now seemed on the edge of tears. "Aye," she said. "That's right." But Tom thought there was something strange in her expression.

To comfort her, he said, "I know you were a friend of my mother's. I've been wanting to thank you for that. I'm sure she appreciated it."

Then he wondered why Fiona looked so stricken as she nodded quickly and hurried away.

Not feeling ready to go back into the shop, Tom wandered down towards the harbour, enjoying the feeling of the drizzle on his face. Through the mist, he could just make out Jura in the distance. He remembered standing here with Nicky when they were children, competing to see who could throw pebbles the furthest. Nicky usually won, but he was always magnanimous if Tom ever did, saying, "Well *done*, Tommy. Good throw!"

What a kind man he would have grown into, Tom thought.

Carefully, he tried to summon up his mother's face, calling the old photograph to mind; it was almost all he had of her now. Part of his father's legacy had been to draw all the attention towards himself, to put himself at the centre of everything. A few years back, Tom had finally looked up the news coverage. He never got beyond the first few paragraphs. Always, the focus had been on his father, on his supposed devotion to his family, his commitment to his community, speculation over his motives and what could have made him "snap". Tom's mother had been wiped out, painted over with the different faces that belong to murdered women: the helpless victim, the martyred saint, the wayward wife who somehow deserved it.

But Tom wanted his mother back. He was tired of his father's company.

Though he was ready to leave the island, he knew that he could keep moving on forever and still never feel safe, never stop fearing men and distrusting himself around women. The old dread was returning, as it always did. There was no getting away from what had happened—not ever. He'd lived most of his life inside a wardrobe and he felt so tired and cramped; he longed for light and space. But again and again he came up against his father's brutality. What kind of man could you be when that was your inheritance? You could not change if you had learned no alternatives.

Then he turned and saw his uncle coming out of the shop. Malcolm was a little stooped and shabby in his old waterproof, Heather's canvas shopping bag slung over his shoulder; everything about him was familiar to Tom now. Malcolm smiled when he saw Tom, and Tom raised his hand in greeting, surprised at his rush of relief as he went to join his uncle.

Three days later, Malcolm stood with Tommy on the harbour watching the ferry approach. A couple of cars were waiting in the queue to board, but no other foot passengers that he could see besides Tommy.

It was a larger ferry than usual; they'd told them that as Tommy bought his ticket. The normal ferry was out of service. And now it approached, it did seem absurdly large to carry just a handful of people across the sea.

"Do you need money?" Malcolm said, annoyed with himself for not having thought of it before. "Until you get settled? I can help."

Tommy shook his head. "I have savings. I'll be fine. And I have a friend there, from university. I can stay with him a week or two while I look for my own place." Seeing Malcolm's surprised expression, he smiled. "I do have friends, you know."

"Of course you do," Malcolm said hurriedly.

They watched as the ferry docked, unwieldy and mechanical, as incongruous on Litta as a tower block.

Malcolm said, "You'll come back, if it doesn't work out?"

"Yes, I'll come back."

"O.K.," Malcolm said. "Good."

Tommy added, not looking at him, looking out to sea, "I thought I might come back for a visit anyway. In summer, maybe."

"Aye," Malcolm said, managing to match Tommy's casual tone. "I'll have your room ready."

The bow doors had opened now and a few vehicles were emerging, islanders returning from Oban with their cars full of shopping, followed by the Royal Mail van. Ross was the only foot passenger to come down the steps from the deck. He paused as he reached them.

"You off now, Tommy?"

"Yes."

"But you'll be back to see us soon."

"Aye," Tommy said. "Summer, probably."

"Good lad," Ross said, clapping Tommy's shoulder, and Malcolm forgave him in that moment for all the irritations he'd ever caused him. Ross smiled, windswept and open faced in his waterproof. "It's been great seeing you," he said to Tommy. "And Malcolm, will we see you in the bar tonight?"

"I'll come for one."

"Great," Ross said, moving off. "Well, I'll be seeing you later then."

There was a short silence after he'd gone, then Malcolm said, "Well, I suppose you'd better embark."

"Wouldn't want to miss it." Tommy hoisted his rucksack on to his shoulder and put his hands in his pockets. He seemed awkward now. "Thanks for everything," he said.

Malcolm nodded. "You take care." He felt this wasn't really enough, that there was more he needed to offer Tommy. But it had always been so difficult to say what he meant.

"You too," Tommy said. They looked at each other for a few moments, then Tommy said, "Well—bye." And he made to move off.

"Tommy," Malcolm said, reaching out to touch his arm. "It's . . ." He stopped, hesitated. "You probably know this already. But you're nothing like your father."

He watched his nephew pause at these words. Then Tommy nodded, and smiled briefly. "Thanks. I don't want to be."

Malcolm remained where he was as Tommy boarded,

waiting for him to appear on deck so he could wave goodbye. He remembered seeing Tommy and Heather off on the ferry twenty years earlier, waving to his nephew as he left the island for the last time. Jill was meeting them in Glasgow to collect Tommy, and then Heather was to return to Litta alone. Tommy, small and pale and stern beside Heather on deck, had not waved back at Malcolm. And who could blame him?

Malcolm wished more painfully than ever that Heather was alive to meet Tommy again. It would have made her so happy. But you couldn't live your whole life only looking to the dead. Life was a hard struggle, a long dark night, and we had best be thankful for those left to us to love.

When Tom boarded, the ferry seemed even more ridiculously oversized than before. It was almost empty. As he waited for the engine to start up, he got his bearings by walking from empty lounge to empty lounge, each almost indistinguishable from the one before, all of them carpeted in tartan and faintly suggestive of a conference centre: a series of large, abandoned rooms with long windows in which Tom stood alone, surrounded by sea.

An elderly couple came to join him in the lower lounge, each holding a coffee cup. Tom didn't think he recognized them, but left anyway in case they tried to speak to him. He bought a coffee from the counter in the corner, served by a man so old Tom was worried he wouldn't survive the crossing. Then, feeling the juddering as the ferry started up, he went out on deck to look back at the island as they moved away.

He was surprised to see Malcolm still standing where he'd left him on the shore, and raised his arm briefly to wave. Malcolm waved back, and then remained where he was, watching as the ferry moved unhurriedly away from land.

Tom breathed in deeply, inhaling the freshness of salt. He had a clear memory of leaving the island the last time, tightening his hands on the cold rail as he stood beside Heather and thinking, furiously, that he would never return. Or he thought he remembered this moment, but what, in the end, could be relied on? Many of his memories he knew he must have changed or embellished, as everyone did: drawing our fragments together into a pattern that made sense, telling ourselves the story of our lives.

Malcolm's figure was growing smaller now, the shoreline blurring, replaced all around by open water. Tom watched the gannets flying back and forth on to the black rocks further from shore. The islanders had never been awed by the sea, though it defined the limits of their existence. But they had always turned away from it, looked inland. Perhaps this wasn't weakness after all but defiance.

As the sky started to clear, Tom leaned on the rail and stared out at the water churned up in a white trail behind them. A moment later, the sun came out, turning the sea a rich, deep blue. He could no longer see Malcolm, but he could just about make out the landscape of Litta, its ragged moorland rising up in crests and ridges, its cliffs leaning over the sea. The island was receding fast now, its terrible beauty fading. A few moments more and it would vanish completely. As he watched it go, Tom was not surprised to feel Nicky beside him again, and then his mother, with Beth in her arms. They were mute, his companions, watchful and patient. He didn't know them well, not at this distance of so many years, hardly knew them at all in truth, but they remained with him. Quiet strangers. He no longer wished to chase them away. Oh my ghosts, he thought. My lovely ghosts. Come with me; we'll try Glasgow.